Dreaming again...

It was dark, just like always.

His head fell forward, his black hair made it hard to see his face. When he moved, she would see just a little curve of his cheek, a reflection of light from his eyes. She wanted to reach out and push that hair behind his ears, but she didn't. Why didn't she?

At least she could hear him breathing and feel his arms as they came around her. So warm. So soft. So hard.

"Stay with me," he begged.

"I will. I promise."

"Stay with me, just until the end. Then you may go."

" 'Til the end of what?"

" 'Til the end, lass. You'll know when it's over."

Frantic desperation hung in the air all around them.

"I'm not who you think I am," he said.

That was what she was supposed to say.

"Neither am I," she confessed.

He pulled her closer, but there was something between them, again. She needed to get closer, to feel his hard chest against her cheek, to know, just for a minute, that she was safe.

But something was stopping her.

NOT WITHOUT JULIET © 2013 Lesli Muir Lytle
All rights reserved

Cover Art © 2013 Kelli Ann Morgan
www.inspirecreativeservices.com

Interior Book Design by
Bob Houston eBook Formatting
http://about.me/BobHouston

ISBN: 9780615824772

Reviews for Going Back for Romeo

"...a delightful, fun read for lovers of time travel romance...LL Muir is an author to watch..."
–Melissa Mayhue, author of the
Daughters of the Glen Series

"I really laughed myself silly reading this and couldn't stop turning the pages to see what happened in the end"
–Grave Tells Recommended Read

"I can't believe how much I enjoyed this book! The author must indeed be a witch...to have made such an impression on me"
–Melissa's Eclectic Bookshelf

"...vibrant, heroic and tragically lonely characters who's souls seemed to call out to each other."
–Cocktails and Books

"L.L. Muir has created a novel that I put high on my favorites list and will be happy to read this one again and again...and again!"
–Reviews by Molly

Dedication

To a real life Romeo & Juliet—

Dan McMillan

and

Leanne (Annie) Moreland McMillan—

a couple whose time together was cut tragically short

and who deserve to be together forever...

if only in a book.

NOT WITHOUT JULIET

By L. L. Muir

PUBLISHED BY

IVY&STONE

www.llmuir.weebly.com

PROLOGUE

Gordon Land, Scotland, 1496

They rose from the heather like dead men rising to complain of their bumpy purple graves, and Quinn knew by the sneers on their faces, he was the dead one.

"Greetin's, Laird Ross." A long-legged man sporting an ill-fitting Gordon plaid offered a mocking bow, not bothering to knock the dirt from his body. "Ye be a long drink from home this day, but we heard ye're no longer sensible of boundaries, since summer last."

Quinn wished he could have called the survey folk to come spray-paint the bloody borders of Ross land, but he couldn't have afforded the extra charges to bring them all the way back to the fifteenth century. And oh, how he hated being babysat by young boys who knew from birth where Ross land ended and Gordon land began.

"I beg pardon, sir." Quinn nodded. "I trusted my horse to keep me on home ground. I'll be sure to punish him accordingly."

He laid the reins against the scapegoat's neck to turn back South, but when more Gordons blocked his way, he turned again to Long Legs and awaited the filthy man's pleasure. If they killed him, at least he wouldn't be around to watch Ewan's eyes roll back in his head when he learned of yet another of Quinn's foolish mistakes. All that rolling surely gave the new laird migraines.

"I be ridin' the horse, yer lairdship. And you be walking."

"I've no doubt you ken I'm no longer laird of the Rosses," Quinn said clearly so they all would hear and maybe reconsider harassing him.

"We do," said Long Legs. "But once a laird, always a laird. Ye were a shrewd mon to give yer clan over to Ewan Ross though." He pulled Quinn from the saddle, not caring whether or not he landed on his feet. "If ye hadn't, they'd be leaderless this night, I reckon."

Long Legs shoved, but Quinn stood his ground easily enough. The man snorted at him and mounted. He motioned another Gordon forward who tied Quinn's hands before him, then handed up the slack. Quinn felt the comforting weight of the knife in his boot and decided to bide his time. No sense taking on the lot of them at once when it might not be necessary.

The sound of approaching hooves turned all attention to the meager road. A horse was coming fast, seemingly riderless but for the two wee legs flapping at its sides.

Dear Lord! It was Orie, the smithy's son.

Quinn turned to Long Legs.

"Hold your men. You will not harm this child." He spoke quickly while he held the man's gaze. "Do what you will to me, but if this boy is not allowed to return home without so much as a scratch, I will call upon the devil himself to see you and your posterity swept from the face of the earth." He glanced over his shoulder. Orie was closing. "You remember my sister, Isobelle, was a witch. Do you doubt I can do it?" Quinn stepped close so no others could hear him. "Satan himself came with

Isobelle in summer last, to dance with her upon her own tomb. Did no one tell you?"

Long Legs' eyes were wide as he raised a hand, freezing his men where they stood. Orie and his horse kept coming, and he'd soon see the ties around Quinn's wrists! It would be too late!

"Is that what drove ye mad, Laird Ross?" The man swallowed. "Did the devil take yer wits? They say—"

"Laird Ross, sir!" Orie waved one hand and slowed his horse. "You forgot your sword, sir. And you forgot me." The boy looked around at the Gordons spread about the field of heather.

"'Tis all right, Orie." Quinn looked to Long Legs, who nodded and discreetly cut the ropes from his hands.

"If ye touch yer sword, the ladboy dies no matter," the man whispered.

Quinn nodded and turned to the boy, who looked him over, his small brow furrowed. A patch of dirt-colored hair poked up from the back of the lad's head and a well-defined line ran all the way around his small face showing he'd at least tried to wash up. Grime stayed to one side of the line, pink skin to the other, like he was peering out through the only clean spot of a filthy window. The next chance Quinn got, *if* he got one, he'd toss the boy into some good clean water.

"No worries. We are but cutting flowers." He gestured to the Gordons who then looked for a nod from Long Legs before bending and using their bare blades to chop at the blossom-covered branches. Tiny purple balls began flying. "We're taking them to Morna's grave. I will have no use for my heavy blade this day. The Gordon lads will see to my safety, will you not?" He turned to Long Legs.

"Aye. We will, that." The Gordon man grinned.

"Laird, why does he sit yer horse?" Orie pointed, as if Quinn hadn't noticed. All the Gordons stopped cutting flowers and waited. Quinn could feel them all itching to get their hands on the child.

"Twisted his foot is all." He waved away Orie's concern. "I'm sorry I did not wait for you, but I couldn't take such an important lad all the way to the Gordon Keep. Go home now. Have the stable master take my sword to my chambers, and I'll see you when I return." He dared not step closer to the boy and the sword, but bent instead to gather the heather another man had cut, holding his breath and praying for obedience.

Thankfully, the boy was quick to follow orders, and Quinn continued his acting until the sound of Orie's retreat faded to nothing.

Long Legs' sudden burst of laughter sent a chill up his spine.

"A grand idea, that. Ye'll be carrying the flowers, but they'll be for yer own grave, not yer sister's."

Quinn was content with the irony that Morna was neither dead, nor his sister, but was living happily ever after in the twenty-first century. A year before, Morna had faked her death and then been taken into the future, along with the real Montgomery Ross. Quinn had volunteered to switch places with him, due to the plain fact Montgomery had the love of a fine woman to live for, and Quinn had naught.

And if Isobelle, Morna's sister, danced, it wasn't with the devil as she, too, was alive and well, though it was uncertain where she hid. It was a fine trick the Rosses had played on their neighbors, and all for the health and happiness of their women.

Ultimately, if Quinn was about to die, history would play out as it should, and no one would know the Gordons would be killing the wrong man.

CHAPTER ONE

Something dripped on Juliet's head.

"I swear, if it rains on me one more friggin' time..." She looked up and watched a squirrel disappear against the trunk of a pine tree. The small branch he'd run across still bounced, flinging little drops of moisture from its needles. "Damned rodent."

She was sure he'd done it on purpose, but she wasn't going anywhere. He'd just have to deal with having his forest invaded for a while longer.

She stood among the trees on a hillside that ran along the west and north sides of Castle Ross, close enough to keep an eye on the place while she worked up her courage. She'd been working it up for two days, arguing with the same stupid squirrel. At least, she thought it was the same one.

Using her voice had felt good. She couldn't remember the last person she'd had an actual conversation with that wasn't a waitress or something. But that was about to change. As soon as the gray Hummer returned to the castle grounds, she was going to suck it up, march down there, and say what she'd come to say. It wasn't her fault *that woman* was always taking off with her husband every time Jules was ready to confront her. Even getting up early that morning hadn't helped, either. The Hummer was already gone.

What were they doing? Shopping their brains out? Trying to spend all the money?

The thought of all that money disappearing made her nauseous.

No way, she told herself. No way could they spend even half of it in the year since *that woman* had inherited it, even if they bought a real life Scottish castle—which she knew they hadn't—it belonged to the husband's family. And a whole fleet of Hummers wouldn't make a dent.

"It's okay," she told the squirrel. "Half is all I want." She looked back at the castle. "And I'm not leaving here without it."

She rolled her shoulders and worked out the kinks from sleeping, folded up, in the front seat of a car for two miserable nights in a row. She'd have stretched out a little in the back seat, but if someone caught up with her, she needed to be behind the wheel.

Sticking earbuds in her ears was a luxury she couldn't risk, no matter how frightening it was to sleep alone in the woods at night. And thanks to her wild imagination, she'd imagined all kinds of animals breathing on the car windows every time she closed her eyes.

The only thing she should really worry about was the FBI catching up with her or one of Gabby Skedros' men. But even that concern was second on her list. Her biggest fear was what kept her on that hillside—the probability that *that woman* and her big Highlander would decide that they weren't going to give her what was hers.

She'd dreamt of him again last night. Exactly the same dream she'd been having for the last six months. Only this time she knew who he was...

It was dark, just like always.

His head fell forward, his black hair made it hard to see his face. When he moved, she would see just a little curve of his cheek, a little reflection of light from his eyes. She wanted to reach out and push that hair behind his ears, but she didn't. Why didn't she?

At least she could hear him breathing and feel his arms as they came around her. So warm. So soft. So hard.

"Stay with me," he begged.

"I will. I promise."

"Stay with me, just until the end. Then you may go."

"'Til the end of what?"

"'Til the end, lass. You'll know when it's over."

Frantic desperation hung in the air all around them.

"I'm not who you think I am," he said.

That was what she was supposed to say.

"Neither am I," she confessed.

He pulled her closer, but there was something between them, again. She needed to get closer, to feel his hard chest against her cheek, to know, just for a minute, that she was safe.

But something was stopping her.

Finally knowing he was a living breathing man, and not some guy her subconscious had conjured up?

Good news.

Realizing he was married, and to whom he was married?

Bad news. Bad, *bad* news.

Wondering how the hell her mind knew about a man across the ocean, six months before she'd ever seen him?

Freaking insane.

Water dripped on her head again. At least she hoped it was water. She didn't look up because she really didn't want to know. If the little thing had peed on her, she had no place to wash her hair anyway. Not until she got her money.

She wished she had her gun...if only to kill her a friggin' squirrel.

"I hear you taste like chicken," she said, still not looking up.

It was time to resume the position.

She felt the ground. Thankfully, it was no more damp than before. Not much of the last little rainstorm had made it through the thick branches. She was on a little plateau, so she stretched out on her belly, propped her elbows up, and looked through the old field glasses she'd bought in a second-hand store, in a little town just outside Glasgow. She wasn't about to go shopping in East Burnshire, the village down the road. Running into *that woman* in a public place was not the plan. And if the FBI figured out where she was headed, they'd be watching East Burnshire for any sign of one Juliet Bell.

She'd tried not to get her hopes up about the Rosses helping her, considering what she planned to say to the new lady of the manor. The big Scot seemed so...courteous...from afar, she tried to keep worst case scenarios out of her head. She only wished she could say the same about her fantasies. The guy was just too gorgeous.

Just one more reason to dislike his wife.

Below her, Castle Ross protruded out of an ancient hill, a massive wreck resisting its lush green grave. The main body of the castle was about three stories tall. The towers, on the corners, looked more like arms reaching for the sky. Just a few fingers left on each hand.

As she studied the place for the thousandth time, a stone tumbled away from the west wall that was painted liberally with the orange light of the setting sun. She raised her field glasses to see what might have shaken loose a building block placed hundreds of years ago.

A couple of blue-grey figures stood on the battlements. Of course she didn't believe in ghosts, but there was something about Scotland that made you believe you weren't in the real world anyway.

She rolled the focus.

Two old ladies—identical in every way—were fighting over a pair of binoculars. Jules would lay odds on the one on the right since the strap was around her neck. Every time the one on the left pulled at the prize, her twin was pulled forward.

Jules couldn't help laughing.

Nothing to worry about. Even if they'd been a couple of ghosts, they couldn't scare her off. The only thing capable of raising her heart rate now was a sexy Highlander or someone with the power to stop her—like the people she'd just escaped. The FBI was staffed by a bunch of mean sons-o-bitches who didn't take too kindly to sole eye-witnesses squirming out from under their thumb. And if she could get away from them, a couple of Scottish ghosts shouldn't even raise her heart rate.

She moved back into a thick cluster of pines, hoping against hope that the fighting sisters had poor eyesight too. She steadied the boughs bouncing around her and hoped her black leather jacket and new dye job would blend into the shadows. Then she looked through the binoculars again.

The old women weren't fighting anymore, and the one on the left was gesturing over her shoulder with her thumb, toward the North. Jules was just relieved the old girl wasn't pointing her way. The other one took the strap from around her neck and handed over the binoculars, then she looked over her sister's shoulder while that one turned and aimed the lenses up at the road running along the ridge behind Castle Ross.

Whatever it was, the sisters found it fascinating. But when the sisters suddenly ducked down behind the wall,

Jules swung her own binoculars to the North to see what had scared her would-be ghosts.

The trees were in the way. She had to inch out a bit, but kept well below the boughs that would give away her progress. A prickly branch reached out and snagged her coat, as if it would hold her back. She unhooked a sticky pinecone from her precious coat, rubbed her thumb over the scratch it had made in the smooth leather, then crawled forward, grateful for the lengthening and deepening of the evening shadows around her.

At first, all she could see was a car tire with a shiny hubcap. She kept losing track of it between branches heavy with pine cones and dense green needles. When she pulled the glasses aside to get a natural perspective, she realized the car was well off the road, intentionally hidden.

Like hers.

Through the binoculars, once again, Juliet followed the hill as it sloped away from the car. Spindly black legs stood on a visible patch of grass. A tripod. Then, a man's knees as he squatted behind it.

"Shit!" Her voice sounded like a gunshot in her ears. She clamped her lips between her teeth and held her breath until she realized she was too far away for him to have heard her.

A Skedros. It had to be. If he were FBI, agents would have been skulking around the castle, hiding on the roof and taking over the big manor house where human beings actually lived. They wouldn't care about disrupting lives while they waited for her to show up.

She tried to calm the panic ringing in her ears, telling her to run, reminding her that every second she waited lessened her chances of getting away. But she didn't want to run. It had taken her days to get psyched up to confront *that woman*. If she ran, she'd never get that chance again. And no one could be expected to run away from all that money, let alone the chance to look into that man's face just once.

She tried to think rationally, to keep her heart from jumping through her ribs.

Maybe the guy was a photographer. Castle Ross probably smiled for a couple dozen cameras a day. Maybe the North side was its good side. Maybe the FBI had decided to give her what she'd asked for—just a little time to take care of some personal business. Maybe the Skedros family had no clue she'd left the country. Maybe she was just being paranoid.

Yeah, and maybe Gabby Skedros hadn't murdered Nikkos right before her eyes. "You're like a son to me," he'd told the kid, just before he shot him. And how many times had he told Jules she was like a daughter? Yeah, she could live without that kind of family affection. She was better off as she'd always been. On her own.

Paranoid? Yeah, right. Paranoid was a way to stay alive. And she wasn't the only one freaking out. Those old sisters had disappeared fast, as if their footing had given way.

No. They were hiding. And Jules wasn't hiding well enough. Even though she was well hidden beneath branches and shadows, she wanted to inch back into the trees, but she couldn't move. Her arm and legs were frozen with fear, as they had that night when Nikkos fell to the floor. She hadn't moved then either. She'd blended in. Gabby hadn't even looked around to see if any of his restaurant employees might have been working late. Freezing in place had saved her then. Apparently her body thought it was a good enough plan to try again.

Great.

She took a deep breath, then another. She just had to relax. It was just like the bears she imagined outside her car windows. They weren't real. Maybe the danger she felt wasn't real either. She just had to be brave enough to look.

From the corner of her eye, she saw movement to her right. There were now two blue forms at the entrance of the castle grounds, jumping up and down. Weren't they a little too old for that?

Thankfully, she found her arms willing to move once more, and she raised her glasses for a better look at the pair of lunatics.

At the bottom of her hill was a road and beyond that, a wide parking lot. Between it and the crumbling outer wall of the castle was a bridge of land the width of a car. Once upon a time, there would have been a moat and drawbridge, she figured. Where the wall began, there was also a large gate that opened inward. Next to this gate bounced the blue sisters.

Juliet realized three things. First, the sisters were looking right at her. Second, they weren't doing jumping jacks; they were flapping around trying to get her attention. And third, the man on the North hill couldn't see them.

Or so she hoped. She swung the glasses in his direction to be sure.

The tripod hadn't moved. The knees were gone, but as she scanned the area, she found a man's torso. When he ducked to take a bite of something in his hand, she saw him.

Sunglasses. It was already too dark for those. The sun was nearly down. Dark shadows had already started creeping up the side of Castle Ross. It was too late for a good shot—at least with a camera.

The man straightened and moved. She watched patiently for a better glimpse of him.

"Don't be Greek. Don't be Greek," she chanted.

Finally, she saw his head. It was covered with long orange curls. For a minute, she thought it was just the trick of the sunset, until she realized the bright hair was all natural. Not a Skedros, then.

Not a photographer. Not a Skedros. Either a hired hitter, or the FBI. FBI agents tried to blend in. This guy, with his lion's mane of bright hair, wouldn't blend in anywhere—maybe not even Scotland.

A hitman then.

She was dead. Her chances for survival just rolled away, down the hill, out of reach. The smart thing to do would be to get in her car and drive away. Act as casually as possible as the road would either take her down the hill and past the castle, right where he was watching, or up and back the way she'd come, about twenty feet from where his car was parked. Maybe he wouldn't consider she'd blackened her hair and wouldn't give her a second look. Once she was out of sight, she would have to hightail it to Edinburg, turn herself in to the police and hope the FBI could come and save her. It was her only choice.

Fire or frying pan?

She was out of money. Nearly out of gas. And if she didn't think of something quick, she'd be out of hope.

She looked back to the sisters. They'd seen the man. They'd seen her, and yet they were still waving. She had absolutely no idea what they could have deduced from that, but they seemed to be beckoning her inside the grounds. Did they sense her danger, or were they out of their minds? Why would they want to help her when they had no clue who she was?

Maybe they'd seen the man's gun and freaked out. But she couldn't just run down there and let them help her. She'd be putting them in danger. A hitter wouldn't think twice about collateral damage.

But with no gas money, what choice did she have?

For just a second, Jules allowed herself to imagine the large dark Highlander, coming up the hill to rescue her, kilt and sword swinging as they had the previous day for his crowd of tourists. But the "see us tomorrow" sign had already been hung, the parking lot chained off for the night. And his Hummer was still gone.

The sisters waved limply, their arms at their sides now, no longer over their heads, but it didn't look like they planned to give up. If they didn't get out of there, there was a good chance they'd get shot. Maybe it was her Christian duty to make them go hide.

Jules waved her hand, then gave them a thumbs-up.

They stopped their antics and one grabbed the field glasses from the other to take a good look.

Again, Jules gave a thumbs-up.

She received two very broad grins in return—smiles that in other circumstances would have made her think twice about taking shelter at Castle Ross. They looked a little too pleased. Like they might have a pot of stew on the fire and were waiting for a bit of meat.

A chill went through her. She figured it was just adrenaline overload.

The jagged tips of the ramparts let go of the sunset and the famous Scottish gloaming settled over the glen with an almost audible sigh.

The car hadn't moved. The tripod hadn't moved.

Jules took a deep breath, appreciating for the moment that she was still breathing at all. She turned to look north again, to check the hitter's location one last time and found herself staring into the guy's small binoculars, aimed right at her.

Air locked in her chest and expanded, like whipped cream from a thoroughly shaken can. She couldn't look away, couldn't drop her glasses and hope not to be seen. It was too important to know what he would do! Did he already have a gun in hand? Had he already seen her and was looking to see if she was alone?

Time froze.

He only stared.

She didn't dare hope he mistook her for anything or anyone else. They conversed silently.

Ah, there you are.

I can't believe you found me.

Believe it, baby.

Now what?

You make the first move. Then I kill you.

It seemed like whole minutes ticked by without him twitching a muscle. That mean square jaw never softened, those lips never curved in satisfaction. A long orange curl swayed in a breeze that never reached her side of the crescent hill.

Calmly, in a less-than-dramatic act of defiance, she raised her left hand next to her binoculars...and flipped him off.

His head snapped back as he laughed—and she heard it, faintly. But the break in eye contact, such as it was, was all it took to shake her into action. She jumped to her feet and looked down at the gate. Blue. Still there.

She judged the distance to her car. He was much closer to his. He could drive over to her car before she could make her way up to it. If she ran flat out for the gate, she'd be an open target, but a moving one. If he tried to come after her, she'd reach the castle before he could drive to it, considering how the road twisted and turned down the mountain. He could drive like James Friggin' Bond and never reach her in time.

But whom would she endanger?

She faltered. Would he take out everyone here? There were children in the manor, or at least there had been yesterday. The more modern home was a good football field away from the castle, but could she honestly expect to take shelter in the old structure and not endanger the people in the new one?

She recalled photos on the website depicting ancient weapons in the great hall. Maybe she could defend

herself without any Highlanders needing to come to her
rescue.

The start of the man's car startled her like a shot
fired. Her legs took all decision from her and propelled
her down the hill. She made a bee-line for the parking lot
since he couldn't be trying to draw a bead on her and
drive at the same time. He was coming after her, then.
Maybe Gabby Skedros was in the area and wanted to do
the deed himself.

And maybe, just maybe, he wouldn't get the chance.

Her cowboy boots slid on the moist grass like skis
on snow, so she braced herself and let them slide. One
heel hit a stone and she rolled. How she got down the hill
didn't matter—down was down. On her feet again, she
cleared a gauntlet of shrubbery she never could have
named then jumped a hedge of purple heather before
touching down on the solidly packed road.

Cowboy boots weren't designed for running, and her
sprint wasn't pretty. She tripped but she didn't go down.
Two steps later, she realized she'd lost a boot in the
gravel of the parking lot, but she didn't slow. The roaring
engine of a sports car gave her an added shot of
adrenaline and she flew across the lot, then the land-
bridge, and past the gate before the car ever made the last
turn out of the woods.

She slowed, looking for a bit of blue. It was there at
the back corner of the castle. Both sisters were waving
her on and she obliged, limping, cursing her lost boot
until she'd rounded the corner, out of sight of the road.

The sisters clutched at her, pulling her toward an
open door, ignoring her resistance and her need to catch
her breath. After they'd taken a dozen steps into the dark
castle, she heard a strangled sound, as if a certain small
car were four-wheeling from road to rocks, by-passing
the chains, then barreling across the bridge and toward
the back of the castle.

"Those people in the manor house!" She grabbed a boney forearm and forced one woman to stop. "He'll kill them! Can you call them? Tell them to run and hide?"

"No one is at home, dear. They've all gone to the city. How else would we have been able to break in?"

Juliet shook her head. Her relief was a tidal wave, but not complete.

"*You* have to hide," she told them. "I need a weapon...from the great hall...and you two need to hide!"

A flashlight materialized and the sisters led the way, silently. After a couple of turns, Juliet didn't know up from down.

"Hang on. Did you understand me? You two need to hide—"

A door crashed open behind them.

"No use for it, sister. We'll have to put her in the hole." The light was dimmed against a blue sweater, but two nodding heads were still visible.

"You want to hide me in a hole? And where are you going to hide?" Juliet whispered, but the man stomping around in the dark castle wouldn't have been able to hear much.

"Juliet Bell!" The hitter's voice echoed around them, but he seemed to be coming no closer. "I know ye're in here, lass! I found your boot in the car park, all but pointin' the way!"

Great. Skedros had hired a local. No wonder he'd had red hair. If he'd have worn a kilt and hung around the ruins, she might have walked right up to him!

One sister grabbed her hand and pulled her along. They finally came to a staircase and Juliet got a funny feeling. Deja vu, maybe. Not really a foreboding, but...yeah, a foreboding. She'd gotten them often enough, she should have recognized it for what it was.

When she'd tried to explain it to Nikkos once, she'd told him it was like playing the Hot & Cold game. Only

something in her gut would tell her whether she was
getting closer to something important, or moving further
away. She'd felt like she was getting warmer the second
she'd touched down in Scotland. Now she was burning
up.

Either the hitter had stopped stomping around, or
they were moving so far underground they couldn't hear
him anymore. After the hallway made a hairpin turn, the
lead sister took the flashlight away from her sweater and
shined it on the ground. A minute later, they hurried into
a small room with a single large barrel in the center.

"Up on the barrel, dear, if ye please." One sister
offered a hand for support, but in this light, with shadows
playing in the deep wrinkles of their faces, the pair
looked too old to support their own measly weight, let
alone hers.

The other shined her light on the odd ceiling. A large
slab of stone capped the room, and in the center of it, a
hole had been carved but was now plugged with a
perfectly fitting block of wood.

"Just push up on the wood, dear. I assure ye there are
no bodies inside the tomb."

"A *tomb*? Are you friggin' kidding me?" Jules
couldn't have whispered if she'd tried. That foreboding
had turned into a loud clown orchestra with bells and
whistles and all kinds of alarms going off.

"Shh." A cool boney hand clamped down on her
mouth, but Jules carefully removed it before glaring a
warning at its owner.

"That's the hole we're going to hide in?" She had
lowered her voice and tried to sound calm considering
the noise in her head.

Both sisters shook their heads.

"We're not allowed inside, dear—"

"We gave our word."

A Portrait of The Black Hole at The Center of Our Universe

Liam Carter MacCormack

ISBN: 9798844027208
Published 2022 by Anthroponcene.

Cover typeface: Aldritch/PT Mono Bold
Interior typeface: Minion Pro

Printed by Amazon.

First edition through December 2022

For Jean -
who dared to see

"Humanity which, beginning with Homer, once used to be the object of contemplation for the Gods, has now become the contemplation of itself. Its alienation from itself has reached such a point that humanity experiences its own destruction as an aesthetic sensation of the highest degree."

Walter Benjamin

Our entire reality is being devoured. In the absence of any clear path forward, modern man has reached the point of devouring its 'self'.

There are plentiful illustrations of this but we shall start with the lighter. Two more recent cases can be seen in game shows: Bullsh*t a game show in which contestants must answer questions, to which if they do not know the answer, they must act as is they know. Several other contestants then try to determine if the contestant is lying; the one who guesses correctly the most replaces the first contestant.

The second case is that of The Circle, yet another game show which takes the premise of Big Brother, quarantines all the contestants in isolated apartments, and forces them to interact only digitally. Big Brother is of course a concept that has become universally accepted:a condensed version of a human amusement park, ghetto, solitary confinement, and Exterminating Angel. In the Circle, contestants are confined to a single bedroom apartment, alone; their only interaction with the outside world is via a television which is connected to a chat with the other contestants. Participants may choose to "present" as a different person entirely, one which may be better perceived than their physical form (on the most recent season several contestants chose to play as their parents in a move that would make Freud proud.) Slowly eliminating each other one by one, from the confines of the virtual womb, each of their daily actions are recorded by closed circuit surveillance in multiple locations in each room. All competition is also closed circuit, as the image of what the others construct are all that are absorbed, never the true aura of the experience.

It is here, when everything has been given over to viewing that one realizes that there is nothing left to see. It is the mirror of flatness, where, contrary to all objectives of a real which the show claims to show, it becomes the proof of the disappearance of the "other," and perhaps even the fact that the human is not a social being. The equivalent of a readymade - an unchanged transposition like that of The Circle, which itself is rigged by all the dominant models. A synthetic banality, fabricated within a closed circuit and under a controlled screen.

In this manner, the artificial microcosm of The Circle is identical to Disneyland, which provides the illusion of the real external world, while if one looks deeper, one realizes they are one and the same. The entire United States is Disneyland and we are all on The Circle. No need to enter into the idea of the virtual double of reality, we are already there - the televisual universe is nothing more than a holographic detail of global reality. All the way up to, and including, the most daily parts of our existence: we are already within a situation of experimental reality; It is precisely from this that we have the fascination, by immersion, of spontaneous interactivity. Are we dealing with a pornograph ic voyeurism?

No. Sex can be found everywhere, but it is not what people want. What they profoundly desire is the spectacle of banality, which today has become the real pornography, the real obscenity - of nothingness, insignificance, and flatness. There is a form of cruelty which can be seen there as well, in consumption of goods at such a pace that many must go without or are directly harmed. At a time when the media itself are less and less capable of reckoning the unbearable events of the world, they discover daily life and its existential banality as the most violent actuality; perhaps even the most perfect crime. And in actuality - it is. People are fascinated and terrified by the indifference to their own existence.

All of this is reinforced by the fact that the public is itself mobilized as judge; that it has itself become Big Brother. We are way beyond the panopticon, of visibility as the source of power and control. It is no longer about rendering things visible to the external eye, but rendering them transparent to themselves, via a perfusion of control within the masses, and in erasing any trace of the operation. So it is that the spectators are implicated in a gigantic negative counter transfer of themselves, and once again, it is from this situation that we see the dizzying attraction of this spectacle.

In the end, all of this comes from the desire to be Nothing and Something simultaneously. There are then two manners of proceeding: complete refusal to participate in society, or we immerse ourselves in the delirious exhibitionism of its decline. We blackmailed make ourselves a straw man - a digital effigy against the necessity of existing and the obligation of being ones self.

The worst part about this obscenity, this shameless visibility, is the forced participation, this automatic complicity of the spectator who has been into participating. It is this which is the clearest objective of the operation: the servitude of the victims, but a voluntary servitude, one in which the victims rejoice from the pain and shame which they are made to suffer. The complete participation of a society in its fundamental function: interactive exclusion - it doesn't get better than that! ***

Everywhere, the experimental supersedes the real and the imaginary.

Everywhere, it is the protocols of science and verification which have inoculated us, and we are in the middle, under the cameras scalpel, dissecting the dimension of social relations, outside any language or symbolic context. Bullsh*t is one such example of the experimental. All pretenses of sincerity are swept aside, leaving only a perpetual verification of deceit, which ultimately is rewarded handsomely. In the end, there isn't even deceit; the presumption that the first contestant is lying almost undoes the surprise, and thus damage of any such deceit. I say almost as we are still hardwired to trust, there is no way around this fact besides actual torture. Perhaps we are on our way there, but not quite yet. If that is the future, such torture will not be televised: it will be lived. The VideoDrome will come to life, and it will no longer be us devouring ourselves. Such nightmares feel right at home in our age of Kali.

Before the horrors, comes the society built on lies. Now, there are two misinterpretations of lying that must be addressed: the first is the idea of a fundamental truth. There can be no lie unless it is established as ultimate fact. As I'm sure many know from personal experience, and is ever more proved by our quantum physicists, is that reality is largely, if not totally, subjective. Such is the power of our echo chambers; by trapping one in a separatist world view, the individual can be lead to wild lengths they would never go to on their own. Such is also the power and allure of the cult. The fact that there is no concrete truth is what drives individuals into these echo chambers in the first place - out of fear and out of a desire for comfort. This is where we see the problematic pretension with bringing everything into the real world; of claiming that everything should be accelerated into an integral reality. And somewhere, we see, this is precisely the essence of power itself. "The corruption of power is to inscribe into the real everything which is found in dreams…"

It is here that we must address the absurdity of a societal liberation. For such a "liberation" is nothing but an indoctrination into a set of beliefs, and any set belief is a chain that binds. If liberation were the goal, varying viewpoints must be heard and considered. Yet this will never happen within our current iteration of digital interaction (social media based), not because it is not desirable, but because it is not profitable for the truth to be revealed. In fact, it is the desire itself which is profitable, as desire unfulfilled is perhaps the strongest driver known to God and man. In the end, it is not even desire. Desire becomes something else entirely; repetition. All that remains is the endless repetition, within an act of accumulation, of consuming copious information with no regard to quality; of regurgitating the same information into the minds of others.

This is the total foreclosure of reality. The only question one could possibly ask is, "What's next?" But it is exactly this question which brought us here. The modern disenchanted vision of the world lives within the realm of appearances; it is a complete misinterpretation and the total opposite of truth. It is the process of ever removing veils, only to find the object still unrevealed. It is our desire which brings us further from the truth, that enigmatic secret, that pure object whose mystery can never be revealed and has no right being uncovered. We would like to get a glimpse of the worst - absolute raw and violent reality - but we never get there. There is an impermeable wall which rejects even our glance. The best course for humanity is to accept that there is simply nothing to see; to sit with that knowledge and be comforted by it. There is then the course we are on; the course which claims the very idea of the enigma as sublime and desirable. Such a path leads down and into a black hole.

The problems with 'The Circle' are threefold and are indicative of larger societal issues: nullity, falsehood, and spectacle. The events within the apartments during the contestants' isolation, in themselves, are ultimately uninteresting. Despite this, or perhaps because of this, there is an immense fascination with the transpiring events. Stepping even further out, this fascination is itself a fascination for our critical gaze. And what is even occurring? Quite literally nothing; the type of nothing which makes up market data, political opinion, and insider analysis (which are each, in themselves, spectacle.) But, the market is the market, and all commentaries themselves become part of the cultural and idealogical marketplace. All that remains is this mysterious contagion, this literal viral chain that functions from one end to the other, and to which we are all accomplices even in our analysis.

The contagion of spectacle becomes a Tulpa, uncontrollable and immeasurable. The fact that it resists intelligence is its very allure. Those who love intelligence, then mock those who are drawn to the spectacle by animalistic impulse; but this impulse is the same drive which forces the ivory guard of academia to mock those very people. To feel better than is the impulse. On the one hand you have, generally, a class of people which has been so drained of their energy and income that they cannot afford to live a life of their own. Thus, they are drawn to the spectacle as a form of vicarious experience. In viewing the spectacle, the need for connection is also met. In a world with communities that are rapidly moving closer together, we are moving further apart emotionally, mentally, and spiritually through the experience of spectacle. This is no better shown than through the academic class which places ridicule and scorn on those who are trapped in the cycle of spectacle. As opposed to offering pathways into a higher understanding of media criticism, they often choose to subjugate and critique those who had nothing to do with the process they are entrapped in.

There is a stupefying effect to the spectacle, which is its falsehood. In the face of the unreal, we often have no choice but to stare as we try and comprehend the logic of the unreal; which is, of course, impossible. Thus falsehood itself is a chain that binds. Within both of our previous examples, Bullsh*t and The Circle, falsehood is built into it inherently. This is clear in Bullsh*t, But within The Circle it is less clear. One of the stipulations for the show is that players may choose to play as another person (a 'catfish') with photos that are not there own, as all interaction is text based (as is the norm with most social media interactions.) In this way, the show is far more insidious than Big Brother, not only implicating the audience and their social connections, but introducing the normalcy of 24/7 surveillance by your fellow citizens. What is to be gained by this? For many, nothing; but for the one who "proves" themselves, a small cash prize of $100 thousand USD. Likely desperately needed seeing as housing costs far outpace income as of 2022 in much of the world, not to mention consumer held debt. At this pinnacle of spectacle we can see that all participants are losers, except perhaps those who run the production houses, but even those…. I digress. In The Circle there is no equivalence between merit and glory; in fact there is neither. It is everything in exchange for nothing.

The Circle insures a virtual glory to everyone in terms of the absence of merit itself; this is the end of Democracy. Complete in-equivalence. But there is only so far this can go. The system behind democracy is based on the belief that there are some who are better fit for certain positions of power, based on field expertise and a proven track record of accomplishment. Yet, this has long since eroded in the United States, the poster child of Democracy. As far back as Kennedy can one see that elections have been treated more like school superlatives than the induction of a king like entity. It is because of this that the democracy of the United States has continued to erode further, even going as far as a democratic nihilism; much of the populace who are eligible to vote choose not to. Even more that do participate, still feel like they are not considered by those they elect. Like most failing empires, the United States has over extended itself wonderfully, having more foreign outposts than any nation in history. There are currently proxy wars only our grandchildren will hear about (due to the 60 year confidentiality limit.) The Circle is both the mirror and tragedy of an entire society caught up in the race towards meaningless, swooning in front of its own banality.

It began with television: that supreme operation of consensus building, that kidnapper of consciousness, that unheralded success story of illusion integration that stoked the spectacle like bellows on a fire. We are now trapped in this global non-event; "A total social fact" as Marcel Mauss says. Television has shown itself to be the strongest power within the science of imaginary solutions. What is meant by imaginary solutions? A distraction would be most concise, but it is ultimately that which draws you from yourself and your potential. But if this is the lure and catch of the television, it is not by insidious design, it is because we ourselves desired it. There is no use in accusing the powers of media, or those of wealth, or even some public stupidity in order to allow for some sort of hope of a rational alternative to this technical, experimental, and integral socialization in which we are all engaged, and which ends in the automatic coordination of individuals within irrevocable consensus processes. Let's call television the integral event of a society which, from then on, without a contract or rules, nor system of values other than reflexive complicity, without any other rule or logic than that of an immediate contagion of a promiscuity, blends us all together with an immense indivisible being.

We've become individuated beings: non-divisible between ourselves and others. This individuation, which we are so proud of, has nothing to do with personal liberty; on the contrary, it is a general promiscuity. It is not a promiscuity of bodies in space - but of screens from one end of the world to the other. And it is probably screen promiscuity which is the real promiscuity, the indivisibility of every human particle at a distance of tens of thousands of kilometers - like millions of twins who are incapable of separating from their double. It can be the promiscuity of a whole society with "the event" of the day. Even more so, it is the idea of an "interactive" other, the parasocial relationship between a follower and an "account." This has many insidious forms, whether it be the lone stalker who's built a false idea of a false idea, or the average person looking for genuine connection. Scammers and "catfish" are well known ills within the sea of digital interaction, but there is another far more treacherous beast many can not yet even see: this is the parasocial relationship between the paying customer and the digital sex worker.

For those who would not normally seek out such content, the proliferation of pornographic material in the early 2000's has been a full on assault. Not only is such content readily available via most search engines, certain social medias allow such content to be shared on their sites. This deluge of pornography into the everyday has relentlessly torrented against the bed rock of our society, washing away the very things which keep us stable. What used to be relegated to fantasy (or perhaps in art for the more wealthy,) has been taken to its immaterial end; here too, the quality of merit erodes into a democratic sludge, swallowing all those who dare desire. As the accessibility increased, so did the amount of participants. It does not seem however, like they are participating out of a genuine want to be seen. Instead, the common reason is financial distress. What is left when one has nothing? Why, the body of course; and so the spectacle takes that too.

It is from this perspective of financial necessity that we must address sex work, if we address it at all, for the financial incentive is the prime reason for the interaction. Here we see all three of our problems. First, there is the nullity, which includes both the inaccessibility to genuine wealth for the sex worker, as well as the absence of love in a "John's" life resulting in an overabundance of wealth from what is likely a pointless job. If we were to stop our analysis here we could perhaps have a fairytale ending, but alas, this is life: the second issue is the falsehood. This is ultimately seen in the illusion both carry that what they are doing is not, to use a lighter term, a transaction (although it may later be seen as such,) but an expression of gratitude or veneration; merit returns wearing a new face - reborn it claims there is only the illusion and desire for the illusion. This brings us to the spectacle, which like the financial element, is essential to the business. The spectacle is driven by desire - and where does desire go when it is fulfilled? Nowhere, it wells up again; this is why the spectacle, in whatever form it takes, is so potent and ever growing.

Consider this: what evokes the spectacle? In the past it was spread by words, infecting mind after mind with grandiosity beyond imagination. Now, it is spread by objects, devices; what was once spurred by human interaction is now associated with a form of self soothing via objects. I would like to recall my previous statement as I've strayed a bit from it: "there is another far more treacherous beast many can not yet even see: this is the parasocial relationship between the paying customer and the digital sex worker." As more and more people are forced into sexual subjugation due to financial necessity, the more these same people will be viewed as objects by those consuming that content on their own personal devices. Not only this, but because of the snowballing nature of the spectacle, recurrent desire will bring those consumers back to the same account over and over out of a sense of parasocial relation: they begin to see the subjugated worker as one of their friends. Many of those indicted in the "Me Too" movement would go on to state that they did not feel there was a power dynamic, and saw themselves on the same level as those they assaulted. I recall this because the same dynamic is likely still playing itself out across the United States and beyond. Viewing themselves as equal, seeing the person you have subjugated as a close friend, but yet not viewing them as fully human; for their face has been neurally linked to other objects of desire and fulfillment - hardwired into objectification.

Must there be an other? is Hegel correct in his approximation that to individuate, one must first separate themselves ontologically? No, ultimately there is no "other," it is all a variation of self; a variation of life. Each of us is a synthetic image of what we believe (and desire) ourselves to be; our gestures, speech, and even those we keep close to us are as close to prefabrication as one can dream. But it is only through our individuation that we can learn this.

For those who have yet to raise themselves to such a metaphysical standing, the "other" is quite real and quite alluring; incisive even. Now, combine this with desire and you have yourself quite the bonfire. This ever renewed sense of digital connection will remain even if (and though) it is only the shadow of the other person they are interacting with. This shadow is nowhere near the three dimensional being that sits behind the screen, while, to use Baudrillards word's on Catherine Millet, "subjected, by her own choice, via serial fucking, to the same sensory deprivation - giving way to the same radical, unique, minimal activity, which, by its repetition alone, becomes virtual. Not only does she get rid of any dual exchange or sexual participation, but also any obligation of orgasm or choice - in the end she simply gets rid of her own body. we can see this in the refusal of choice as with any sort of elective affinity, a type of asceticism, a flaying of free will (which we know, is merely a subjective illusion), which would make Catherine Millet, as some have said, a saint..."

Millions of saints, nuns, and monks holed up in their own personal convents, deifying the absolute minimum. A rejection of the body and desire at the price of being chained to both. If doing away with desire and its concept can be characterized as a nihilism of will, then this reiterated proof of the existence of sex by sex can be considered as a sexual nihilism. The immanence of banality in this, the more real than real, is integral reality.

By its absorption in information and the virtual, behind the murder underlying the pacification of life and the enthusiastic consumption of this hallucinogenic banality, reality is a process heading towards completion and it is lethal at every dimension. A return to limbo, to this crepuscular zone where, by its very realization, everything is coming to an end.

In the end, it has nothing sexual at all about it. It is a curiosity of the visceral, organic, and endoscopic order. This evokes the Japanese striptease where clients are invited to plunge their nose and to gaze into the woman's vagina in order, apparently to explore the secret of her entrails - something quite different in its focus than sexual penetration. Not too different than the endoscopy of the internal body by micro-cameras; this too is not that different than the caliph who, after the dance of the stripper, cuts her open to find out just a bit more what's underneath. Sex and sexual knowledge are superficial compared to this: the real danger of the spectacle.

Beyond sensory deprivation, which is what the screen aims to induce (or we wish to induce with it), we find total sensory and social elimination. "Othering" to the extent of fear and disgust towards all, derived from a fear of the self. This fear of the self is natural, as it is quite uncomfortable for anyone to sit with certain thoughts they have. Besides this, there is the viral aspect of our nature which desires to participate in group conversations and activities; such is how we and many of our ancestors are designed to survive. In this world of digital screens, however, these same mental pathways will reform to desire interaction with content as a means of dopamine release. When the body priori tizes dopamine release over survival, not only does ones quality of life rapidly diminish, illnesses and diseases will abound. At a point, with so much conditioning, it will be difficult to reform those pathways to be normal again, craving interaction; it may even be impossible. This is the subtlest form of extermination: murder by banality.

The most incredible thing about it all is that this properly unbearable situation is provided to the gaze of the crowds, and getting them to relish the event as an orgy with no tomorrow. A beautiful exploit, but it hasn't ended there. Following the same logic, we are now proliferated with "true crime" content, the lightest of bloodsport. Just at precisely the same point in history in which we are trying to exterminate death, it makes its return to the screen as an experience of the extreme.

Our recent history has experienced many a crime - Hiroshima, Auschwitz, slavery, systematic poverty - but the one that stands before them all is the second fall of man; the fall into banality. Where is the secret to this banality? Of this overexposed nullity, enlightened and informed from all sides, and which leads nothing more to be seen except for transparency? It is both the object of a veritable horror, and the dizzying temptation to plunge into this limbo - the limbo of an existence in a vacuum and stripped of all meaning: the spectacle itself. There is a murderous violence in banality, precisely due to its indifference and monotony. A veritable theater of cruelty, of our cruelty to ourselves completely played down and without a drop of blood. Banality abolishes all stakes and erases its own traces - but above all, in this murder of reality, we are both the murderers and the victims. It is only with suicide that the victim and the murderer approach the same level, and in this regard the immersion into banality is indeed the equivalent of the suicide of the species.

But all of this is just a running gag between the screen and reality, which is over.

So where do we go from here? Questions such as this and "Whats next?" should be banished from our language; for asking whats next, is the equivalent of saying, "all of this was not enough." If there is one other thing to learn from our individuation, besides Oneness between all people, it is that we only have this current, sacred moment. What we do with it shall define us for the rest of history, and indeed has for many millennia. Merit has and will continue to define the generations.

While reality may be a deceased creature, we do not have to go down with it. In its place, we must no longer wonder how we wish to reshape things to better automate our lives, but we must ask, "what is best for us?" and "what do we need?" For as the veil of illusion that has masked governments around the world, begins to fall, the social contract will erode quicker than ever before; in fact it has already long been going disappearing. State agencies are already hard at work reshaping definitions, just as Orwell predicted, to make issues disappear like a magic trick. Not only this, but the United States attempted to establish a Bureau of Disinformation. Such moves towards to totalitarianism are safe from critique however, as any promotion of anarchist belief systems or even stating, "The United States is moving towards tyranny" are labeled as 'domestic violent extremism' and punishable by law.

It is in times like these that we must remain the most vigilant in protecting our rights, and the rights of all human beings; for it is now clear, in a moments notice, the right to free speech can be taken away. We must also aim to rebuild ourselves for the tasks ahead: of building thriving self-sustaining communities, of re-establishing law and order to be simple, plain, and based in a love for all.

Beyond reality, there is truth. The goal of all people across all time has to been uncover it, even at the risk of self immolation. Now, in our time beyond reality, we must know this truth with our whole hearts: all are one and all individualism is simulation. The drivers of love, fear, desire - shall always be there; so how do we do what is best for us in the face of these?

Such is the work of history...

72535476R00021

Jules didn't get it. "Then where will the two of you hide? This guy isn't messing around. He's going to kill me, and he's going to kill you if he knows you're here."

"Oh, don't worry about us," said one. "There is a place for us just on down the hall, but ye'll be safe here."

"Yes, it won't take us a moment to hide. But we'll see ye safe first."

Great. She'd come to save them and they ended up saving her.

"Fine," she said. "Let's move."

Jules did as ordered—they were a bossy pair—and pulled herself up into the hole. She couldn't think of it as a tomb and still crawl inside. Once she was out of it, she'd ask questions.

She stuck her head out and watched the pair turn for the door.

"Wait a sec," she said.

"What is it, dear?" asked one.

"You're not ghosts, are you?" She pretended she was joking.

They both chuckled. One of them winked in the light from the flashlight shining on her wrinkled face. "Not yet, dear. Not just yet. And don't forget to plug the hole."

When she'd first stuck her head inside, Jules had seen a stash of flashlights and candles against one wall. She felt for them now, praying at least one would have live batteries. The first one she tested worked. Then she did what the old chick had done and put the bright end against her shirt. If the guy came looking and found the little room, the last thing she wanted him to see was light shining down through the ceiling.

Oh, she was in a tomb all right, and it took a lot more courage than she thought she had to nudge the plug into the hole with her foot.

But which is better, dead or just temporarily buried?

A room—she'd just think of it as a stone room.

It was oblong. Its walls were black stones of all shapes and sizes that fit perfectly, like a puzzle. The ceiling was high enough to let her stand, as if the guy who built it expected a tall crowd inside.

Jules had read every word on the website, but hadn't paid much attention to the fairy tale crap. She'd been more interested in the current Lady of Clan Ross, not the marketing aimed at the tourists. Now she wished she'd read it more carefully.

She ran one hand along the wall. The mortar and cobwebs felt old and genuine, not like a recent set design. The air smelled dusty and stale and she hoped it had nothing to do with the decomposed body of some Ross woman who'd been buried alive by her brother. At least the body had been removed. A ghost she could handle. A skeleton? Not so much.

"Joooliet! Come out, come out, wherever ye are."

The hitter's sing-song words were muffled and came from her left. He must have been standing in the great hall. No way did he know she was inside unless light was finding its way out some crack, but there was no way she would turn off the flashlight now. What if it didn't turn back on? Then, he'd know exactly where she was because she'd be out of her friggin' mind and screaming her head off.

Just the thought of it pushed her heart rate up. Freaking out wasn't far off, so she bit her lip and breathed through her nose, not trusting herself to keep quiet. Any little sound and he'd start blowing holes in the walls.

The sneeze came upon her so fast she couldn't do much more than try and muffle it with the sleeve of her jacket. Still, the sharp whisper echoed around her before settling.

Shit!

There was movement against the wall, like rats running up and down it. He'd heard the noise and was looking for a way in! She could imagine him clearly as he felt every stone for weakness. He was thorough, right to left, top to bottom, in sections, twice around the tomb. Rougher sounds followed and she imagined him trying to pry the stones apart. Then she heard the slide of his body on the roof.

He cursed and she braced herself for the blast that would soon follow. Scrunched down in the far end, she shut her eyes and willed herself to become invisible.

But the blast never came. The noises stopped altogether. A hitter wouldn't just give up, though. He'd go looking for a basement. He would have realized it was the only way she could have gotten in.

Well, if he was coming from below, she'd just try to get out through the stone wall. There'd been a crowbar among the flashlights. She exchanged it for the flashlight in her hand, but left the light shining on the floor. Next, she took a big two-handed swing at the wall, hoping a big chunk would break away, but it was like banging against concrete. The force got absorbed into the bones of her arms and she nearly dropped the bar. But there was no time to recover. She had to move fast.

She jammed the sharp end under the lip of a stone and pushed down. The edge of the stone broke off. The mortar hardly gave up any dust.

She tried the same spot again, struck the mortar to get under the stone a little better, but the stuff wouldn't give. She turned around. Found another shadowy spot. Jammed the crowbar into it, but nothing held. The only thing the crowbar was good for was making noise. She would have pounded on the wall in frustration, but pain still ricocheted in her arms from that first blow.

I'm such a wuss.

But no. The crowbar couldn't damage the wall, but it could damage something else!

She toed the flashlight so it was up against the stones. The light made a little circle that only stretched about six inches up the wall, but it was enough to keep her from freaking. Then she lifted the curved part of the bar over her right shoulder and held on with both hands, like a golf club. Whether it was a gun or a head that lifted up the plug, she was ready to swing.

CHAPTER TWO

Jules waited forever.

Maybe the guy was lost in the dark.

She considered climbing out, but she couldn't risk dropping into the killer's arms. And there weren't any other places to hide. If there'd been room for her down the hall, the old broads wouldn't have made her climb into the tomb. If she stayed, it was just a matter of time.

She closed her eyes and prayed, like she hadn't prayed for years.

"Dear God, I'd even give up my revenge if you could just get me out of this." And since who knew when she'd ever get the chance to pray again, she added, "And I'd give just about anything for a lovely Highlander, just like that Ross guy. Amen." Too bad the last part would have been an easier miracle to pull off than the first.

Jules opened her eyes and realized the flashlight had died. Before she could start feeling around for another one, there was movement. Someone was in the room below her. Orange light filtered around the edges of the wooden plug. Apparently it hadn't fit as snugly as she'd thought. There was a heavy thump. The barrel? Or a body? She would peak through a gap, but a bullet in the face would be just too painful.

The man's voice made her jump.

"God...or Jillian...if either of ye can hear me," called the man from below. "I'm in sore need of a miracle if either of you have one to hand."

Except for a florist in Queens, Jules hadn't had anyone to speak Gaelic with since her mom had died. She assumed she'd forgotten most of it, but when the man had spoken, it was as if a file had opened on the computer screen of her mind. It was all there, just as she'd left it. Every word, every note of it, was tied to a memory of her mother. And if it weren't for Jillian, her mother would still be alive.

But this was no time to turn up the flame under that particular pot. She would have plenty of time to deal with her Jillian issues when, or if, she survived the day. She mentally hit rewind and listened to the man's words again.

It didn't sound like something a hitter would say. Or an FBI agent.

Jules got down on the floor to take a peek. She hesitantly moved her head over the gap, still half-expecting to find herself staring down the barrel of a gun. Sitting on the keg below the hole, however, was a large blond guy with a heavy beard. His folded hands were empty, his head was tilted back, and his eyes were closed.

Oh, man! The hitter would be there any second!

"Hide!" she hollered at him, the front of her tongue shaping easily to the Scot's language. A muscle memory. "A hitman is coming! He'll kill us both. Now hide!"

The blond jumped to his feet but didn't go anywhere. In fact, he peed his pants—or he would have, if he'd been wearing any. From Juliet's viewpoint she could only see the man's kilt and the puddle beneath him expanding. Thank goodness for a dirt floor. His boots got it, though—probably because he couldn't seem to take his eyes off the hole.

"Sorry I scared you," she called. "But you need to hide. You don't want this guy to find you. He's a killer. Go!"

The man didn't budge. "Jillian?"

Jules was temporarily frozen by the fact that he'd mistaken her for *that woman*, but she shook it off.

"No, I'm not Jillian. It's God. Now go!"

The man burst out laughing. "Oh, Jillian. I've missed ye. Come down and give us a kiss before Monty can stop it."

"I tried to warn you, you idiot. Not my fault if you won't hide."

Juliet didn't want to see this strange Scot or anyone else get killed because of her. Maybe if she removed the plug she could drop down on the hitter and knock his weapon away. Or maybe it wasn't too late for the big lug to climb up inside with her. The hole might not be big enough for him, but they could at least try.

She tried to move the plug, but it only wobbled, even when she used the crowbar. She needed light, so she felt around for the little pile of supplies. It had to be there somewhere, but she kept missing it. She was so turned around she couldn't remember which direction she'd been facing before the sneeze, but the flashlights were gone—even the one that had died.

Which is impossible.

Finally, she found a handle. It turned out to be a hammer. Then she found a small tin cup, a couple of candles, a leather bag with a cork in it, but nothing she remembered seeing when she'd had a flashlight. The hammer wouldn't get the plug out of the hole any better than the crowbar, but at least it was another weapon.

The little room lightened and she turned back to the plug, to find that it had been removed. She was so surprised she nearly fell through the hole.

The light from below jumped and flared like firelight and the big blond stood directly beneath her, where the barrel had been, with his arms held out like he was planning on catching her. A large tree trunk was tipped against the wall behind him, next to the barrel. The end of it looked like it was just the right size to plug the hole. Maybe it was the source of the original plug.

The foaming puddle of urine was now only a shadow on the floor.

And still, the hitter hadn't come.

She whispered, in case he was listening just outside the room. "When he comes in, I'll jump on him and bash him with this hammer. Just don't look up!"

The blond man's face fell.

"No one is comin', lass. Daniel's guardin' the steps. Ye're safe, ye are. Now come down and give us a hug." Again, he raised his arms.

Great. They were both going to die. Why couldn't she have just backed up into the trees and waited Gabby's man out? She had enough chocolate in her pockets to keep from starving, and she'd left a couple bottles of water against that stupid squirrel's tree. She should have crawled back...but no, she'd frozen. She'd let fear cripple her and now she and at least two others would die for it—this one, and whoever Daniel was. Unless she could prove herself one last time and take the hitter down.

"I dinna ken what's running through that head of yers, Jillian," said the man. "But since you dinna seem to be goin' anywhere else, ye may as well come doon."

She'd never get the drop on the hitter with this big bear staring at her, and since it didn't look as if he was going to listen to a word she said, she gave up.

"I'm not Jillian, by the way." She dropped her legs through the hole and was caught against a large chest, then lowered to the ground. She stood on one foot, refusing to lower her stockinged foot to the ground until she had hopped side-ways away from the dark circle. Then she discreetly wiped one boot on the drier dirt.

"I don't suppose ye brought along Monty darlin'?"

"No, I'm alone," she said.

"And ye say ye're not Jillian. Then just what are ye doin' in the witch's hole, wearing Jillian's own face?"

Jules huffed out a breath and summoned up the courage to answer.

"I'm the sister, the sister she conveniently doesn't remember she has."

She'd been practicing that line for a while, only she'd hoped to say it to Jillian's face. Now she'd never get the chance. That was, unless the hitter was so stupid he couldn't find the basement. If she hurried, maybe she could get out of the castle without being caught, but she wasn't about to run away and let these people take a bullet meant for her.

Then she got an idea.

She grabbed the barrel and started tugging.

"Please, Mister," she said. "Do me a favor and climb up into the hole. Just for a few minutes. I wasn't kidding—a killer is gunning for me, and he can't know you're in here. There's nothing you can do for me, so you may as well save yourself."

She stopped trying to move the barrel. The guy was shaking his head, standing there with his arms crossed like she'd said something to piss him off.

"I'll never stick so much as me nose in that tomb, lass. And no man is coming. Daniel would have made a great clattering if someone tried to get past him."

Great. Well, at least she'd given it a shot. It wasn't like she could force him into the friggin' ceiling. Although...

She still had the hammer in her hand. It didn't feel very heavy, so she'd have to put her weight behind it. And she'd have to get him to turn around.

"Give me that, Jillian." He pulled the hammer out of her hands as if she wasn't resisting at all.

Considering the look he was giving her, like he wanted to tell her that little girls shouldn't play with such things, she thought it would be no use asking him to reach into the hole to get the crowbar for her. Since she'd been in New York, working alongside a lot of Greek men with the same attitudes, she knew better than to beat her head against the wall trying to convince this guy she could take care of herself.

"I'm hurt, I am, that ye'd think of clouting me with it," he said. "I'm Ewan. Do ye not remember me, lass?" His bottom lip, plump and pink, was suddenly visible in the middle of all that hair on his face.

"Oh, don't go getting your feelings hurt. It wasn't *your* head I was thinking about bashing," she lied. "And I told you, I'm not Jillian. My name's Jules."

"And ye left Jillian back there?" The guy kept looking up into the dark hole above their heads.

"Back where?" she asked.

"Back in the twenty-first century." He looked at her and frowned, like he wasn't buying the sister act and thought she was just Jillian, messing with him. And now he was messing with her.

What the hell. Life was short and getting shorter by the second. She'd play along.

"Oh?" she said. "Have I *left* the twenty-first century?"

"Aye, lass. Ye have. Welcome to the Year of Our Lord, fourteen hundred and ninety-six."

Well, if that were true, if the big Scot wasn't out of his gourd, that would explain why the hitter hadn't ever made it to the basement. And she wouldn't be responsible for anybody's death today. Not even her own. Too bad it couldn't have been true.

Then again, she *had* prayed for a miracle. Did that mean she might find a nice Highland warrior for sale too?

She laughed. Too bad all she had tucked in her bra was a Visa, and there were about eleven dollars left before it was maxed.

"Fourteen ninety-six?" she asked.

"Aye, lass."

Well, he certainly smells like a medieval Scot should. She snorted. *And he'd peed on the floor without so much as blinking.*

She looked at the dark outline in the dirt.

And the floor hadn't been dirt before.

She tried to remember. Maybe it had. It'd been pretty dark.

There was a torch hanging on the wall, for hell sakes.

Since she knew nothing about torches, that meant nothing.

And there had been that foreboding...

No. The warnings in her head were due to the fact that a hitter was minutes away from taking her out.

But the flashlights had disappeared.

Trying to think in a straight line was taking the fight right out of her and she wondered how long she'd be able to stay on her feet. Gabby's hitter would burst into the room any second, and she wouldn't be able to put up any kind of fight. How pathetic.

Wuss!

As her head grew lighter and she started to collapse, she prayed the blond would keep her from landing where he'd peed.

CHAPTER THREE

Hell hath no fury like a Gordon scorned.

When Quinn Ross exchanged places with Montgomery Ross, so the second man could live with his twenty-first century bride, in the future—without leaving a gaping hole in the past—he'd been amazed by the civilization of fifteenth century Scotland. That was, until he'd been taken prisoner by the mighty Clan Gordon. At that point, he realized that civilization related more to the people than to the modern conveniences he had so long associated with the word. Just because they didn't have indoor plumbing didn't mean they lived a mean life.

Except for the Gordons.

For all the clan's grandeur in size and strength, both of land and men, they were sorely lacking in the finer things of life. A washed bit of table, for one. An absence of foul odors, for another.

Dogs lived better, cleaner lives. In fact, every time the great door opened, the beasts would make a run for the outdoors, as if they had risked their very lives to come scrounge for food beneath the long tables, and had since thought better of it.

Quinn had been placed in the corner furthest from the fire and forced to kneel upon filthy rushes. He tried not to wonder at the sharp and pointy bits that pressed into his knees. His arms remained tied behind him and mere children had been placed as his guards, each one of the four possessing a finely sharpened short-sword, the tips of which were held to his neck, his back, and both shoulders. If he flinched away from one biting blade, he'd push himself against its opposite, and it took only a few painful slices into his skin to inspire him to remain as absolutely still as possible. If he stood and tried to bully past them, he was afraid of what those blades would accomplish when only waist-high.

The children laughed and waited for him to relax his posture once more, but he wouldn't give the little monsters the satisfaction. He marveled at the patience of ones so young. They took to their duty as if their suppers depended on it, which they may well have. When night fell and food started piling on the tables, only then were the monsters distracted from their bloody play.

The door banged open and a horde of ragged people poured through the opening. The last to enter, and casually, was a broad man with a red tinge to his gray beard that grew up the sides of his balding head. He looked immediately at the corner and locked gazes with Quinn.

Act as if you know him, Quinn reminded himself. Monty would have spoken with the man at least a dozen times, and it was still important for The Gordon to continue believing him to be Montgomery Ross.

"The Mighty Ross no longer resembles his statue, aye?" Laird Gordon, the Cock o' the North, swaggered over for a closer look. He sounded as if he had rocks in his throat. "Are ye ailin' mon? Is that why ye gave up yer clan to that cousin o' yers?" He bent low, looking into Quinn's eyes, then looked down at his neck and dabbed a dirty finger on the blood he'd found there. "Have our bairns been playing roughly with ye, Laird Ross?"

The Gordon had spoken carefully, as if to a child, or an elder that might no longer be right in the head. Is that what they all thought? That he'd lost his senses a year ago, when the switch had taken place? That could prove useful. In the old days, people with mental illness were given a wide berth. *Oh, aye, and burned as witches,* he recalled.

"Laird Gordon, is it?" He blinked a few times. "I know you, don't I?" Witch or no, he was likely about to die anyway. What harm could it do to mess with their heads?

"You used to know me, Ross." Still The Gordon used a kind tone.

"Yes. Before Isobelle's spirit came. You don't suppose she followed me here, do you?"

The hall fell silent. A moment passed before The Gordon threw his head back and laughed.

"Ye're a sly one, Montgomery Ross. That ye are. You've made a fine foe for many the long day. You'd have made a fine son-of-the-law if your sisters wouldna ruint it." And with that, the man turned and made his way to the high table. "Come. Enjoy yer last meal if ye can, with me bairns watchin' o'er ye."

The blades were drawn back, but the little monsters followed his every move as he straightened, stretched his legs then tested their ability to walk a straight line to the laird's table.

Once he was seated, the devil's wee army set up camp around his feet, aiming their blades in four directions as before. It was the North blade that worried him the most. The Gordon had known his business when he'd said, "Enjoy your meal if you can."

The meat was greasy. The trencher of bread looked as if a few meals had been served from it before, but Quinn couldn't be picky. His hands were cut loose and he ate whatever looked edible and even a few things that didn't, but he managed to keep it all down. The Gordon was famous for his dungeons and if the man wanted to give him a grand tour for a week or two before he died of hunger and thirst, Quinn would be wishing he could have this disgusting meal back again.

I should just stand and fight. Die with my boots on. Wasn't that the whole reason for trading Monty places? To put an end to my own suffering?

He'd expected to die from grief, after losing his wife, Libby. If he died now, he'd be with her all the sooner. Why drag it out? He'd been trying to picture her in his mind all evening, anticipating their ethereal reunion, but her image was never clear. Even remembering her photos wasn't working.

It had to be the stress. If he could relax, he'd remember every detail.

"I'll show ye the dungeon when ye're finished, Ross. Ye'll be impressed, ye will."

This was it. The chance to stand and die. He might be able to wrench a nice sharp blade from the boy in front of him, slit the throat of The Gordon, then be quickly skewered by his numerous full grown sons glaring at him from the other side of the table. And it would all be over.

Why did he hesitate?

Did he truly *want* to live? After years of mourning, was he ready to live again? How cruel was Fate if that were true, taking away his life just as he'd decided to embrace it?

His tense muscles relaxed with one deep, accepting breath. He would go where he was bid and no doubt use every last moment mourning the years he'd wasted. When he met her in Heaven, he was sure Libby would have a few choice words for him as well.

The thought of his wife brought to mind the wife Montgomery Ross would have had a year ago if his wedding hadn't been interrupted by a charming lass from Quinn's own century.

"How fares yer daughter, Gordon? Any chance—"

"Silence! Ye'll nay lay eyes upon the lass, let alone anything else." Gordon glanced at Quinn's crotch. "Ye had yer chance."

The laird ate faster then, more anxious to show off his dungeons, no doubt.

"I can honestly say, Laird, that I'm not the man you knew a year ago. I'm a kinder man. A forgiving man, even."

"Aye. 'Tis best ye left yer clan into Ewan Ross' hands, then. A laird canna lead with kindness and live long." Gordon eyed his sons, as if he expected one of them to attack him before the enemy at his side might do so. Six men, including Long Legs, glared back as they chewed, as if they were considering doing just that as soon as the food was gone.

Someone was missing.

"Hey, now," Quinn said. "Where's my brother of the law, then? Where's Cinead?"

The laird choked, then took a long pull of wine from his tankard. When he set the drink aside, Quinn realized the man was furious, but trying to control himself. Oh, he was going to end up in the dungeons all right. But at least there wouldn't be small boys cutting his flesh to ribbons there. Or so he hoped.

Finally, the other man spoke.

"Ye've no brother of the law here, Ross. When yer sister chose Neptune's arms over Cinead's, the marriage was nulled." The Gordon took a deep breath and the redness that had been climbing up his neck receded. "The man is above stairs, with his bride."

"Ah yes, I remember now." Quinn couldn't contain his excitement as histories began to bubble up in his mind.

Gordon frowned and leaned forward. "Ye remember what?"

"Morna's husband, Cinead, took a second wife and had nearly a dozen children, one of whom ruled the Gordon Clan after...you...died."

Oops.

Judging from the fury on the faces of Cinead's brothers, Quinn had hit a sore spot. But their anger wasn't directed at him, but at their father, as if they'd just had some suspicion verified. The fact that Quinn had been telling fortunes hadn't seemed to impress them at all.

The older man growled at the pack of wolves rising to their feet and Quinn realized the rocks in the man's voice was likely due to a lifetime of making that same noise.

"The man's no witch, ye dolts. He's tryin' to stir ye up so he can get away in the confusion." The Gordon turned a wild eye on Quinn. "Ye've not The Sight, Montgomery Ross. Otherwise ye would have known what yer sister Morna would do, and ye would have stopped her!"

Quinn snorted. "I knew enough of what would happen here that I gave Ewan the Clan, did I not?"

The Gordon snorted and banged his tankard for a refill.

What else? What else could he remember to make them think twice about keeping him prisoner? There had to be something. Something that happened near the year 1496!

"The grandson of the current King James will be handed the crown of England." They needn't know it would be given by an English woman.

"What do we care of English politics a hundred years from now?" Gordon snorted again. His sons' hackles were back down and they were now laughing at their father's comment like he was the king and they were pretending to kiss his arse.

"One day a man will walk on the moon," Quinn offered, sure that would give them pause.

Gordon's nose curled to one side. "I care more who walks onto Gordon lands, and today, someone did."

Another sore subject then.

"What would you like to ken of the future, Laird Gordon? I will trade any information for my freedom. I'm more surprised than anyone to find that I'd prefer to live."

"Ach, now. Bad timing that," said a strange voice very near his ear. He turned to see a small man, who had to be Cinead Gordon, forcefully lowering a club to his head.

CHAPTER FOUR

"Jillian. I beg ye to cease yer teasin'."

Jules was still sitting against the wall where the big man must have propped her up after she'd passed out, clearly due to a lack of food. She should have shoved a chocolate bar in her mouth before running down the side of the mountain. With no calories to burn, her body must have burned some brain cells instead, because nothing made sense. The hitter still hadn't found the room, hadn't shown up at the door, and hadn't shot his way into the tomb. He sure as hell wouldn't have given up.

Unless too many people had suddenly showed up for an evening tour...

Maybe he'd retreated and planned to come search for her later. If so, she wasn't going to wait around for him. But she couldn't seem to rouse herself. Maybe that chocolate would help. Better late than never.

She pulled a bar from her pocket and ate it quickly.

Mm. Better.

"Jillian," the big man said again.

Jules pointed to herself. "Jules. Okay? Jules. You call me Jillian again, and I'm going to have to hurt you."

"Bah!" He turned away, then turned back. "If ye be Jillian's sister, why did the lass never mention ye, let alone a sister who looks just like her?"

"I don't know if she knows about me, actually. I mean, it would be an obvious excuse for her to use, but it's not like she wouldn't remember me, right? I mean, I remember her just fine. And if we're identical, her memory should be just as good as mine."

"She may not ken? Surely, when she saw yer face she realized—"

"She hasn't seen me yet." Jules held up a hand in the universal request of *help me up*.

It took him a second to take the hint, but then he pulled her to her feet.

"Hasna seen ye? And how did ye come to be in the witch's hole then? I was of a mind Jillian and Monty would be guarding it a bit close, aye?"

It was a little embarrassing to admit to breaking and entering, but she'd had good reason.

"Two old women showed me how to get up inside, to hide. You know, from the guy who's going to be coming through that door any second now?" She moved over to the wall behind the door and tried to flatten herself against it.

He just stood there in the middle of the room with his hands on his hips like he still didn't believe there was any danger. But he looked none too pleased.

"Old women?" he asked. "Twins?"

Oops. They'd probably saved her life, or at least postponed her murder, and she'd ratted them out.

"Yes, twins. Like eighty or ninety years old, going on a hundred? They said they had another place they could hide, but the hole was my only option. You obviously know them, so that shoots your little fifteenth century story to hell."

He was nodding his head, but not like he was agreeing with her.

"Muirs, and no mistake. Far too many twins among them. Every century has them, it seems."

"Every century. Right," she said and rolled her eyes.

He looked at her sideways. "If I didna ken that Jillian was both a MacKay and a Ross, I'd have worried that the pair of ye might be Muir witches as well, aye?" Then he just waited, like he was expecting a confession.

"Witches? Now I know you're messing with me."

"Messing? I doona understand."

"Oh, give it up, would you?" She almost wished the hitter would come and get it over with. She was tired of arguing with Bushy-head.

He tossed his hands in the air. "Ye'll see, soon enough I reckon. Whenever the hole's been opened, the Muirs ken it. Somehow." He shrugged and rubbed the back of his neck. "Too bad yer set of Muirs didna think to trick Monty back into the hole. I could use his aid. I'm right desperate for it."

"And Monty is Montgomery?"

Ewan frowned as if by not knowing Monty she'd spouted some sort of blasphemy. "Jillian's husband. The former laird of Clan Ross and my cousin. I'd be ever so happy to see his gob, but e'en more so, now that I've..." He grimaced, reached for the torch, then turned to the door.

"You've what?"

He sighed and raised the light higher. His shadow swung around on the wall behind him as he turned back to her.

"I've lost his great nephew."

Jules shook her head. "I don't understand. His *great* nephew? How could you have lost someone that can't possibly have been born?"

"Jules, is it? I told you plain. 'Tis the year fourteen hundred and ninety-seven, and so it is. Monty is from this century. The nephew is from yours."

The wall wasn't much to hold onto, so she leaned sideways onto a stack of smaller barrels. She started shaking her head but then couldn't seem to stop. If she hadn't eaten the chocolate, she probably would have been passing out again.

"So I've somehow gone through *time*? This tomb is like some kind of *tardis*?" She'd watched only a couple of episodes of *Dr. Who*, but apparently it was a couple too many. She wouldn't have even known the word *tardis* if the bookkeeper at the restaurant and one of the waiters hadn't been big *Dr. Who* geeks.

"I dinna ken the word *tardis*, lass. But they go inside, they doona come out. 'Tis all I've seen. I'll not try it myself, mind ye."

"You're Montgomery's cousin? He's from...here? No wonder." Then she realized what this Ewan had been trying to tell her. "And a little boy is missing?"

"The lad's name is Quinn. But he's no wee laddie."

She was so relieved. The thought of a little kid— from the twenty-first century—getting lost out there in Medieval times, was just too sickening to think about. If, of course, she believed that Medieval Scotland was truly out there.

"Quinn's a man grown. Looks to be Monty's own spit, he does. So when Monty needed to go to your time, to be with Jillian, Quinn came back here, to take Monty's place. And now, The Gordon has 'im."

No friggin' way! There was another Highlander, just like Jillian's husband. *Just* like him.

Maybe, just maybe, I should say my prayers more often.

Above their heads, there was movement. Not from the great hall, but from the tomb.

"Where the devil are ye?" a man muttered.

The hitter!

How the hell had he gotten inside the tomb without going through the bottom, like she had? No way could he have broken through the wall, or she'd have heard it!

Her missing boot fell through the hole and landed on unholy wet ground.

Holy shit!

Jules snatched the boot up and put a finger over her lips, then motioned for Ewan to hurry out of the room with her. Thankfully, he followed without argument, bringing the torch with him. The door opened outward and Jules shut it behind her, then leaned against it.

"Can we block this door?" she whispered. "That's the man who's after me. He's got a gun. I'm sure he'll kill anyone who gets in his way."

The Scot nodded, handed her the torch, then rolled yet another barrel out of the dark and in front of the door.

"This should hold him for a mite," he said. "But your only way back home is through that tomb, lass. If ye and Jillian are to meet, ye must face this man first, and no mistake. Sooner or later."

"Later sounds good to me."

The hitter beat on the door, having found his way out of the tomb with little light to help him.

"Juliet Bell! When I get my hands on ye... Listen, lass. If ye let me out now, it will go much smoother for ye. Ye have my word. No harm will come to ye."

She could hear him breathing against the door. He was probably listening to her breathe too. After a few seconds, he went back to beating on the door.

"He'll just blow the hinges off," she warned the Scot.

"Truly?" The big man rolled his eyes in the torchlight. "Perhaps you underestimate the quality of a Scotsman's carpentry, or the strength of a full barrel of whisky. He'll not get out so easily. Now come up into the light. Let me get a good look at you, and I'll decide the message I wish you to give to Monty, once ye've got the courage to go back, of course. But tell me, why does yer pursuer call ye Juliet *Bell*?"

"Bell is a long story. And I don't let anyone call me Juliet."

The door seemed to be holding up well to the pounding, so they moved away. Ewan took back his torch and led her along the dirt-floored hallways. She was so turned around, she had no choice but to trust him.

Dirt floors. God, help me. I've lost my mind.

"But mayhap you could find your courage sooner, rather than later," Ewan said. "As Quinn may not live long enough for Monty to be of any help. I would send others to bring his wandering hide back to Ross lands, but none else kens who the lad truly is. I fear a close look by our own lads might give the game away. We've been careful to keep the clan from getting too close. I imagine word of an imposter would be the type of tale to pass through the generations, aye? And Jillian was ever one to go on and on about the dangers of changing history."

Jules snorted. "Yeah, I'll bet she was."

Ewan stopped and looked at her. "What do ye mean, lass?"

"She's got the world at her feet. Why would she wish anything different? She's probably thrilled with the way things have turned out. Changing the past would screw up her little fairy tale, right?"

And just like that, Jules was glad she'd gone back in time. Maybe there was a reason she was there. Maybe she could fix all kinds of things. Screw Jillian's rules about changing history.

"Lass," said Ewan. "Jillian has a kind and gentle soul. If she believes that changing history will ruin lives, I have no doubt it is not her life for which she fears. She loves Monty, and yet she was willing to give him up so that Morna and Ivar could be together. You'll find no selfishness in Jillian's heart."

"I hope so," she said. It was the nicest thing she could think of to say since Ewan was clearly on Team Jillian.

Finally, he stopped yakking and started moving again.

But inside, there was a giant scrapbook of pain, and it had Jillian's name written on the front in big jagged letters.

CHAPTER FIVE

Quinn woke to a painful throb at the back of his head. He was lying on a cold dirt floor, in the dark.

For a moment, he thought he was still stuck in his dream and waited for the softness of his mattress to register, but it didn't. Then, as he had hundreds of times in the last year, he remembered which century he was in. But this was the first time he'd awakened on the ground.

And it was still night?

His last memory was of going stir crazy inside the castle, of sneaking away without his young escort... And then he remembered the heather. He could still feel the scratches on his arms from gathering the branches. Then he remembered the scratches from sharp little knives.

"Shite."

He rolled to his side to take the pressure off the back of his broken skull, and every muscle in his body complained. At first, he wondered if they'd beaten him, after he'd lost consciousness, but then he remembered all those hours of kneeling at attention to keep those blades from breaking his skin. The pain from a beating wouldn't have gone quite so deep.

A smell wafted around him when he moved—the smell of a tomb where a body would have rotted away

for years. The smell of stale urine was a pleasant relief—
he only hoped the urine wasn't his.

No. His kilt was dry. Thank goodness the ground
below him was dry as well. The blade was gone from his
boot.

So, this was the famous Gordon dungeons. They
were so close to the sea, he expected it to be damper—
not that he was complaining. But if he was going to die
here, he could wish for harsher conditions that might
speed along his demise.

And even as the thought presented itself, his
stomach tightened.

He remembered now. That moment at Gordon's
table, when he realized he wanted to live. Lord help him,
when had that happened?

Quinn sat up and searched the darkness, straining to
capture even the smallest hint of a reflection. He needed
to know what surrounded him, but he would not go
feeling about. He could only wait for someone to come
with a light. Of course, he might be able to persuade
them to come sooner...

"Gordon! Gordon! You can either grant me some
light or I shall have the devil call up a fire, here, beneath
your home. Which do you prefer?"

There was movement, but he had no idea how far
away it had been. Were there other's sharing his dark
hotel?

"Who's there?" he said.

When there was no answer, he tried again in Scots.
Still no answer.

The pain in his head bid him lie down again, and he
did so, but gently. As he was just about to drift off to
sleep, the room grew lighter. Someone must have heard
him after all.

He suppressed a groan as he pushed against the floor
and forced himself up to sit. There was nothing in his

ten-by-ten cell to sit upon, so he stayed put. A young lad with bulging eyes carried a torch to light the way for a tall, thin man. At the entrance to the dungeon, about thirty feet off to the left, an old man took a seat. Considering the bandages across his eyes, Quinn guessed he was blind—a natural babysitter for a prisoner kept in the dark. He must have been the one to carry his message to The Gordon.

Quinn was also pleased when he recognized his visitor, Long Legs.

"Why Long Legs! What a pleasant surprise ye make."

The thin man laughed." Ah, but ye were not so pleased at our first meeting, were ye, Laird Ross?"

"Mmm. No. I can't say as I was," he admitted, wishing now he had taken his stand back in the heather and perhaps gotten away before Orie could have come along.

"You were bellerin' for something?" Long Legs raised a patient brow and folded his arms.

"Yes," Quinn said cheerfully. "The Gordon promised me a tour of his dungeons and I had no light by which to see it."

"Well, then, look yer fill. I suggest you be quick about it." Long Legs turned to go.

Desperate for a few more minutes of light, Quinn looked about him, searching for some topic of conversation. His eyes caught the white reflection of bare bone in the next cell.

"Perhaps ye could pass on a request to The Gordon," he said.

It worked. The man came back, and his light-bearer with him.

"Aye, sure. What would ye like, yer lairdship? New straw fer yer mattress no doubt? A better wine with yer supper?"

Quinn gestured to his left, to the only other cell between his and the entrance. "A bit of housekeeping is in order, aye? Seems this one's overdue for a grave. Was his crime the same as mine? Stepping on Gordon soil?"

Long Legs expanded as he filled himself with a deep breath. His eyes, in the shadows, flickered with some emotion Quinn could not identify. If it were possible, the young man grew taller and looked down upon him as a hawk about to rip apart the mouse in its grip. And Quinn found himself grateful for the bars between them. Otherwise, he might be forced to kill the man in defense of himself—that was, if he somehow found the strength to get to his feet. It had been a mighty mean blow he'd taken to the head.

The light moved as the small lad stepped to the side and raised the torch. Shadows quivered as the boy took in the sight of a skeleton wearing meager rags and even less flesh. It sat at the back of the cell with its arm raised, its wrist dangling from a ring in the wall.

Long Legs, Quinn noticed, turned his head away, but slightly. And though he refused to look at the body, it seemed as if he were concentrating on it just the same.

Quinn could not resist prodding. There was a story here. He would hear it.

"Would you look at that?" he said. "He's thin enough now to free his hand, and yet he willna flee. Perhaps he has come to love The Gordon's famous dungeons and prefers to stay."

Long Legs swallowed. When he spoke, his voice was heavy with emotion, though he tried for nonchalance.

"Famous? My father's dungeons are famous?"

So. Long Legs *was* a son. And here was yet another chance to mess with a Gordon's head. Besides, the damned prophecy, the one that had shaped his life, might make the difference for him. If they believed he had real power, they might free him in the end. He needed only plant enough seeds of unease. And if they wanted to be rid of the unease, they'd need to be rid of him. He only hoped they would believe it was safer to release him, than to burn him.

And Long Legs had already proven that he was a sucker for rumors.

"Aye. Famous. Five hundred years from now, folks will still speak of these dungeons by the sea. Tell me of this fellow," he pointed to the skeleton. "Perhaps he is also famous. Or will be."

The light quivered harder than before. Apparently he'd done a better job of scaring the young one than an emaciated corpse had done.

Long Legs stood for a moment, staring into Quinn's eyes. He opened his mouth once, but thought better of it, Quinn supposed, because he soon turned and walked away.

"Come," he said to the torchbearer.

The lad backed away, as if he was too frightened to turn his back on Quinn.

"Leave the light, Son of Gordon. I care to stay awake for a wee while. And I meant what I said, about getting firelight from the devil if I must."

Long Legs snorted and spun around. "It is my leave to deal with you as I will. You are *my* prisoner, not my father's. So I will leave you the light—if you answer my question with the truth."

"Ask it," Quinn said, pleased a seed was already taking root.

Long Legs nodded to the lad who walked to the wall and dropped the torch into a loop, then he shooed him to the entrance and the lad hurried up the steps and away. "Leave us," he said to the old man, who followed, albeit slowly, after the boy.

Long Legs walked back to the cell but stood away from the bars as if Quinn might jump to his feet and get a hold of him. Quinn tried not to smile.

"You want to know if what I said was true, if the Runt's child ends up ruling your clan."

Long Legs shook his head.

"Truly?" Quinn was surprised. The sons of clan chieftains often fought wars over their father's power. Why would the Gordon's sons, of all people, be different? "What do you wish to know?"

Long Legs shook a dismissive hand. "Cinead is an ambitious bastard. He has much to prove, as ye well ken. I was not surprised to hear his seed would one day rule the clan, but I would know how ye ken this is to be. And do not think me daft. I will hear the truth of it, not silly tales of the devil whispering in yer ear. For if the devil is all the threat ye have, ye'll get nothing, including yon torch. The devil will be easier to appease than my father."

So much for playing on the man's superstitions. But there was a weakness there, to be sure. If he told this man the truth, would he win an ally?

Suddenly he was struck with an idea.

"What is your name?" he demanded.

"Percy."

"Percy Gordon, I will tell you the truth, if you think you can bear it?"

The man smirked. Close enough.

The only sound was that of the fire, fighting itself at the end of the torch. Percy was as quiet as the guest in the next cell. Quinn felt the urge to cross himself against the blackness at his back, lest the devil feel he'd been invited, but he could not show such weakness.

"My name is Quinn Ross. I am from the future, from the year twenty-twelve. Muir witches brought me here, to stand in the stead of Montgomery Ross."

"And they changed yer face to look like the laird?" Long Legs looked unimpressed. He'd have to do better.

"There was no need to change my face. I am Montgomery's great nephew twenty times over. I carry his...looks." He'd almost said DNA.

Long Legs weighed the information for a minute. Indeed, a year ago, it took Quinn days to digest it all when Jillian MacKay disappeared in front of him, when she'd first slipped back in time to fulfill the prophecy. The fact they'd been standing in the tomb when it happened, had not made it any easier to believe.

"Even if this is true, how can you be of any use to me?" Percy stepped closer.

The man may not believe him, but if there was something in it for Percy, he would at least be hopeful Quinn was telling the truth. It might be enough to win the Gordon's son to his side.

"Because I have the ability to move between the future and the past. I can change the future. Because I know what will happen, I can change it from happening."

Okay, that wasn't quite true and wasn't the most logical argument, but it was all Quinn could think of at the moment considering the bump on his head and the pain in his skull. His best chance of rescue might be from within Clan Gordon itself. And what better reason could Long Legs appreciate than to have Quinn change the future so that Percy Gordon ended up with the Gordon scepter?

"You think me simple." Percy shook his head and backed away. "I can change the future, simply enough, by slittiin' Cinead's throat before he has his offspring."

Quinn wasn't about to point out the man's new bride might already be pregnant. He wasn't going to be the reason behind the murder of an innocent woman.

Or was it already too late?

He'd broken one of Jillian's sacred rules. He'd told the Gordon brothers who their enemy was, and now Long Legs was considering killing his brother to change the future. Quinn had promised Jillian a hundred times over that he would be cautious. She was going to kill him unless he thought of a reason why Long Legs and his brothers should keep their hands off The Runt.

Then he had it. God and Ewan might damn the Muir witches, but they were often the answer to his problems.

"There is one thing you should know, Percy," he said gravely, "about the man who kills Cinead Gordon."

Percy took a deep breath and waited.

Quinn stared him in the eyes. "It's part of the prophecy."

Percy rolled his eyes. "What prophecy?"

"Oh, come now. Even the Gordons ken about the prophecy given by Isobelle before she died."

Percy nodded once. "I've heard a bit. Tell me the whole of it, then."

Oh, but that was the easiest request Quinn had ever heard.

He'd been an attorney, back in the real world of the twenty-first century, but after Libby died, he'd walked away from it, gone back home. And for all the years since his wife's death, Quinn's role at Castle Ross was to tell the tourists all about the prophecy. It was almost a relief to get to tell it again, even though he'd told it a thousand times before. It had been over a year since he'd done it last, and he was eager to see if he remembered the script. Of course he could not tell it verbatim. Percy Gordon would not know of Shakespeare and the tale of Romeo and Juliet.

"I will tell you first how the prophecy came to be." Quinn moved to the side of the cell to lean his back against the bars there.

Percy walked toward the stairs and returned with the chair used by the blind man. He sat at an angle and Quinn got the impression the man did so to avoid the sight of the dead man more than to face Quinn head on.

"In the year 1494, the duty to one's clan was far more important than any notion of love."

Percy snorted.

"I must tell in the manner it was taught to me. You must bear with me if you would hear the whole of it."

Percy nodded and waved impatiently.

"...far more important that any notion of love," he repeated, getting a run at it. "Clan meant survival. Allegiances meant survival. And when our fair Morna's hand was the price we had to pay for aligning ourselves with the powerful Gordons, Morna did her duty. Her true love, Ivar MacKay, understood. By the way, Ivar and Morna were not so understanding after all, but I'll explain that later."

Quinn returned to the script, to the part that always excited the crowds.

"Isobelle Ross was a witch...and Morna's sister. And even though she was a strange and opinionated woman for those times, Isobelle loved her sister dearly. She would have changed places with Morna, but the Gordons would not consider a union with the wilder sibling who was already suspected of not being right in the head. But Isobelle couldn't bear to see Morna suffer over the loss of her Ivar, so she placed an enchantment on a simple torque."

Back in his day, Quinn would have pointed to a copy of the necklace they displayed upon a bed of black velvet. The crowd would have leaned in. Aye, but he missed the crowds.

"Isobelle promised Morna that one day soon a faery would claim this bit of silver, a faery bearing the Immediate Blood of both the MacKay and the Ross clans, one who would have the power to reunite our Morna with her Ivar. They needed only be patient."

At that point in the show, he would have paused for a drink of water. He only hoped his little story would earn him the same when it was over.

"Unfortunately, innocent women were burned as witches, let alone strange sisters who spewed prophecy. Instead of Isobelle's plan easing her sister's aching heart, it broke the organ entirely. Word spread like the plague, and The Kirk came to put Isobelle to the witch's test.

"Montgomery was laird and as such held some power. But there was no power to equal that of The Kirk in those times, or rather, in your times, Percy. Thus Laird Ross, my great uncle twenty-one times removed, was unable to spare his sister from condemnation. He was, however, able to change the manner in which she was to die."

"The oddly shaped construction on the stone dais is truly Isobelle's tomb, built by Montgomery for both his sister and the accursed torque, built there so she would always be near him. Isobelle was spared from a stranglin' and a burnin', but she could not escape her death sentence. Before the last stones were set, his very-much-alive sister and her offensive creation were sealed inside the wall by her brother's hand."

Quinn hoped that speaking of Montgomery as someone other than himself might help Percy come to picture them as two separate men. He struggled with the twist of his gut that reminded him that he'd promised never to tell the tale. But he wasn't about to tell the most important secret of all. That secret would have to accompany him to his grave. He only hoped that grave was not destined to be a pile of ashes tossed into the North Sea, at the hands of a Gordon.

"Montgomery thought only to spare his sister the horror of being burned," Quinn continued. "He had no idea that he'd sentenced them both to madness. Day after day he sat next to the tomb, listening for any sound from his sister within, tormenting himself, regretting his interference. But The Kirk would not allow him to take back the bargain he'd struck. And during that time, Montgomery would cross and re-cross that invisible line into lunacy, thrilling over every little sound Isobelle made, only to cry to God to end her suffering. More than once, he tried to tear down the stones to put her out of her misery, only to be halted by The Kirk's henchmen who stood guard until the witch was clearly dead. After ten and two days, the little sounds ceased...and the haunting began."

At this point in the presentation, the crowd would have been startled by the squawk of bagpipes starting up a melancholy set. The next part of the story involved himself.

"My family, in the future, will be caretakers of Castle Ross. It will be my duty to see that the history of Montgomery and his sisters is retold."

Percy laughed. "Aye. I can see where ye have the gift for spinning tales, Laird Ross. But I heard no mention of my brother Cinead, as yet."

"Ah, but I'm not finished with the telling. For one day, in my time—over five hundred years from now, mind—a lass comes to Castle Ross with the Immediate Blood of both Ross and MacKay clans runnin' through her veins. With the help of a pair of Muir Witches—for there are Muirs in my time as well—we helped the lass into the tomb, gave her the torque to wear, and sent her back here, to save Morna and Ivar."

He wasn't about to tell The Gordon's son that Jillian had actually reunited the couple and taken them back to the twenty-first century, since the Gordons believed that Morna threw herself into the sea. Nothing good could come from telling a mighty and prideful man that he'd been fooled by a neighboring clan, let alone a woman.

It was a cowardly thing he'd done, to tell Percy his own secret in hopes of saving himself, but his tongue and his wits were the only weapons left to him.

"And she failed, this woman from the future." Percy snorted, but Quinn could tell the man was eager to hear the rest.

"Aye, her good intentions went terribly wrong. Even Isobelle came back from the grave to try and sort things out. Her ghost cried out from the tomb on the day Montgomery was to marry yer sister, as ye may recall."

"I heard of it. I was not there."

The sad note in Percy's voice made Quinn look up.

The man was staring into the next cell. After a moment, he shook himself and turned his attention back to Quinn, who pretended not to have noticed.

"After Morna was brought back here," he said, "ye ken what she did."

Percy turned angry, but Quinn couldn't guess why.

"Then the prophecy was not fulfilled after all," the man snarled and got to his feet. "And whatever prophecy there might have been for the one who kills Cinead is worthless as well."

Quinn shook his head calmly.

"Nay. As soon as Ivar heard the news, he came to Castle Ross and threw himself from the northeast tower. They *were* united. In death. Had the woman not come, they might have gone on, pining away for each other for the rest of their lives. The prophecy said nothing about reuniting them in *life*. Only that they would be reunited. And the rest of the prophecy states clearly that as compensation to Cinead Gordon for the loss of Morna— for he was destined to lose her, one way or another—a curse was placed on the head of the one who would spill his blood."

"Pah!" Percy paced for a moment, then settled back on his short stool. "Tell me this curse."

Biggest fear. Biggest fear. What did every man fear? What would make this man frightened enough to—

"Impotence." Quinn even managed to say it with a straight face.

"What mean you?"

"The man who kills Cinead Gordon will be impotent for the rest of his days. He will have no power. Over anything." When it looked as though the word had little meaning to the man, he realized he must elaborate. "Neither will be able to bed a woman. Ever again."

Percy's eyes widened and he stood and walked away. He was buying it. The only risk, which Quinn realized too late, was whether or not Percy was interested in bedding women. One never knew.

Percy paced, which stirred up the smell from the poor man in the next cell. He seemed to notice it too, for his nose curled and he stopped pacing. A moment later, he nodded, as if he'd come to some conclusion, then he walked to the torch and removed it from its ring. Instead of coming back to let Quinn out, which was too much to have hoped for anyway, he headed for the archway.

"Wait a moment," Quinn called. "I answered your question. We had a bargain."

"Nay, Ross," he called, without turning back or slowing his step, "I have yet to decide whether or not I believe ye."

Quinn was once again left in the dark.

He tried to remember the details of his cell and crawled to his right, putting as much distance between himself and the rotting corpse as possible. In truth, he was getting used to the smell unless someone stirred the air.

He rested his back again to alleviate the soreness of his stomach muscles. He was thirsty, but alive, and if all went well, his little prophecy would keep Cinead alive long enough for history to unfold as it was supposed to. And hopefully, he'd planted enough fantasy in Percy's brain that the man would be coming back to place a request for the future—hopefully before Quinn was thin enough to slip through the bars, but too dead to do so.

He closed his eyes, content to sleep for a while.

***

Quinn hadn't quite drifted off before the inside of his eyelids turned red, then orange. Someone was coming.

Only it wasn't Percy. It was the violent little man, Cinead.

Shite!

Two large guards entered Quinn's cell and took him by the arms.

"I've just saved your life, you know." Quinn needed the future head of Clan Gordon to think kinder, gentler thoughts about him. The fact that the man had come so closely on the heels of his younger brother gave Quinn hope he might have overheard the end of their conversation. The rough handling by the guards took that hope away.

The small man seemed none too proud to carry his own torch and held it aloft while Quinn was brought before him.

"I'm aware of that," he said. His voice was quite normal, though Quinn didn't know what he'd been expecting. "Percy willna be killing me in me sleep, but that willna keep the others from killing me in the bright light o' day, will it?"

So. The man had heard the conversation after all.

As Cinead stuffed a rag into Quinn's mouth, he noticed swelling across the smaller man's face. There was a good chance the curve of his nose was new.

Quinn nodded, accepting the blame for the other man's beating. He just hoped Percy might share the prophecy with the rest of his brothers. Of course, if he hoped his brothers would become impotent in all things...

Shite!

"It's time to meet yer maker, Laird Ross, be he god or devil." Cinead led the way out of the dungeon, and as relieved as Quinn was to get away from the smell, he'd gladly go back and wait for Percy to come 'round.

The little parade proceeded out of the castle proper, past the inner bailey, and into the wider outer bailey where a makeshift gallows had been erected in the moonlight. Next to the gallows, a pole rose out of a stack of wood and Quinn had seen the drawings of enough such constructions to know it was meant for the burning of a witch.

And witch burning seemed all the more barbaric when one found himself to be the witch in question. He should have kept his mouth shut. The Gordon hadn't been impressed by his fortune telling but he'd recognized a grand opportunity to rid himself of an enemy. But why send Cinead to do the deed in the middle of the night? Or was it only that the little man wanted his own revenge and would take it out from under the old man's nose?

Perhaps there was good reason Cinead Gordon would end up leading his clan.

The future laird looked up into his face and grinned.

"I know what ye think, Laird Ross," he said. "But if we doona allow you to speak, you canna call the devil to your rescue, aye?" He stopped just below the noose and jumped up to swat at it, like he was proving he was tall enough to reach it.

But he wasn't.

The noose hung perfectly still. The men holding Quinn stifled their laughter.

"Get on with it," Cinead hissed. "Someone's coming,"

Quinn tried to turn, to see if maybe Percy had finally decided to act, but the guards pushed him forward. One had a fist full of hair at the back of his head that kept Quinn from seeing anything but the closing proximity of his head to the noose. With his arms tied behind his back once again, there was only so much bucking he could do. His only hope was to bob and weave to keep that noose off his head. And pray for a miracle, of course.

A forceful blow stunned him for a wee second, but it was enough. The rough rope fell on his collar bone, then tightened against his neck as he plowed his body into one of the guards. Unfortunately, he picked the wrong guard. It was the second man who held the tail end of the rope, and he pulled down hard to bring Quinn to heel. The abrasive rope cut into the delicate skin below his jaw. The growth of two days' beard did little to protect him.

"Climb up there," The Runt demanded, pointing to a short stool.

Quinn just glared down at him, wishing with his eyes that the brothers would have beaten him to death and damn the future consequences.

"Just a moment, brother!" A woman's voice came from behind, from the direction of the castle. "As his former fiancée, I would have words with the bastard before ye kill 'im."

Oh, jolly.

At least his death wouldn't be in vain; the Gordon lass would have some closure. And while he waited for the woman to appear, he wondered what he might have requested for a last meal, had they offered him one.

A deep fried Twinkie sounded just the ticket.

CHAPTER SIX

Jules followed the blond and the torch up out of the cellars and into the light. At the top of the steps, another man turned. He looked her up and down but showed no reaction. She tried to do the same and not stare at his plaid costume.

"Daniel," said Ewan. "This is Jules. Guard her with yer life. She's kin."

Kin?

The statement sent a little chill through her chest, even though it was an exaggeration.

Daniel gave a quick bow. Then, while he looked past them, down the steps, he pulled a tiny pouch from around his neck, kissed it, then tucked it back into his poorly fitting shirt.

"Dinna be daft, Daniel," said Ewan. "Have ye seen the Muirs anywhere about?"

"Nay, yer lairdship."

Jules jumped when she heard footsteps behind her and turned, ready to launch herself at Gabby's man since she had nothing she could use for a weapon—Ewan still held the hammer. She only hoped a tumble back down the steps would break the hitter's neck and not hers.

But it wasn't a man at all. It was a matching set of women in long dresses, dresses that looked more like medieval costumes. Like Daniel's.

Holy shit! Was it really 1496?

Maybe the hitter really had entered the tomb the same way she had—from another century. Maybe she really wasn't dreaming. Maybe she was going to be sick.

As the look-alikes climbed the stairs, she realized the women were much younger than the ones who had put her in the tomb. Fiftyish. Long, straight, strawberry blond hair that was turning gray in all the same places. They even held onto their skirts the same way. It was like watching a woman walk up the steps while someone held a mirror next to her.

Very freaky.

There was something unnerving about their matching smiles, though. Jules didn't trust them for a second.

Ewan let out a deep sigh and she couldn't tell whether he was glad to see them or really disappointed.

"Speak of the sisters and they'll appear," he muttered. "Ye'll see I spoke the truth about them."

The women in question reached the landing. One of them looked surprised to see Jules. The other one kept her eyes on Ewan and gave him a little bow.

"Laird Ross," she said. "Ye've a busy cellar this day it seems."

Ewan shook his head slightly. "Hopefully, ye're the last to come out of it. Won't the pair of ye sup with us this e'en?" The last sentence came out through his teeth.

The second woman gave him a sly nod. "Such a kind laird ye are, Ewan. We'd like nothing more than to sit and have a grand chat with Jillian."

The way the woman was eyeing her, Jules knew she understood perfectly well she wasn't Jillian. Was she hoping for an introduction? Or did she expect Jules to lie about who she was? She had to admit, it was a little intriguing to know that her sister had known these people. She just wondered why Jillian had come to be there in the first place.

Jules had been about nine when she'd demanded to know why her grandmother had stolen Jillian and disappeared. They'd been searching for six years and the only explanation her parents had given was, "*Ivy MacKay is mentally ill.*" But at nine, Jules wasn't buying it anymore. Finally, they'd told her what the paranoia was all about, that the old woman was certain there were people in Scotland who would try to kill Jillian, who would try to bury her alive. The crazy part was that Grandmother claimed that she'd traveled to the future and been there when those murderers were planning it.

Since Jules' mother couldn't believe her, the old woman had taken Jillian away, to protect her. And back in the days of no internet, it was much harder to find someone who didn't want to be found.

Now that Jules realized she, too, had been convinced to climb into that Scottish tomb—and apparently traveled through time—she was beginning to think her grandmother wasn't as paranoid or crazy as her parents had believed.

But even if she hadn't been, that didn't excuse her for the hell she'd made of their lives. No amount of money could make up for that. And half a fortune wasn't going to excuse Jillian for not trying to come home.

No. She wasn't Jillian. She'd never be Jillian.

Jules put her hands in the pockets of her jacket. "My name is Jules. I'm not Jillian."

"Of course ye're not Jillian." The woman winked. "How silly of me. I can see the difference now."

Jules resisted the urge to ask what the woman saw that made her so different. She never wanted to look like

Jillian, of course, but she didn't care for the feeling that she was lacking in some way. She wasn't jealous.

Well, maybe just a little envious—it didn't help that Jillian was married to the mouth-watering Highlander that had started to haunt her dreams for no reason whatsoever. The website for Castle Ross Tours said the man was Quinn Ross, but it must have been the name he used for tourists. Jillian's husband was Montgomery Ross, or Monty, as Ewan called him.

In her dreams, she'd never known his name, only that they had to stay together or...something bad would happen. And she'd always been pretty sure it would be bad for them both. Pretty melodramatic for a dream with a stranger, but anyone who'd laid eyes on Montgomery Ross wouldn't laugh. Even the shot of him on the website took her breath away and made her heart stutter—and this from a girl who never got breathy over anything but a great dessert.

Every night, when she'd fallen asleep, she'd willed herself back into that dark dream. She'd make it there, too, but only every couple of weeks when she went to bed early. Maybe their dreams only linked up when they were both asleep, and time-zone-wise, that meant earlier in New York.

Holy shit. What if the guy was really dreaming about her too? What if he might be sharing the whole emotional ride?

Jules shook her head and sighed. It wouldn't make any difference if he was—he'd just think it was a dream about his own wife. And that thought made her instantly sad.

She dragged along next to Ewan, hoping he'd take her somewhere quiet where she could sit down and shut her eyes for a minute. What she really needed was to just confront her sister and get the hell away from her, and her husband, but the woman was even farther out of her reach than before. Over five hundred years away. And the only short cut back was through that tomb, now inconveniently guarded by Jules' personal Angel of Death.

It was just so surreal. What had it been, an hour since she'd started running down that hill? She couldn't have made it into another time zone, and yet she'd traveled centuries? What a crock. Maybe, after she'd rested a bit, she could figure out another explanation. And it was a great plan...

...until they rounded a corner.

CHAPTER SEVEN

Since she'd come through the back entrance to the castle, Jules had never seen the great hall except in a photo gallery on the internet. But this was no polished museum. It was a madhouse. Tables filled every corner except for the raised dais where three large items were the only decoration. The tomb—the one she had to have been inside. A giant carved throne which looked a little too imposing to sit in. And a massive statue of Jillian's husband, in his kilt. It looked so much like him—or at least what he looked like through binoculars—that she expected him to walk right off the stage.

But the most shocking part, and the thing making her nauseous again, was the crowd.

They were all dressed in medieval garb. Every last one of them. Women, children—even the dogs looked a little barbaric.

She turned back to Ewan and took a good look at his clothes. His kilt was nothing like any kilt she'd ever seen in real life. In the movies, yes. But modern day Scotsmen did not dress this way, not even for their Highland Games and Scottish Festivals. She knew. Her parents had taken her to them every year. They'd always been searching the crowds for some reason. When she was big enough, she realized they were searching for Jillian.

Always Jillian. Their lives had centered on finding Jillian. If her parents hadn't been driving across that long stretch of Wyoming highway, hunting down one more lead, they would have still been alive. But they'd been sure they were going to find her that time, just like every other time, and Jules had refused to go along. She found a friend whose parents would let her sleep over for a few days. She hadn't even told them goodbye.

Of course, if she'd have gone along, she'd be dead too. No one could have survived, even with seat belts. She still wasn't sure how she felt about that. But she'd been pretty damn sure how she felt about Jillian.

Out of habit, and a sort of homage to her parents, she'd kept going to the festivals. She'd even looked for Jillian, but her reasons were different. She wanted her sister to know she was responsible for their deaths, responsible for how they'd wasted the short lives they'd had—looking for a girl who never looked back.

Watching the Scots gathering around for their evening meal, all the anger came flooding back, swirling in her nearly empty stomach like the ghost of a rotten meal—anger so sharp it brought tears to her eyes. She nearly turned around and headed back to the cellar, ready to confront her sister, mad enough to rip off the hitter's head and spit down the hole. But she'd never get past him. Not without a gun. And she wasn't sure these people even knew what a gun was.

She let out a harsh breath. It was no use fighting it. She really was Dr. Who, and there was a monster inhabiting her tardis. She had to figure out a way to capture that monster so the friggin' episode could end— so she could turn off the nightmare.

Or maybe the Monster would go back the way he'd come, see Jillian, and kill her instead, mistaking her for Jules.

One of the Muir sisters gasped, as if she'd read her thoughts. Then she frowned at Jules and shook her head. What was with her?

"Mind your own business, Witchy Poo," she snarled.

I didn't say I wanted it to happen, she thought, and she thought it hard, just in case someone was listening in. And she'd be damned if the woman didn't nod.

Holy shit. I'm not in Kansas anymore.

She and the sisters were led toward the dais. She couldn't tell which disturbed the people more, the Muirs or the fact Jules wasn't wearing a dress like all the other women. Ewan gestured for them to sit at his round table, just in front of the dais where the giant chair, the tomb, and the statue stood like three pink elephants in the room that everyone pretended not to notice. The crowd quieted when Ewan took his seat. But they weren't looking his way anymore. They were looking back at the doorway, the one that led to the kitchens—and the cellar—where a very angry, though slightly confused hitman stood with his forearms braced against the walls to either side of him. In one hand, he held a shiny black gun. His black leather coat and blue jeans stood out as badly as her own. It took three seconds for him to locate her.

Ewan reached out and squeezed her hand. Under his breath he said, "Stay calm, Jules. We'll catch him and cage him. Just ye stay calm."

Calm? He didn't know what he was talking about.

A baby cried off to her right. She noticed a toddler on his father's knee. From behind layers of her mother's skirts, peeked a little girl. Jules couldn't let these people get hurt because of her. But if she surrendered, she was dead.

Ewan stood and Daniel fell in step beside him as they ambled toward the red-headed stranger. The man laughed as he tucked his gun behind him, then rubbed his hands together and egged them on. The fact that he hadn't shot them was a damned good sign.

She'd have only a minute or two, so she'd just have to move fast. And going back to the cellar, back into the tomb, was not an option at the moment. Her only chance to get him away from these people was to run.

She was a great runner. She'd dragged the FBI babysitters around by the nose, insisting they let her run or she wouldn't testify. It was the best way to pretend she was free of them. Eventually, they realized she was dead-set on testifying no matter what they did, so they'd stopped dancing to her tune. They'd made her settle for a treadmill. Still, over the months, she'd become quite the long distance runner. All she needed was a little head start.

Ewan growled and attacked. Men jumped up all around her, suddenly ready to fight. The crowd blended quickly and in a matter of seconds, all those men were standing in the center of the room with the women and children to their backs and their enemy before them. The women were shuffling along the wall and taking the children with them, out a half-hidden doorway near the statue of Montgomery. It was like a dance they'd danced before, or a fire drill.

Ewan had flung his arms around the enemy's stomach and plowed him into the side of the archway, but the big man just laughed. When he noticed the small army waiting their turn for a piece of him, he laughed harder.

Jules had to move. Now.

She hustled to the giant wood door that stood open to the night air, then paused. It was covered with metal and rivets and looked like a shield for a giant. It was probably part of that Scottish carpentry that Ewan was talking about. But that's not what made her stop.

She realized if she slipped away, Gabby's man would keep searching for her there, among all those innocents. They might be slaughtered. She needed to go, but she needed the hitter to follow.

Jules searched the back of the room for those long red curls.

"Hoo hoo!" she hollered. "Hey! Red!"

The red head popped up and he scanned the crowd until he saw her. He looked none too happy to be pulled away from a good time, like he was in the middle of a neighborhood basketball game and she'd told him he had to come home for lunch. He really was enormous. Ewan looked like a kid hanging on his back with one arm around his neck. The hitter was all but grinning. Ewan, on the other hand, looked furious.

"I'm going now," she called, as if she were popping out to the store. "Give me a few minutes' head start, Laird Ross. Would you?"

Ewan sputtered like a fish.

"Bell! Don't do it!" The hitter's voice died in her wake. And she made damn sure she left a wake. Dogs scattered. She pulled a pile of wooden buckets over next to a wagon, making sure a mess pointed the way out of the torch-lit inner bailey, through the opening where the old Muir sisters had been waving at her.

She was standing on the bridge before she remembered about the moat. But it was no land bridge, just a wide, sturdy piece of construction built across a large creek. The cheerful gurgle of water over rocks was not the toxic water full of vicious creatures she'd always imagined a moat to be.

Once she was on the other side of the bridge, she realized that old crumbling curtain wall was now perfectly intact, probably two stories tall, and caging her in. And more importantly, caging in a hitman among a clan's worth of collateral damage.

She kept moving.

Little buildings were scattered around the edges of an expansive outer bailey that had once been, or rather, *would one day be*, a huge parking lot. Light glowed orange from behind a window here and there, but for the most part, the structures were random gray shapes in the blackness. The air was cool against her face and the combined smells of grass and manure reminded her of Wyoming, but she pushed the memories away—not out of pain this time, but from necessity. She had to stay alert.

Thanks to torches lit on either side, she could see where the massive main gate was closed up for the night. It stood where, not long ago, the chain had hung between two modern posts with the little sign that read, "See Us Tomorrow."

The long stone battlements had torches burning every fifty yards or so. Some of them moved back and forth—probably carried by guards. Above the gate, the torches held still while men moved back and forth just below them.

Jules hurried toward that gate, past the buildings and out into a dark stretch of ground that seemed to move in waves. She walked right into something short, nearly toppling onto her face. When her hands shot out to steady herself, she felt something soft—and mobile.

Sheep.

The wool-covered creatures bumped around her for a second or two, then moved away when they realized she wasn't one of them. She said a little prayer, grateful they'd stayed quiet, then she got moving again, bracing herself to step in sheep dung.

The wall was gigantic. She couldn't believe there wouldn't be more of it left in five hundred years.

Something that big couldn't just erode away. People would have to tear it down and carry the stones away. But why?

She moved more carefully as she neared the light of the gate torches, but the two guards manning the wall there were facing outward. A grid covered the wide opening, and on the inside, giant doors stood open. Apparently, they weren't expecting an attack. Too bad they didn't realize it was going to come from within.

Off to the left, there was a staircase that led to the top of the wall. What could she do, climb up there and explain things, then ask them to lift the gate and let her out? Oh, and leave it open until the killer left too? Wouldn't they be a little suspicious when she described the guy as being dressed just like her? Jeans and black coat?

Yeah, she needed a better plan. And she couldn't just wait around for something to come to her. She moved silently until she was next to the stairs, then plastered herself flat against it, in the shadows, while she figured out what to do.

Come on, Jules. Think!

If it had been the twenty-first century, she could just pass herself off as Lady Ross, and they'd do what she told them.

A woman's scream rang out from the inner bailey, maybe the castle itself. Had the hitter gotten free? Had he killed someone?

"Go!" a man shouted from somewhere above her. Then fast footsteps on the stairs. Then more muffled strides as a man struck out across the dirt and grass toward the castle.

One man left. Or at least, she thought it was only one.

Her only hope was to sway one man into helping her. She just hoped she had a good idea by the time she got up the steps because she couldn't waste any more time.

She ran to the end of the staircase and started up. The stairs were suddenly well-lit. The problem was, a man was standing at the top holding a torch, looking right at her. He glanced in the direction of the other guard, probably wondering if he should call him back, so she distracted him.

"Hello!" She smiled and gave a little wave.

He didn't wave back, but she had his attention. She knew the moment he realized she was wearing pants, because he caught his breath. As she made her way up the stairs and stepped onto the wall walk, he moved back and rested his butt against the battlements. She figured he didn't think a woman—even a woman in pants—was much of a threat. He set the torch in a ring, folded his arms and smirked at her, like some club bouncer who wasn't going to let her in.

"And just where do ye suppose ye're goin', lass?"

"I'm just coming to pay my penalty," she said, hoping her accent wasn't too horrible. But Ewan hadn't had any trouble understanding her.

"Oh, aye? And what penalty might that be?"

She looked out over the wall, to gage how far she'd have to run to reach her precious hillside, but she saw only darkness. She would have the distance of at least a road before the beginning of the slope. The man followed her gaze and tensed, pushing himself away from the wall.

"Who be ye?" He looked toward the castle, then back at her.

"I'm just visiting. With the Muir sisters," she said coyly.

He froze and his eyes bulged for a second.

"Oh, I'm not one of them," she said, and he looked relieved to hear it. "But I did lose a wager. And my penalty is to find a guard and give him a *Glasgow Kiss*."

By the guy's reaction, she could tell he didn't know what she meant, that he assumed a kiss was just a kiss. She looked down the wall walk, to where another torch was perched against the stone. She saw no guard there. Maybe all of them weren't manned. The sentry followed her line of sight.

She gave her best impression of a pout. "But if you'd like me to find another man, I can—"

He was already shaking his head. "Och, nay. There's none on this wall with me tonight that would be worth the kissin', lassie. Ye're right lucky ye found me first."

He stepped up to her. She looked behind her, to make sure she wasn't too close to the edge, since there was no railing of any kind. The man grabbed her arm gently, like he was promising to keep her from falling.

She blinked a lot, trying to look innocent. Hopefully, he thought she was a harmless idiot.

"If you're sure," she said. "You're such a tall one. You'll have to bend down a little." He didn't resist when she put her hands on his furry cheeks and angled his head down. "And I think we're supposed to close our eyes."

She closed hers for a couple of seconds, then peeked to make sure he'd fallen for it. Then she reared back and gave her first Glasgow Kiss ever, putting her weight behind it to make sure she got it right. A half-hearted head-butt would only get him mad.

The impact surprised her, but she was most surprised by the fact she was still able to stand. Everyone in the castle had to have heard it, like someone hitting a coconut with a hammer. She was just grateful her head got to be the hammer. Her forehead was numb, but at least she wasn't falling to the ground, like the sentry was.

Unfortunately, he crumpled forward without time for any reaction whatsoever. She had to ignore the gong sounding in her own head while she broke his fall without them both pitching over the side, onto the steps. It wasn't easy getting out from under him.

She'd been trying to leave a trail of breadcrumbs for the hitter, and Kissy-face was going to be the last crumb. His body, with his arm dangling over the edge of the walkway, was well lit. Anyone looking toward the gate would see it.

Perfect.

She walked carefully to the center of the gatehouse—carefully, because she was pretty sure she'd just given herself a concussion—and found the mechanism for raising the metal gate. It was much easier than she thought it would be to turn the gears to bring the thing up. Unfortunately, she couldn't figure out how to keep it suspended if she let go. In the end, she jammed the handle of a torch between cogs and it held.

It had taken so long, she was expecting the hitter to meet her at the bottom of the steps, but he wasn't there. Of course, there was a chance Ewan had managed to get the man locked up again, but she couldn't risk going back to find out.

She ducked beneath the nasty-looking spikes along the gate's bottom edge and started running. The hitter would have to have pretty poor eyesight to miss the fact that it was open, but it was the last bit of help she was going to give him. Once he was away from all those people, what he did was no longer on her head.

I've done what I could. Now I have to start protecting myself.

She knew the crescent hill pretty well after three days. She could think of a few places to hide. And when Gabby's man got far enough away, she would run back to the castle and have Ewan help her get into the tomb. After that, she planned to click her heels as many times as it took, but that friggin' *tardis* would take her home. If she didn't return soon, she'd miss the trial. In a text, she'd warned the DA that she had some business to take care of, but she'd be back in time to testify. She'd be damned if she was going to miss it. They were idiots if they called it off.

Her FBI babysitters had drilled it into her head that she'd have to start a new life, that she'd have to leave her old one behind. She'd played along, of course. No use ranting and raving to deaf ears. But the world was just too small a place to hide in unless you had a helluva lot of money. Luckily for her, though, she knew where she could get more than she'd ever need. And it was rightfully hers.

There were just two people she had to deal with first—Gabby Skedros and Jillian Ross. As soon as she made the two of them pay, life was going to be good. But Jillian first. In ten days, it would be Gabby's turn.

Ten days. Plenty of time.

And by the time she'd finished that thought, she was running up into the trees—or rather, where the trees should have been. In the starlight, all she could see were stumps, and dirt, and patches of grass.

The trees had been there only hours ago. *Hours* ago. She'd have given her last candy bar to see that stupid squirrel and his tree again.

She wanted to sink to the ground and convince herself she wasn't going crazy, but it would have to wait. She had to put a lot of space between herself and that castle, and she had to be careful not to get lost while she did it. The trees had probably been cleared so the Scots could easily see their enemies approaching or something.

At the moment, it was more useful for a hitman to clearly see his target.

Jules turned and looked into the outer bailey/parking lot just in time to see a large dark figure run across the bridge and head for the gate.

She turned north and started running.

CHAPTER EIGHT

Jillian was giddy on the way home from Edinburg. Quinn's brother, and his wife, Maggie had decided to stay a few more days in the city, with their kids, so she and Montgomery would have the manor house to themselves. She would have to call the butler and tell him to give the staff a few extra days of vacation too.

Holiday, that was. Scots didn't call it a vacation. She had to remember that so she didn't sound completely American every time she opened her mouth.

She noticed her husband watching her instead of the darkening road and she raised a brow.

"Are ye finally thinkin' what I've been thinkin'?" he asked.

"Aye," she said in her best Scots accent. "I'm thinking we should have a grand barbeque and invite the staff... And their families, o' course."

"Truly?" His brow worried into a pucker.

"Wasn't that what you were thinking?" She looked back at the road and tried to keep a straight face.

After a moment, she looked back at him. He was still speechless, though at least he was watching where he was driving. She took pity on him.

"Or maybe you were thinking they'd rather have a longer holiday."

His head whipped around. His boyish smile made her heart flip. She really shouldn't have teased him. Sarcasm was not as common in the fifteenth century.

"Of course that means we'll have to take care of ourselves," she warned. "Or maybe we could take care of each other. Would you like a bath?"

He laughed. "I thought ye far too generous with the servants, madam, but only because ye might mean to give yer attentions to them instead of me. I am relieved."

"I thought you might be." She held out her hand to him and he took it, pulled it up to his lips and kissed her knuckles. She was embarrassed her skin wasn't smoother, but she'd become an obsessive compulsive lately and washed her hands constantly. There was this stuff her grandmother used to use on her hands when they got chapped doing chores around the farm. Cornhuskers Something-or-other. It looked like snot, but it worked. If they couldn't get it here, she'd have to order some.

"Bitches!" He dropped her hand and grabbed the steering wheel with both of his.

In the beams from the Hummer, Jillian couldn't see what might have spooked him. No sheep or anything else in the road. When it turned out not to be life-threatening, she laughed. He had taken up modern cursing like it was a sport, but he was still getting things a little mixed up.

"I believe you meant to say *son of a bitch.* And it's not a nice thing to say, just so you know."

He shook his head and instead of taking the upper road to the house, he drove a bit farther and turned into the castle's parking lot. She thought maybe some tourists had ignored the closed sign again, but there were no other cars to be seen. When he stopped the car, she finally understood.

"I said *witches*, Jillian, not *bitches*. Though I suspect you were not far afield."

She couldn't argue with that.

The Muir sisters, Loretta and Lorraine, stood just beyond the reach of the headlights, at the corner of the crumbling inner wall. Jilly's first thought was that the sisters were much too old to be running around at that hour. Then she remembered they were much too old to be doing any of the things they did, the time of day didn't matter.

Muir twins were never good news, no matter what century they popped up in.

"Be nice, Montgomery. If it weren't for them, we'd have never met. Remember that." She was reminding herself as much as her husband.

"How do they always find their way into my castle, I'd like to ken. Some mornings they're already inside when I unlock the bloody doors."

"Maybe they're not witches. Maybe they're ghosts," she joked as she got out of the car.

"Not ghosts yet, Jilly dear," called Lorraine. "But funny you should use those words today."

Jilly almost climbed back into the car. Monty was right. It was never good news when those two came around. And why did they have to pop up when she and Monty finally had a chance for some privacy—enough privacy to share her exciting news? She hadn't quite told him the truth about their little shopping trip to the city, unless you could call it shopping when she was hunting for a trustworthy OB/GYN.

Loretta looked at her funny. Her eyes dropped to Jilly's middle, then looked away. Jilly instinctively covered her stomach with both hands, then she forced them to her sides before anyone noticed.

"Why is it odd that she speaks of ghosts, ladies?" Monty left the lights on and walked to the middle of his hood, then leaned back against it, crossing his arms, bracing himself for bad news. Jilly shut her door and stood next to the front tire. She didn't want to get between her husband and the women he considered his nemeses.

"Someone else thought we might be ghosts, just today if you can believe it." Loretta gave Jilly a nervous look. Guilt? Pity?

"I'll bite," Jilly said, against her better judgment. "Who thought you were ghosts?"

"Would you like to sit down, Jilly dear?" Lorraine also stared at her middle.

"No. I don't want to sit down. Spit it out so we can get out of here." She would never forgive the sisters if they messed around and told Monty she was pregnant. How the hell did they know anyway?

"Fine, then. You remember we gave you a chance to sit down."

Jilly glared at Lorraine, daring her to piss her off. Didn't she know better than to mess with a pregnant woman?

"Your sister," the old woman blurted.

"Morna?" Montgomery pushed away from the hood and unfolded his arms. He was alarmed as he always was just because Morna and Ivar lived too far away for him to be any protection. It hadn't quite sunk into his head yet that dangers in the twenty-first century were very different. If they had problems, they would call.

"Not *your* sister, Laird Ross." Lorraine paused and looked her in the eye. "Jillian's."

Jilly didn't understand. She didn't have a sister. But the thought of finding more family caught her breath.

"Yes, Jilly. *Your* sister. We met her today. Lovely thing, too. I'm sure you'll agree—Montgomery, catch her!" Loretta ran forward.

Jilly was surprised to find that she was the *her* that needed catching. She hadn't noticed before, but she was teetering to her left, sliding along the fender with little attention for the ground rising up to meet her. She ended on her bottom, in the gravel, with Monty kneeling beside her.

"Jillian! Ye will be fine." It was definitely not a question, but an order. She'd gotten used to his fifteenth century, bullying ways, but she knew he was only bossy when he was worried. Unfortunately, he worried a lot.

"Yes. I'm fine. Of course I'm fine. I was just caught off guard. I forgot to breathe. I don't have a sister, that's all." But deep down somewhere, it sounded true. Deep down, she wanted it to be true.

After her grandmother's death, and the shock of her huge inheritance wore off, the first thing she'd done was go looking for more family. She'd started at the geneological library in Salt Lake City, but she hadn't even started digging when these Muir sister's had gotten her distracted by the Curse of Clan Ross. Of course, she couldn't be angry with them now, in spite of all their conniving. If it weren't for them, she'd have never slipped back in time to find the one and only love of her life.

She'd been waiting for the right time to tell her husband she wanted to start looking again, but the poor man hadn't completely adjusted to the twenty-first century yet. She had to wait until he was comfortable with his own country before she exposed him to too many Americans.

But a sister? She'd been hoping for a cousin. A sister just seemed...greedy.

And if there was a sister she hadn't been told about, who else might her grandmother have hidden from her?

She searched her memory for some image, for a time when it hadn't been just her and Grandmother, but she found nothing. She remembered a doll she named Necklace. Seeing a bear at Yellowstone. Little else. There couldn't have been a sister. Grandmother couldn't have been that cruel.

"Yes, Jilly. You do have a sister. Didn't we tell you we thought you might have a twin? In the tunnels. Remember?" Lorrain grinned down into her face as if she deemed her news to be the most wonderful surprise. But if it was a wonderful surprise—if Jilly truly had a sister, twin or not—then why did Loretta look like she had bad news?

Did Lorraine say twin?

"*Twin?* A twin s...sister?"

Jilly's mind stuttered as badly as her mouth. She remembered just a flash. A feeling. Her own image, in a mirror, looking up and smiling at her. She'd always remembered what she looked like as a small child, but maybe it hadn't been a mirror after all.

Then there was another memory. A white room with a low table in the middle. She and the girl with the smiling face. She was wearing a maroon jumper. *They* were wearing maroon jumpers? Little cups of water on the table, each holding a crayon. They were taking the papers off and soaking the bright sticks—trying to color the water. Then grandma came in and spanked her for ruining the crayons. She remembered that spanking, but she always remembered it as an observer, seeing herself being swatted on the butt. But it maybe it hadn't been *her* butt.

Why hadn't she remembered before? And why would her grandmother never have told her about a sister? And a twin? Why would she tell her nothing more than her parents died in a car wreck and there was no one else?

Jilly took a deep breath and let her anger with her grandmother wash away from her. She didn't want to upset the little life inside her with the spite she felt for the old woman. She shook her head and held out her hands. She had to get up.

Montgomery pulled her to her feet.

"Where is she?" She brushed the rocks from her rear end, then the dirt from her hands. "When was she here? Is she still here? Are you sure she's my sister? What was her name?"

She looked around the car park. No other cars. No cars parked up at the house either. Then she noticed Monty. He was glaring at the Muirs and taking deep breaths, like he was building up enough air to start yelling at them. And that never did any good. She put a hand on his arm and pulled him close, both to restrain him and for a bit of needed support.

"Juliet, I believe," said Loretta, then she bit her lip.

Juliet? Juliet. Juliet.

Jilly said it a dozen times in her mind, but it didn't ring any bells.

"Where is she?" she asked calmly. All happy thoughts vanished when she'd read their guilty faces.

"Dinna worry yerself, Jilly dear. She's hale and healthy, we're almost sure of it," said Lorraine.

"Where?" Monty's patience was gone.

"Well, the last we saw her was when we put her in the tomb. Then of course we had to hide ourselves, what with that man chasing her." Loretta put an arm around her sister and patted her shoulder, as if they'd been through some terrible experience.

Jilly smelled a rat, like she usually did when those two started over-acting.

Montgomery squeezed her hand. "A man was chasing her?"

"Yes," said Lorriane. "Now we don't want to worry you, Jilly. Not in your condition. But the man was carrying a gun."

"I wouldn't call him a gunman, sister, just because he carried a gun," Loretta offered.

Lorraine frowned. "I didn't call him a gunman."

Loretta waved away the argument. "Of course ye didn't. I'm just saying I wouldn't call him a gunman, that's all. Some men just look the type. He didn't look the type."

"Heavens to Betsy, sister," Lorraine chided. "Ye can't expect Jillian to stay calm if ye go on spouting the word gunman."

"Spouting? Why ye—" Loretta's face turned red.

"Shut it!" Montgomery had pulled out his best Gordon Ramsay impersonation to get everyone's attention, and it worked. Even the insects shut up. "Now then, the pair of ye will disappear for a moment whilst my wife explains this condition of hers."

With bulging eyes and thin, tightly shut lips, the blue clad pair walked off, but stopped about ten feet away.

Jilly burst into silent tears as Monty's arms came around her.

"Ye were about to tell me ye carry my son, were ye not?" he asked.

"I was not," she said with a hiccup.

He pulled back. "Then I misunderstood?"

"I was going to tell you we're going to have a baby. It might be a girl, you know."

He laughed and lifted her into the air, then spun her around until she thought she was going to puke. He put her down immediately, smart man.

"But that doesn't matter now," she said.

"The hell it doesn't." He started pulling her toward the car door, but she pulled back.

"I mean, what matters right this minute is finding my sister."

"Come, now, Jillian. Just because those two think some woman looked a bit like you, doesna mean she's yer kin, does it? Once ye have a babe, perhaps it will put an end to yer search for more family. Ye'll have me, and the babe. What more could ye need?"

Jilly struggled against his hold and he loosened his arms.

"It haunts me, Montgomery, not knowing anything about my family. And the idea that I have a sister just feels like there's hope, like the haunting might stop. Besides, one day there will be a little girl, or boy, who asks about the American side of the family. And if I do have a sister, she might have those details."

He pulled her tight again and tucked her head beneath his chin.

"Haunted, ye say? How can a man, even as braw and brave as I, fight a haunting, then?"

She smiled against his shirt. "Let's go find my sister."

"Oh, she's gone, Jilly." The Muirs were back. "We checked. She did not come out of the tomb."

"She disappeared?" She was afraid of that. She'd done the same every time she'd been in the tomb.

"And the gunman—er, the man with the gun went in as well. He didn't come out either."

"And she is yer sister, Jilly dear. You look as much alike as Quinn and Laird Montgomery."

For some reason, she resented the Muirs for meeting her sister before she could, and resented them even more for sending that precious woman into the tomb. No one ever wanders into a stranger's cellar, sees a hole in the ceiling and says, *Hm. I think I'll climb up there and have a look around.*

There was no doubt about it. They'd sent Juliet back in time on purpose, just like they'd sent Jillian a year before. The question was why?

The old sisters shrugged and looked away as if in answer.

Jilly tugged Montgomery toward the old castle. "We'll just have to go after her."

Monty stopped walking. "No. We won't. Ye will go nowhere but home. Who knows what might happen to my child?" His eyes went wide. "Not to mention my wife. Nothing can happen to you, my Jillian. Nothing!"

Jilly shook her head. "If you think I'm going to let you go off to who-knows-where without me, you're out of your mind. Where you go, I go."

"But I see a need for haste, here," Monty reasoned.

Jillian narrowed her eyes. "Agreed."

Monty took a deep breath and looked into her eyes. "If I asked you kindly to stay and look after our child—a daughter even—would you—"

"Sure. You go. I'll stay." She shrugged.

He frowned. "Truly?"

He looked a little too pleased. She couldn't wait to let him down.

"Only, be sure to get out of the tomb fast," she said.

"Fast? You mean quickly? Why?"

She crooked a finger so he'd lean close. Then she whispered in his ear.

"Because Junior and I will be right behind you."

He straightened quickly. "Son of a—"

"Don't you dare."

CHAPTER NINE

The pain is worse because I want to live.

The thought was already forming in his head before Quinn woke on the hard dirt ground. Again.

There was not so much as a moment's confusion about where he was this time. His mind was alert—brought to attention by a hard, mean headache. That ache made it immediately clear that he yet lived. Either that, or hell was going to be a bit more hellish than he'd imagined.

He groaned if only to prove his ears worked. When he then heard the shuffling of feet, he supposed it was his blind babysitter going to alert the media that he was awake and ready for the next Gordon sibling to come have a go at him. Why not?

"Has no one ballocks enough to kill me thoroughly this time?" he complained, for even though he'd decided he wanted to live, the pain in his head was convincing him otherwise. What he wouldn't give for some good old headache tablets and a bag of ice.

Someone shuffled in his direction and the darkness was pushed back a bit by the orange glow of single weak torch.

"Why nay, Laird Ross," said a woman. "I haven't ballocks at all. But I do mean to see ye dead. Unless..."

Quinn thought it only right that he sit up, though slowly, and show a bit of respect for anyone offering him but a dram of hope. He'd need something more promising to get him on his feet, however.

Etha Gordon stepped forward. A manservant stood beside her holding the light. The last face he'd seen, before losing consciousness at the gallows, had belonged to this lovely red-haired lass. Unfortunately, the backhand that had sent his abused head back into the darkness had also belonged to her. Either her brothers had taught her a thing or two about defending herself, or he was a soft, delicate man to have been laid low by such a soft, delicate lass. One more blow to the brain would be his last, no doubt. He was in no better shape than a prize fighter who'd lost one too many prizes. And he'd best start protecting himself or he didn't deserve to survive.

Quinn knew two things: The Gordon had but one daughter, and Montgomery Ross had been about to marry the woman when his current wife, Jillian, materialized in the tomb and made such ghostly noises that everyone fled Castle Ross. All believed she'd been the ghost of Montgomery's sister, Isobelle, come to protest the wedding. Obviously, Etha was not the forgive and forget type.

"Etha? Is that you?"

"My name is Betha, ye bastard. Ye were about to speak vows with me and ye failed to learn my name?" Her voice got louder as she went on. A sweet voice, turned a bit ugly at the end.

From what Quinn had heard, she was a quiet biddable lass. Or perhaps she had been, once. It was possible she'd been affected by Isobelle's ghost arriving in time to ruin her wedding. The only thing Montgomery had done wrong was not to have learned her name. Quinn was certain both Monty and Ewan had told him it was *Etha*.

"Forgive me if I heard amiss, but did you say you'd see me dead *unless*? Unless what, Lady Betha?"

She stared at him for a moment, as if weighing the worth of his apology. She gave a nod, as if her mind was made up, then she offered a smile that made him shiver. He didn't care much for the look in her pale eyes.

"Ye will lie with me, Montgomery Ross. I will at least have yer child, bastard or no."

He was not about to explain that one night together had little chance of producing a child, not if keeping quiet meant he might be untied, conscious, and on the other side of those bars. The combination meant freedom.

"As you wish, my lady. Will you then see me free?"

"If ye please me, Ross. But only if ye please me."

Was that her game? Was she only looking for a bit of pleasure, perhaps a taste of what she'd forfeited when she'd run from Castle Ross and a perfectly sound bridegroom? What might be wrong with the woman, other than her family's manners, that kept her from finding another husband all this while?

Suddenly he was much more hopeful that Percy would come through for him. Pleasing Lady Betha sounded like a task he might not be man enough to accomplish. She was pretty enough. Beneath all her velvet and furs, she seemed petite, but in truth was probably an average size for the century. But lying with the daughter of the man who was supposedly his greatest enemy just didn't seem like a wise move to make. If they were caught, he'd die on the spot, he was sure, and the idea of dying with a bare arse would make his martyrdom anything but noble.

He hoped his wife Libby was otherwise occupied in Heaven at the moment, and not looking down on his sorry state.

Since Percy showed no signs of coming to a quick decision, he felt it wise to try and buy the man some thinking time. But in order to do so, he would need food. His stomach had long since ceased to growl, turned outside-in as it was. He needed food, and water.

"Aye, my lady. I'd be happy to oblige you," he said in his most seductive voice. She stepped closer, to be able to hear him. She lifted a pale hand to her face and he was certain she'd gotten a whiff of Skully, as he'd begun to think of the skeleton next door. "But I need my strength to do so, as you might understand. But mayhap a bit of sleep is all I need."

"Boyd!"

At her call, a large man moved into the light.

"See to it this man has food—good food—then a bath. Tell no one. If my brothers ask what you are about, tell them to see me."

"Aye, milady." Boyd bowed before leading the woman away with his torch.

A moment later, Quinn was alone again, basking in the cheer of real hope—for food and a bath, at least. Hope for survival was close, but he didn't dare reach for it. It might just disappear. And if he really thought he might live, he'd have to start thinking about what he was going to do with that life.

What in the world could he do? How could he tell Ewan that he'd had a change of heart and wanted to go home, to live the life he was meant to live instead of hiding in the past and mourning his wife in peace?

The image of the witch's hole popped into his head. Of course he couldn't go back. He had a role to play. A promise to keep. And if he went back, he'd be facing Jillian and her husband. He'd have to deal with his dreams of her.

That cursed dream! It made him want to live, then made the living unbearable.

God help him.

CHAPTER TEN

Chocolate did not make a good weapon when dealing with a hungry animal. When dealing with a hungry child, yes. Wolf, not so much.

Jules wasn't a mace-and-pepper-spray kind of girl. She found that a few wisely chosen insults can hurt a thug's feelings enough to make one back away when necessary. And in extreme cases, dropping Gabby's name had been the only weapon she'd needed to carry. She knew he was considered a tough guy. But reputation and actions were two different things. Or so she'd thought. Turned out he was just a ruthless as people thought he was.

"I don't suppose you'll leave me alone just because I'm like a daughter to Gabby Skedros."

The wolf showed its teeth and snarled conversationally.

"I didn't think so."

Why in the world couldn't she have been a pepper-spray kind of girl! But no. She'd been a physics major, waiting tables at Gabby's restaurant, *Papa's*, in New York. And physics wasn't a great weapon either.

Or was it?

The wolf was stalling. It was containing her. Probably waiting for the rest of its pack to arrive. She'd be ripped to pieces if that happened. Her best chance was against one wolf. And if Gabby's man happened to find her now, even with his gun, chances were he'd let the wolves have her and save the bullet. Besides, he'd already told her she would regret locking him in that dark cellar.

So. One wolf. In no hurry to attack her. So she'd attack him. She could do it—she was so bat-shit scared there was enough adrenaline shooting through her veins she could jump ten feet in the air and land in a tree before the wolf thought to stop her. Of course she wasn't willing to test it.

Out of the corner of her eye she saw a long stick. It had little bark left, so it nearly glowed in the darkness, like a weapon sent from Zeus. And she wasn't about to second guess Zeus.

She circled slowly. The wolf mirrored her steps. Another wolf howled—not so far away this time. The first wolf stepped closer.

"Aw, now, don't jump the gun," she cooed as she bent down for the weapon. It was far too light. There would be little strength in it. Her mind raced, searching for formulas, guessing at torque. If she could get the thing to bite down hard on the side of the stick, she could turn it quickly, maybe twist its neck. Scare the hell out of it.

Maybe. But it was a much more feasible plan than jumping up into a tree.

She refused to consider how surreal this moment was, that she was here, in these woods she'd wandered for days, without fearing wild animals. In the future, these woods had been a bit closer to society. But here, there was no society. The land was still wild.

This isn't real, she thought, as she swung the stick like a baseball bat, wishing it was a crowbar. The wolf dodged away, then came back mad. Its growl could probably be heard a mile away and it promised that his friends were a lot more dangerous than hers.

She didn't have a plan B, so she swung at it again. This time, the jaws clamped down on it in triumph. She tugged at it to make sure the wolf knew she would swing again if he let go—so it would hold tight. And it did. There was no give at all. Its fangs were sharp enough to sink into the wood like it was more like flesh than bone.

But they wouldn't sink into her, damn it!

Twisting her arms as she went, she lunged forward, grabbing both ends of the stick in spite of the short end being so close to its mouth. Then she spun it, using her own body as leverage, putting all her strength into untwisting her arms.

Something snapped. She both heard it and felt it. The wolf jumped back, yipping. It glanced back at her, over and over, while it ran away, as if it feared she might come after it.

She looked down at her wimpy weapon. There, imbedded in the wood, was the wolf's fang. Broken below the gum line. Red blood smeared across white wood.

She'd done it!

Before she had a chance to think better of it, she raised the staff over her head and whooped.

"That's right," she taunted in the direction the wolf had run. "Go tell your friends, baby. Don't mess with a Physicist!"

And what if Gabby's man might have heard her? She had no choice but to change direction again, just in case. She had a weapon now. Well, kind of. No chance she could get the hitter to sink his teeth into it, but it would give her a little false courage to get her out of the forest and to a road.

Surely, there would be a road. If not, she would climb a tree in the morning and get her bearings. If he'd gotten away from Ewan and the Rosses, Gabby's man was in these woods too. If she gave up looking for a road and circled back, could she get to the tomb first?

If she did make it back, she would linger long enough to meet her sister, give her an earful, and get the woman to hand over her share of the inheritance. Then she'd tell the husband that his look-alike was missing and Ewan needed his help.

If she was lucky, Gabby's man would be stuck here. He'd use up his bullets, in the darkness, on an angry wolf with only three fangs. Then, for the rest of his life, he'd have to pick fights the old fashioned way.

When the adrenaline wore off, she felt like she'd been hit by a truck. And she kept forgetting what she'd decided to do. Was she hoping to find a road? Was she hoping Castle Ross would be over the next hill? Although her legs moved just fine, she was having a hard time balancing the rest of her body on top of them, so she searched for a climbable tree. She'd never heard of a wolf climbing a tree and avoiding wolves was the only priority she could manage to hang on to.

Finally, in spite of the darkness, she found a good one. A tall thick pine tree with plenty of lifeless branches at the bottom of the trunk, then healthy ones about ten feet up that were dense with pine needles—a little camouflage after she twisted and squeezed her way up through the natural ladder. Every time she figured she'd gone high enough, she pushed herself up a little higher. The only things that could get to her then were squirrels and birds.

And hopefully, they were all asleep.

She picked a sturdy spot and sat down facing the trunk. She hoped the tilt of the branch would keep her from falling backward. Then she wrapped her knee over one branch and tucked the toe of her boot under the next. If she started to slip in her sleep, her leg should catch. The pain would wake her up and she'd be able to save herself. But there was no question about it, she would sleep. She was lucky she hadn't collapsed already.

Her hair was the most convenient cushion to protect her cheek from the bark. She then hugged the trunk and laced her fingers. Her coat protected her skin. Once she realized she wasn't at all uncomfortable, she tried to imagine her worries, one by one, falling to the ground like so many brown and crunchy pine needles. It was the last thing she remembered.

When she woke, Jules found that she hadn't moved a muscle. The sky had a strange blue glow and mist swarmed like a shallow river against the forest floor. She could almost taste the pine sap in the moist air. She didn't think it had rained. Surely she wouldn't have slept through that.

A bird flapped its wings above her head, then settled again. Dawn wasn't far away, and she was afraid Gabby's man wasn't either. If she was lucky, he had stopped to sleep too, and if she moved quickly, she could put a bit more distance between them. She would head east for a little longer, then turn south toward Castle Ross.

She made her way back to the ground feeling pretty refreshed considering she'd maybe only slept an hour or two. After walking about a mile to the east, she found a small track that could be called a road. The feeling of safety, of humanity, increased with each step on the rutted dirt. Someone had been there. Someone would be there again. Someone with two legs and no fangs.

"Woohoo," she said, but only in her smallest voice, just in case. A moment later, she came around a bend and found herself in the dooryard of a little cottage. It looked almost lived in. Her first instinct was to move away, quietly, before she woke someone. She really didn't need any help, after all. Of course she was starving, but she didn't need anything quite so much as she needed to get back into that tomb.

But.

If someone inside knew a good wolf-less road that would lead her straight back to Castle Ross, she'd be a fool not to ask. Of course, when the sun came over the trees, she'd know which way was east. The problem was, she wasn't quite so sure how long she'd actually gone north. She'd checked the North Star a couple of times, when she'd been able to see through the trees, but there was a chance she'd gone in circles. What if Castle Ross were due south?

Damnit.

All that wondering drained away her confidence and suddenly, she didn't dare take another step without a little guidance. Of course, there was also a chance that no one lived in the little cottage, but she wasn't going to wait until the sun came up to find out.

She walked to the door and knocked. "Hello?" She knocked again. "Anybody home?" Then she realized she needed to speak Gaelic and repeated herself.

The door creaked wide, but it was too dark to see who opened it. She stepped back so she wouldn't seem too threatening.

"Oh, we're home, lassie," the man said as he stepped out into the yard. "It just doesna happen to be *our* home."

The laughter of more men—many more men—came from inside, and Jules stepped back, but the first man hurried around behind her.

Hadn't she just gone through the same thing with the wolves? Easier to escape one than the whole pack?

She had just decided to turn and rush the guy behind her, maybe knee him where it counts, when another man emerged and her chance was gone. This one was a lot taller and had to bend over to get through the opening. When he stood, long curly hair fell around his shoulders and in spite of the blue cast of the sky, she recognized his face. Laughing hazel eyes. Slashing brows.

Gabby's man. Only now, he was wearing a kilt and looking a little too at home in the fifteenth century.

"Juliet Bell." He tossed his head, to swing his wild mane out of his smug face. "You should have let me out."

CHAPTER ELEVEN

Ewan fidgeted in the great Ross Chair. He'd a bad feeling and it wasn't due wholly to the fact that he didn't belong in the chair, but that was part of it. Montgomery had obtained the clan's blessing to put the Rosses into Ewan's care over a year ago, but it didna make the chair or the mantle of leadership any the more comfortable.

None had known Monty was leaving and not coming back. And they still didn't know, thanks to the fact that Quinn Ross had taken upon himself the role of former laird. If they'd not looked so similar, the switch would have never worked. And many a time, Ewan had wished Monty's great nephew had never thought to make his sacrifice, for keeping the man home and hale was taking up far too much of Ewan's time when he had a clan to care for.

Of course he was grateful. Had Monty disappeared a year past, the Gordons would have poured in from the North and taken over with no thought for the blood spilt. But with Quinn on hand, The Gordon was held in check whilst Ewan earned his title. Now, instead of holding off for fear of Isobelle's ghost defending her brother and her clan, they held off for fear that Ewan Ross had an impressive hatred for all things Gordon and would lay to waste any who strayed South. There would be no more alliances between them.

It was also rumored that the Gordons had offered protection to Clan Muir, no doubt to counter the Ross Ghost with a witch or two. Ewan hoped the rumor proved false, though. The Muirs lived but on the far side of the hill to the east. And although he and Monty had been searching since they were wee laddies, they'd never been able to find the existence of the tunnel they suspected of running beneath that hill.

The Muir sisters were forever popping up out of the cellar, as if there were a leak in the floor and they a bit of sea water determined to get into the boat.

Nay, if the Gordons won over the Muirs, I would wake one night with Gordon's boot on me throat.

Since Quinn knew so few names and faces, the clansmen had believed their laird had gone addlepated. They paid him every respect, but their glances were full of pity. Poor man. It was not the easiest way to live, with people speaking to him simply and slowly all the time.

But this day, he pitied Quinn Ross for another reason entirely. This day, the Ross Pretender was in the hands of Clan Gordon. The lad Orie hadn't been taken, praise be, and had been able to ride home to tell Ewan where the wayward man could be found. And considering the many grudges The Gordon held in the name of Montgomery Ross, Quinn might find it a fine time indeed to deny that name, to tell The Gordon that he was not truly Montgomery Ross at all.

And if The Gordon was able to ferret out one secret, he might be able to ferret out the rest, that although Montgomery had buried his sister Isobelle in the tomb that stood inside the great Ross hall, Ewan and Ossian had tunneled beneath and freed her from it while Monty kept the bastards at bay with his rantings. The kirk's henchmen believed she'd died inside, as the clergy had decreed. The priest had ordered the tomb be placed upon stone so such a rescue would be impossible. And it nearly had been. If they'd gotten to her only a few hours later, it would have been her grave in truth. If the kirk discovered the deception, the entire clan would be punished, cut off.

If The Gordon discovered their secret, Clan Ross was doomed. And a clan cut off from the kirk might be unhappy to have lost their souls in order to save the life of one lass. No matter that it had been their laird's own sister.

If the Gordon were to squeeze the truth from Quinn...

Although Ewan blanched at the thought, even as he thought it, the notion came upon him that Quinn's life might not be worth a clanful of resentful Scots, let alone souls—especially if Quinn had taken on his current role of Pretender in order to keep that secret.

Ewan took a long drink of *aqua vitae* before he allowed his thoughts to go farther, for strong drink might prove a fine scapegoat for the argument he saw coming.

Quinn Ross was no' so keen on livin' in any case. Hadn't he said so many a time when he first arrived?

Before Ewan thought better of it, or had the chance to sober, he hollered for Daniel.

"Send Enos to me."

Daniel swallowed, but his feet didna move. "Enos?"

"Have we more than one Enos among us?"

"Nay, praise be." Daniel took the bag from around his neck and kissed it. A superstitious man was his second in command.

For the first time, Ewan wished he had such a talisman around his own neck.

"Then send Enos to me," he said.

"Can we not call everyone to arms and go after our lost laird?"

Ewan shook his head. "Nay. Quinn Ross would tack me bloody hide to the curtain wall if I allowed one man to be harmed in his stead. He's told me so a dozen times."

The young man's shoulders dropped as he left the hall, and inside, Ewan's soul sagged as well. It was an unholy thing he must do. And as he waited, and drank, the weight of the great Ross Chair seemed to be upon him instead of beneath him.

He'd send Enos to the Gordons. Enos would dispatch Quinn Ross to Heaven, where selfless men like him were sure to go. And the secrets of Montgomery Ross would be safe, as Ewan had vowed to keep them, if indeed they hadn't already been told.

CHAPTER TWELVE

Jules walked along the road trying to enjoy the lovely day and ignore the hitman who held her upper arm in his grip. She needed to enjoy the fresh air—the breath she shouldn't still be breathing. Why hadn't he killed her already?

The smell of pines and birch trees warming in the sunlight reminded her of Star Valley, Wyoming, where she'd grown up. She could just imagine the smell of campfires from the hunters, the sound of gun shots ringing out, echoing through the Grand Tetons that had been her backyard. She would have killed to have a shotgun in her hand at that moment. But all she had was her lucky stick.

Why hadn't he taken it away?

If the hitter wasn't all dressed up for a Scottish festival, it would be easy to believe they were just walking through some woods in the twenty-first century. But there was a different kind of quiet there. Was it just because it was Scotland? Or because it was Ancient Scotland? Or maybe it was quiet because everything was lush and heavy with moisture?

The road was uneven and had been cut deeply by flooding rain. The wild growth was so brilliantly green, it looked Photo-Shopped. It was like God was making up for the fact the country was so wet.

Sorry about all the rain. Here, I'll tweak the landscape a little. It's on Me.

The last minutes of her life could have been spent somewhere much worse, but the anticipation was killing her. She didn't really want to remind him to kill her, but she wanted to know who she should thank for her Stay of Execution.

"Why am I still alive?" She turned and watched his face, hoping she'd be able to tell if he lied to her. She didn't trust her own judgment much anymore. Not since Gabby had gone from father-figure to cold-hearted killer in a split second.

The hitter was more handsome than a killer should be, to her way of thinking at least. His hair was gorgeous and wild even though he'd tied it together at the back of his head. The loose copper ringlets were almost painful to look at when the sun hit them.

She tripped, but he caught her and helped her get her balance back. She expected his hands to be cold for some reason, but they were nice and warm.

Nice? Gah!

"Why are ye still alive? That's a fine question," he said, implying that she was a klutz and was lucky to have survived as long as she had.

"You know what I mean."

"Do I?" He cocked a brow.

"Oh. I see. You're going to pretend like you're not a brutal son of a bitch who could snap my neck at the drop of a hat?"

He laughed. "Aye. I suppose I could at that. Though I'm only brutal when it's called for."

What was he trying to do? Get her to let her guard down? Get her to cooperate? Not a friggin' chance.

"I know your kind. I know what you're like," she said.

"Oh, do ye now?" He snorted.

"I do."

After the feds had taken her into custody, she'd begun to suspect the line between law and crime was as fine as that between love and hate, and some of the good guys weren't on the side they thought they were on. In fact, Agent Dixon, on whose watch she'd escaped, had gotten pretty comfortable on that other side. He was willing to ignore all kinds of rules that were meant to keep her safe, especially if there was anything in it for him. He'd even teased her, said Gabby was probably pay a literal fortune to some agent willing to forget to lock a door and leave her long enough to get some take-out, like he'd done a dozen times already. But lucky for her, Gabby Skedros didn't have the address. Yet.

She thought she'd been safe when she'd slept? She hadn't been.

And the next time she and Dixon had been alone and the taunting resumed, she'd egged him on, told him just what she thought of him, gotten him all worked up. And when he'd lost control—grabbed her hair and even reached for his gun to prove how he held her life in his hands—she'd had all the excuse she needed to put a nice heavy pan to the side of his head. Then she'd used Dixon's phone to send an email to the DA, promising she'd be back in time to testify. Then she'd slipped away.

She looked over at the hitter. Yeah, it hadn't been just Gabby who'd taught her what a cold-blooded man was like.

The guy frowned. "Well, perhaps the Scottish version is no' so bad as the American."

She snorted. "Bullshit. A killer is a killer, even if he wears a badge."

If she could have mustered up some saliva, she'd have spit at him. She really needed some water.

His eyes narrowed. He hadn't liked being called a killer.

Well, too bad.

"I'd been warned ye'd be a difficult handful. I believe they might have underestimated ye, lassie. Ye've a hard heart, to be sure."

"Hah! What do you know about hearts?"

She was on a roll. At least she'd be going out in a blaze of pithy glory.

"Ach, now, yer teeth are showin'. Why don't ye tuck in your claws and we'll have a nice wee stroll back to Castle Ross. Were ye aware how you'd gone in circles? Or did ye mean to do it? Did ye think ye could hie home to your witch's tomb and leave me back here, in the past? Ye forget, I'm a local lad. It's a bit easier for me to swallow what's happened to us than it has been for ye. And I speak Scots too, only without the American accent, o' course. Ye never had a chance. Those lads reported yer every footstep.

"I must admit, I'm a mite impressed by you scarin' off the wolf as ye did. But now that we've had a chance to get to know each other a bit, I'm no' surprised in the least. No doubt you could scare the whole pack away with but the venom in your sweet voice."

She was tempted to let him have it with her stick.

"If I didna have a job to do," he added, "I'd leave ye be, here in the woods. But I wouldna be so cruel to animals, aye?"

She ignored his joke, too busy asking herself, *Why didn't she let him have it with her stick?*

He might not have considered it a weapon because she'd been using it as a walking stick. Or maybe it looked a little too brittle to cause any harm. If he hadn't been the one to see her chase the wolf away, maybe he didn't know she'd done so with her glorified toothpick.

She started thinking like a physicist again. Okay, so she'd only had one class, but still. It had worked with the wolf.

Weak stick. Big man. Weak spots.

They'd left the other men behind. Either McKiller was too cocky to think he needed help with her, or he couldn't find anything in his pockets that might bribe them. So she only had to get away from one little man.

Okay, one big man.

The morning sun was up, lighting their wide, well-worn road. In the distance, a ridge had been stripped of trees. Stumps left behind looked like stubble on a giant jaw. It had to be the ridge that ran up behind Castle Ross. She was almost there! But then again, so was Gabby's man. A footrace to the hole would only continue what they'd started. Once they were back outside, she'd be racing up the hill to her car. He'd beat her to it since his car was probably still parked at the castle, or behind it.

As much as she wanted to go back, it would be futile. She'd be handed over to Gabby for the ultimate betrayal. And that wasn't going to happen.

She dragged her foot over a rock and tripped, then stopped to adjust her shoe. McKiller let go of her arm, but stood with his hands ready to grab her. She rolled her eyes and walked on, but as she did, she began to limp.

"Ye're hurt?" He looked at her sideways, suspicious.

"Rock in my boot," she said. Then she stopped in the middle of the road and pretended to remove said rock. While she pulled the boot back on, he looked behind them for the hundredth time. "Better be careful," she teased. "Some FBI agent might have followed us through time. Might be hiding in the bushes."

He snorted. "And that would frighten me, why?"

Her skinny piece of wood might not have had much mass, so thumping him on the head would have done nothing but break the stick. But if she added a bit of momentum and velocity to it...

She spun in a circle, holding her innocent stick away from her body, then pulling it in a little just before it smacked the cocky Scot across the nose. He'd ducked right into it. The stick broke, of course, but before it did, it gave the big man's nose one hell of a whack. She was pretty sure it wasn't just the stick that broke.

He cried out and stumbled back. His eyes were pinched tight. His hand reached for his gun at his back. It was too late to try to push him to the ground and wrestle him for it. She just had to run and hope there were some trees between them by the time he could see straight.

"Get back here, Bell! Ye're a lot safer with me than ye are out there!"

Safe? With a killer? Hah!

Deep and deeper into birch trees she flew, her feet barely touching the ground. When the grasses gave way to rocks, she had no choice but to slow. She struck out east, hoping to avoid those men that had supposedly been tracking her every move before. McKiller kept hollering at her, but it didn't sound like he'd even left the road yet. The first time she'd dared look back, he'd still been holding his nose and groping the air with his free hand.

"Juliet! I'll not go back without ye. Do ye hear? And ye're going to stick out like a sore thumb. I'll know exactly where to find ye. And this time, I'm going to truss ye up like a pig and hang ye from a pole! Do ye hear?"

"Thanks for the pointers," she said softly as she ran. First thing on the wish list would be a change of clothes.

CHAPTER THIRTEEN

After about an hour, Jules rested in a clearing full of tall grass and wildflowers. It was so tempting to lie down and sleep, but sleep wasn't even close to the top of that list. Clothing had slipped to number three, after water and food. It was when she lifted her eyes from the tempting flower bed that she first saw the smoke. A nice, focused trail of it lifting into the sky.

"Civilization. Hallelujah." She headed straight for it.

Sounds of industry reached her ears just as she noticed her feet were following a path through the trees. A lovely little stream came next, where she bent down and drank her fill. Soon, both water and path led her to a thatched house with a water wheel on its side. The wheel had little scoops on it, just a bit deeper than a paddle, more shallow than a bucket—about the size of frying pans. It might not be used for harnessing any energy at the moment, but it was doing a fine job lifting water from the stream and dumping it into a trough at the roofline of the house.

Somebody was thinkin'.

She wondered if the woman who lived in the little house might be a laundress considering the long lines of clothes at the other end of the house. Either that, or a few dozen people lived there among the little cluster of buildings. The yard was still in deep morning shadows, thanks to the giant oak trees that surrounded the place, so Jules felt brave enough to scurry to the clothes on the line, to see if they were dry, hoping her dark coat and jeans wouldn't draw any attention.

She was grasping the hem of a plaid wool skirt when she realized she was being watched.

Shit!

A woman stood at the corner of the house, shaking her head. She wore a solid blue dress with a plaid pinafore over the top and an apron on the front. Catching someone about to steal from her clothesline didn't seem to alarm her, but she was suggesting, rather strongly, that Jules not do it.

Jules put her hands behind her back.

The woman motioned for the would-be thief to follow her.

Why on earth would Jules follow her? Was this one of those centuries where thieves had their hands cut off?

But then again, why on earth shouldn't she? The woman looked harmless enough. And it wasn't as if she or her hands might end up as the meat in someone's giant pot of stew.

Jules shook off the Hansel and Gretel images and followed the woman around the corner of the house where she stood with a door open, pointing inside while she scanned the yard. The fairy-tale-gone-bad images came roaring back until the woman gave her a wink. Evil, child-eating witches didn't wink, right?

The air inside was heavy with steam. Small fires burned around the room, their smoke floating up into a funnel-like ceiling. That had to be the source of the smoke that had led Jules there. On top of the fires sat large copper cauldrons with clothing slopping around inside them. Long paddles sat propped on the edge. They looked like giant bowls of dark porridge with flat spoons at the ready.

A hand descended on her shoulder and Jules jumped. She still had that Hansel and Gretel scenario running through her head and if there were ever caldrons made to accommodate a human being, these were it. The woman was oblivious to the fact that Jules was freaking out. She just kept reaching for her until she finally got her fingers on the lightweight sweater Jules wore under her leather jacket. A pale blue t-shirt made up for the loose and see-through weave of the sweater, but the woman tisked and shook her head. She spoke, but Jules didn't understand and asked her to repeat herself.

The woman did. She even spoke slowly, but it didn't help at all. Whatever her dialect, Jules couldn't understand it. She grimaced and shrugged, hoping the other woman would understand her dilemma. The latter smiled and nodded, then made a gesture that clearly meant Jules was supposed to take off her coat. The same gesture got her to take off the sweater, but the third time, the woman was looking at her jeans.

Jules shook her head.

The woman pointed at the wall behind her. Jules turned and saw a plaid pinafore hanging against the wall. Just a skirt, a square bib, and shoulder straps. It certainly looked like something the locals, in the local time zone, would wear. But before she dropped her drawers, she had to make sure the woman knew she couldn't pay for it. Jules didn't need to speak the language to know this chick couldn't take a Visa.

She hoped the gesture of turning out one's pockets was universal. Apparently it was. The woman waved an impatient hand and then picked up the sweater again. It so happened the gesture for 'trade' was also universal.

The laundress looked pretty pleased when Jules handed over her jeans, but it creeped her out just a little when the woman peeked over the folded denim to see what Jules was wearing underneath. Her blue lace-fringed panties made the woman laugh. Hard. Jules tried not to be offended and slipped the pinafore over her t-shirt.

The woman tisked again and gave her a simple yellow blouse to wear besides, and once Jillian was completely dressed, she realized she looked just like the laundress except for an apron and the pointed tips of her cowboy boots peeking out from under the ankle length skirt.

Sore thumb, eh?

The woman pushed her back outside, then took her over to another little house that shared the same yard. A square table took up most of the space in the center of a modest kitchen. No fridge. No sink. No dishwasher. No countertops. Just a stone fireplace, pots, and the table. Onions and turnips hung in baskets from the ceiling, along with things she couldn't identify. And they still had a thick layer of dirt on them. Jules wondered if maybe that preserved them better, since the rest of the little room looked neat and tidy. She couldn't imagine someone who liked things to be that clean would allow half a garden's worth of dirt to come in with the crop.

She was pushed toward a chair, so she sat. If she was going to be used for stew meat, surely the woman would have conked her on the head before she had a chance to get dressed again.

She chuckled, but it was probably more from relief than from thinking anything was funny. Nine days. She still had nine days to stay alive and make it back to New York to testify. She'd already outrun McKiller, frightened off a wolf, slept in a tree without giving a thought to bears, and escaped McKiller again. And it hadn't even been twenty four hours!

Now she had a disguise and was about to be fed, and both miracles due to the kindness of a stranger's heart.

She re-evaluated the whole *kindness* part when she was served a bowl of mushy, tasteless...well, *mush*. She was pretty sure it would have the texture of throw up.

She couldn't do it.

As grateful as she was, she just couldn't sit there and pretend it was edible. Not for her anyway. Her gag reflex wasn't something she could control. If she forced herself to swallow it, it would come right back up. But how did she explain?

The woman poured her a tankard of milk, then another for herself. Then she sat down opposite Jules as if she hadn't noticed her dilemma.

"Um," Jules said. She looked down into her bowl for courage. "Um," she tried again.

The woman laughed. Then she laughed harder. Then, when she could speak again, she said something incoherent and laughed again.

In Gaelic, as clearly as she could, Jules said, "I've never been able to eat this...stuff. And believe me, I do want to eat it. I just can't."

The woman shook her head. "Life is hardly fair, is it?" She'd changed her dialect to match the one Jules used. "Me sisters all could eat it fine, but it took pride to get me through. God forgive me, I'm a proud woman. Try this."

She sucked some milk into her mouth, then leaned her head back and dropped a spoonful of mush into the back of her throat. She swallowed it down without chewing.

"Sticks to yer ribs half the day. Ye'll see."

And so went their meal. Mush washed down with a swallow of milk and a lot of giggling. Jules had needed a second mug to get through it all. As their laughter died, the woman jumped to her feet in horror.

"Och, I'll be boilin' the colors clean out of their kilts. Their enemies willna recognize them." She hurried to the door, then looked back with a smile that reminded Jules of the Muirs.

A couple hours and some pulled muscles later, the laundry was hung. Jules' hands looked just like the hands of Debra, her mush instructor. They were red and raw and needed much more than just Corn Huskers Whatever-It-Is Lotion.

The woman might stir the clothes with large wooden paddles, but it seemed the only thing to wring the hot water from them, in those days, was a couple pair of hands. With one of them twisting each end of a length of plaid, Deb claimed her work went much quicker that day and together, they were able to sit on the edge of the stream and dangle their red arms in the cool water. Deb said it was a rare treat, that she was able to do it at night sometimes, but when she had to choose between dangling and sleep, sleep usually won.

Since the conversation had turned to Jules' next concern, she asked— and was given—a safe place to sleep and a promise she would be awakened for supper.

How simple it would be, Jules thought as she nestled down in Debra's soft clean bed, to just stay there. Live a simple life. Pretend she was a nature freak and leave civilization behind. But then she needed to pee and that put an end to that idea. It was no use, really. She was a city girl. She would always be a city girl. She just needed to get back to the city.

Returning to the bed after a trip to the *necessary*, she blocked out all thought of what had brought her to this place and what would take her away. Instead, she concentrated on the sound of her own breathing, on the scent of heather coming from the purple bundles hanging and drying next to the wall. She didn't remember falling asleep.

And maybe she hadn't.

He was there again—the big Highlander, the spirit that had finally tipped the scales and made her do anything necessary to come to Scotland. She'd used the excuse of finally confronting her sister and getting her hands on her share of their grandmother's fortune, but it was *him* she'd come to find. How sad, really, that he'd turned out to be her sister's husband. Jules had stayed in the hills above their home for days after that little shocker. But now she realized it wasn't because she was afraid to face her sister, but afraid to face reality. As long as she didn't verify who he was, she could still fantasize about him, without being a sicko, right?

And now he was back.

And if this was truly a dream, she didn't want to wake up.

It was dark. It was always dark. The air around them seemed thick with more than just her anticipation. They were already standing close—toes to toes—and yet, she could not get close enough. His head fell forward, his hair made it difficult to see his face. But she could hear him breathing and feel his arms as they came around her. So warm. So soft. So hard.

"Stay with me," he begged. His voice was edged with worry, ragged. Didn't he know she'd stay?

In some dreams, he'd say it simply, like an invitation to lunch. This time it was different. He was feeling as desperate as she was.

"I will. I'll stay," she whispered. "I promise."

How could she comfort him? It was driving her crazy.

"My own lass. Stay with me, just until the end," he said, then whispered, "then ye may go." He'd said it so softly she wondered if he hadn't meant for her to hear, didn't want her to worry too.

"I'm not going anywhere. And I won't let go. I swear." She was almost too afraid to ask, but she did. "'Til the end of what?"

His hands gave a little squeeze. It was so real, she was sure she felt it, that he was really there with her, and she refused to open her eyes, to prove he wasn't.

"Just 'till the end, lass. You'll know when it's over."

Sometimes the dream ended there, but she wouldn't let it. This time, it was important that she figure it out. And she needed to hurry.

"I'm not who you think I am," he said, when she was the one who should be saying those words.

"Neither am I," she confessed, half hoping he hadn't heard her. Of course he thought she was Jillian. If he knew she was only Jules, he wouldn't be holding her like this, wouldn't be cherishing her like this. It was going to kill her to tell him she'd been Jules all along, through all the months they'd been meeting like this, in her dreams.

He pulled her nearer and bent his head to kiss her. She could feel his hair brush her cheeks, felt his lips press ever so slightly against hers. She willed him to kiss her harder, give her a solid memory to hold onto in the light of day, but there was something between them, always between them. It was so frustrating. She wanted to get closer, to feel his hard chest against her cheek, to know, just for a minute, that she was safe. To pretend she was loved.

Whatever it was separating them was cold. Ice cold. Like bars. Like...a knife.

"Wake, lassie." A man's voice. "Ye be dreamin'. Wake before ye slit yer own throat with yer thrashing about."

"Wake, my lady!" The desperation in Deb's voice brought Jules fully alert.

A man stood over her holding a long dagger against her neck. She looked up his arm and into his face. She was going to remember that face because she was going to make him pay for interrupting her dream, from taking her away from her Highlander when she'd just promised not to leave him.

She was way too disoriented to see it any other way.

"Get up nice and slow-like, else Debra be punished on yer behalf. Ye understand me well enough, aye? Yer the lass that big ruddy bastard was hunting last eve. How did ye slip away from him? Mm?"

"Izatt," Debra snarled, "you harm her or me and you'll be boiled along with your kilt next time." She elbowed a second man who held her. When he let go, she didn't try to run. "Get up, lassie," she said. "These two are harmless, and no mistake. But ye must do as they bid. She'll need her boots and her mantle, lads."

Jules didn't know what Debra was talking about, but she was grateful to be given a chance to get her boots back on. To her, boots might mean the difference between escape and not. They also waited for her to put on her jacket.

Once she was on her feet, the taller one pointed to the door with that same dagger. "After ye, milady."

Debra winked at her as she walked past, then slid behind her and blocked the doorway. "Run, lassie!"

Jules didn't dare turn around to make sure the washerwoman was going to be okay. She hadn't seemed particularly afraid of the men, so maybe she knew best. It killed her to leave her new friend in danger, but she didn't want Debra's sacrifice to go to waste, either.

She picked up her skirts and hit her stride as she went into a curve in the road, then ran face first into the neck of a horse.

"Mon Dieu!" a man shouted.

Jules landed on her butt and raised her arm in case the animal felt the need to defend itself. The poor thing might have been even more surprised than she was. But the rider was able to calm it. The screaming had stopped.

The swearing was only getting started.

CHAPTER FOURTEEN

Quinn was having that dream again, so he knew he was still alive. But the dream was so frustrating he simultaneously wished he would stop having it and wished it would never end. He'd been haunted by it for months upon months, but it was his own fault.

Ewan had ordered Mhairi and Margot to stay away from the witch's hole, so when Quinn had caught the Muirs wandering up out of the cellar again he thought they should be punished. As usual, they'd had a better idea. They thought they should pay for their misdeeds in another way. For instance, how would he like a bit of potion to help him dream of his true love?

Of course, when he'd fallen for their little trick, he'd been hoping to revive his dreams of Libby, to remind himself how she'd looked, how she'd sounded. The memories had been fading since he'd left the modern world and he felt as though he was being punished for fooling with the natural order of things. He'd tried to convince himself that his memories were fading because they weren't memories any longer; it was the fifteenth century, so Libby had yet to be born. But that knowledge didn't take the soreness from his heart and he'd been desperate to get a tighter hold on those precious recollections.

And he'd played right into the Muir's conniving, clever hands.

That night, he'd taken their potion, not knowing if he'd wake in the morning, not caring if he didn't. And he'd dreamt, as they'd promised he would. Only it hadn't been Libby in the dream, but Jillian, *Monty's wife!* And oh, how he'd loved her in his dreams. His heart had wept at the sight of her, as if it had been Jillian who had died years before, only to return to him again in his hour of need. For in his dream, he'd been sick with desperation. Something was about to go horribly wrong. They wouldn't have much time together.

Knowing this, they'd knelt on the floor, in the darkness, holding tight to each other, measuring the moments. But something was between them. He'd supposed it was the thought of betraying Monty, for the thought of doing so—if only in his dream—made him sick. Sick while he was dreaming and after he'd awakened as well.

This time, the dream was no different from that night he'd taken the potion, except for the fact he was finally able to kiss her! Always he fought the urge to betray his great uncle, but the urge to press his lips to hers had been too powerful. Nothing else mattered. When they were alone together, in his dream, this woman mended together the pieces of his soul, a soul that had been ripped and tattered by loss and loneliness. Of course he had to kiss her, possess her, make certain she knew she possessed him in turn.

If they could only move a little closer...

"Wake, Montgomery," a woman whispered.

"Jillian?" he mumured.

"*Who* is Jillian?"

Quinn hid his anguish at being jarred from his dream and rolled onto his side.

Betha stood before his cell door with her man, Boyd, by her side. The man smirked. Betha, even from his sideways view, looked furious.

"I dinna ken," he lied.

Betha considered for a moment, then nodded to Boyd. The man dropped his smile and moved to unlock the cell door.

"Hold!" The Runt himself moved out of the shadows and Quinn was strangely relieved.

After his dream, as disturbing as it was, he was loath to pretend affection for another woman. Of course he would show no affection for Jillian either—even if she weren't more than five hundred years into the future.

Quinn rose from his fresh pallet. Thus far, he'd been allowed to bathe and eat a decent meal, but all within his cell. He supposed the pallet was merely to keep him clean until Betha was ready for him, for the lass couldn't mean to lie with him in the dungeon. He'd seen yet another reason to get to his feet, however—no use lying about—he feared leaving his head within easy reach of the violent little man when it might take little to kill him.

"What do ye here, sister?" Cinead jeered as if he knew full well what was afoot.

The Runt was not alone. Another shadow, much larger, separated itself from the wall and joined them. Either it was The Gordon or else the man had a son that looked just like him.

"Father!" Betha sounded genuinely horrified, but Quinn had to give her credit for not cowering.

"Answer the question, daughter." The man's growl sent shivers up Quinn's spine. It was the first time he'd seen the chieftain truly angry. How did Montgomery manage to survive so many years as this man's enemy?

Quinn took a smooth and slow step backward. It was one of those primal instincts to avoid the attention of an angry animal. Out of all the times he'd had a visitor, since waking in the dungeon, he never felt closer to a noose than he did at that moment.

Other Gordon siblings slithered through the entrance carrying torches and fanned out. The place was lit up like they were about to have a party. Quinn just hoped it wasn't a lynching party, but he was afraid he was wrong.

"I only came for my due, father." Betha squared her shoulders. She was either very brave, or very stupid. Perhaps, she was just very *Gordon*, for she looked overmuch like her father as the pair stood facing each other with their hands on their hips.

"Yer due? Ye think ye're due a romp in this man's bed? Ye think ye have some right to his seed? Nay daughter. Ye've the right to a cell there next to him if ye're as addlepated as to believe that."

She glanced at the cell, at the remains hanging against the wall, and swallowed, but she didn't back down. Once again, she faced the old man and raised her chin.

"Ye promised, Father."

The runt frowned, but quickly smoothed his features. Quinn could understand why no one would wish to reveal their thoughts among such an emotional bunch. The rest of the brothers leaned forward, listening closely.

The Gordon's nostrils flared. "I promised noth—"

"Ye did! Ye promised me that if I bore ye a grandson," Betha pointed at Quinn. "A fine grandson that resembled him, that it would be *my* child to rule once ye're gone."

Her father barked with laughter. The sons didn't seem to find humor in their sister's words. Perhaps it had sounded like something their father would promise.

Finally, the old man stopped laughing when he noticed his sons' faces.

"Ye daft wench," the man spit. "Ye thought I'd place a bastard in my stead when I have sae many sons?" His voice boomed louder with each word. Betha finally took a step back, shaking her head, edging away from the bars as if she now believed she might end up on the other side of them. Then she stopped and lifted that chin again.

Was she crazy?

"He wouldn't be a bastard...if I marry him." Betha lifted a shrewd eyebrow, but her father never noticed, busy as he was, glaring at Quinn.

"He's no longer laird of his clan. There is nothing noble about him, lass. Look ye. Look ye past his breeches and ye'll see for yerself. He's a broken man. Hardly worth the rope to hang him." The Gordon leaned close to the bars. "And mark ye well, Ross. Ye've caused enough grief between me bairns. Make yer peace with God. Ye hang on the morrow." Then he turned to make what was sure to be a grand exit.

Quinn lunged forward. If this was his last chance, he'd have his say.

"Why, you mewling warty bastard!" He spit through the bars.

That got the devil to turn at least. The siblings stood perfectly still, only their eyes followed their father as he retraced his steps.

"I pity you, Gordon," Quinn jeered. "You have neither their love nor their respect. You have only their fear. But if that's all you want in this world, you've got it. Do you know how history will remember you, Oh Mighty Cock O' the North?"

Quinn had everyone's attention and it was going to his head. He couldn't have stopped had he wished to. Momentum was pushing him hard and fast, down a hill that might end at that scaffolding sooner than planned.

But it was more than probable he was going to die. Today or tomorrow would make little difference.

The Gordon rolled his eyes, but there was interest there. He was still listening, waiting to hear about his legacy, even if he didn't believe Quinn had The Sight.

"You will not *be* remembered," Quinn announced. "The world will hear the name Cock o' the North and have no idea what it means or who you were. In fact, lairds of Clan Gordon will use the nickname when it suits them. History will remember nothing of you." It might not be true, but it might give the arrogant man pause.

The man's face fell the tiniest bit, then recovered.

"Ye're as daft as yer sisters," he said. "What do I care about history?"

His wide shoulders turned away once more.

But Quinn had seen it, that spark of anger in the bastard's eye and the set of his jaw when he heard that others would use his cocky nickname.

"That could all change, you know."

It was a desperate promise, to get the man to turn back, to change his mind about hanging him tomorrow, but perhaps The Gordon had recognized it as such. After all, the man had seen no proof that Quinn was able to tell the future, and he wouldn't be around to see if the Runt's offspring took his place or not.

One by one, the Gordon siblings, including Betha, tossed a look over their shoulders before following their father out. The funny thing was, Quinn knew he wasn't the one they'd been looking at. It had been his bone-thin companion in the next cell.

CHAPTER FIFTEEN

It was morning again. As Jules and her kidnappers entered through the massive open gates, a whirlwind of emotions entered with them, nicely contained in her gut. First of all, she was relieved they had arrived anywhere at all. Her butt was sore and she was anxious to see if her legs would even work again. Secondly, she was intrigued by the sight of the huge castle perched on a plateau that hung over the sea, and it looked as if she was going to get to see inside. Next, she was pissed that she'd been taken so friggin' far North, away from Castle Ross and her little escape hatch—so pissed she was going to make her new set of captors effing sorry they'd ever laid eyes on her!

And last but not least, she was nervous and excited to see what Fate had in store for her. For the last mile or so, she'd had the growing sensation that something very important was just ahead. It was like the foreboding she'd had before climbing up into the tomb, only this time it was a *good* foreboding. And since her premonitions were pretty reliable, she was almost giddy. But she wasn't about to give these Bozos any points for escorting her there.

She threw an elbow into the ribs of the tall one sitting on the saddle behind her. "Get me off this friggin' horse."

He took a long deep breath, like he was trying to control his temper, and she realized she might be messing with the wrong guy. Just because she'd felt ten feet tall and bullet proof since she'd gotten away from the Feds, didn't mean it was true. Besides, these guys didn't use bullets, they used blades. And they all had at least one.

"Please," she added.

The guy laughed and jumped to the ground. He was still smiling when he reached up for her, thank goodness.

When some ragamuffins ran forward for a good look at her, her captor told them she was a witch. The kids scattered. A few minutes later, there was a mob.

"We're havin' a hanging and a burnin' in the morning, Cheval. We can easily add this one for kindling." This news came from a grubby looking Scot with either a kilt that was too short or skinny legs that were too long. When he got close enough to see her face, he looked surprised. "Or perchance she'd be a poor choice for kindling after all."

"Bonjour, Percy," said the man she'd ridden with, apparently named Cheval.

"The fire might smell a mite better," someone hollered.

Oh, hell. In what century did they burn people as witches?

She tried to think, tried to put years to movies she'd seen, then realized they probably burned witches in all of them. But they couldn't burn her. She had a date with the New York District Attorney in eight days. And the only way to make that date was to convince these people she was worth more than a little firewood.

She laughed loud, to get everyone's attention.

"Burn me? Are you kidding? There is a huge red-headed man near Castle Ross who would pay a fortune for me. And you want to *burn* me?"

She'd broken her stick on the redhead's face, but thankfully she'd slipped off the wolf's tooth first. It was the tooth, held tight in her hand, that kept her from worrying too much. She'd gotten out of a lot of tight spots in the last day. What was one more? Wolfproof. Bulletproof. Fireproof. It was all just the same delusion; she just needed to keep it up.

She was getting mixed looks from the crowd. The kids were slack jawed. Some adults looked worried, like they expected her to burst into flame on her own. But some of them just looked...hungry, and she got that *stew meat* feeling again.

She was pushed and pulled through a door built for yet another giant, but before she got a good look at the vaulted ceiling, she was shoved into a side passage that eventually led to a stairway.

Going down. Again.

Maybe these guys have their own witch's hole.

She picked up the insults where she'd left off when the castle had come into sight. Cheval, the Frenchman who'd insisted she come to this party, had tried to dish them back, but his were all in French. When he'd get pleased with himself, she'd just laugh because she had no idea what he'd been saying. Eventually, he stopped talking to her. Why he never thought to gag her was a mystery.

Izatt was still a viable target, however.

"I hope, Mister Izatt, that when Debra boils your balls, you'll be able to feel it, even in your shallow grave." Jules spit the words over her shoulder as she was pushed through the mother-of-a-castle's mother-of-a-cellar.

She wanted to make sure the man remembered Debra's promise, that if he harmed Jules, he'd be boiled along with his clothes next time. After riding sidesaddle for hours the night before, then again that morning, she was a little cranky and wanted her captors to be as uncomfortable as she'd been.

She should have kept her jeans. In a skirt, she'd had no choice but to ride sideways or the inside of her legs would have been rubbed raw by horsehair. Now her right thigh was sore and her left butt cheek was in a knot from trying to grip the strange saddle. Walking straight was impossible. Add a hump to her back and she'd make a great character for a horror film.

She was lucky the floors were flat since her eyes were having a hard time adjusting back to torch light after all that bright sunshine. After a few minutes, she wondered if her vision was stuck.

They went down another stairway, then came out into an actual dungeon.

Jail cells? Basement of a castle?

Yep. Dungeon.

"Percy Gordon wants this one locked up," Cheval announced.

An old man came out of nowhere and juggled his keys, though he didn't look at them. Cheval gave her a gentle shove, telling her to follow the guy. After the key man managed to open a cell that looked far too shiny to be medieval, he turned a sad smile in her direction. His pupils were white.

"I'm sorry, miss," he said, as Izatt pushed her through the opening.

She reached out and gave the old man's arm a squeeze. "Don't you worry about me."

Izatt grunted. "I thought you was blind, Martin Woolsey."

"I am. Dinna tell me ye canna smell how pretty she is."

Izatt slammed the gate shut behind her. She was sure he stole a little whiff in her direction before he released the bars and headed for the stairs.

"I smell naught," he muttered.

"Maybe you should wash more than your kilt, Izatt," she jeered.

Then she remembered, in Scotland, they didn't call them balls, they called them—

"Ballocks! I meant ballocks! When Debra boils your *ballocks*, I hope you feel it! Every bubble!"

Izatt groaned on his way out. Jules started to laugh until she realized he was taking the last torch with him.

"God have mercy, let me be dreaming!" The anguished shout came from behind her and she spun around and backed against the cell door. She could see nothing in the dark.

"Who's there?" She still had a voice, but the bravado had fled with the light.

"Jillian? Tell me 'tis not you!" The man's voice was deep, the brogue Scottish, but he spoke English. The chills it produced danced against her skin like musical notes.

It was *him.* It had to be.

Then her heart sank. She was dreaming again. But in her dreams, it had never been pitch black. She needed to see his face!

His breath was ragged, like he'd just returned from a run. He was waiting for her to say something.

"Mister Ross?" she whispered.

His breath caught, then he moaned. "Jillian! Tell me it's not you, lass. Make me believe it!"

"Okay. I'm not Jillian."

There. The truth was out there. The fact that she'd been flippant and he wouldn't believe her wasn't her fault, right?

CHAPTER SIXTEEN

Castle Ross, 1496

Ewan Ross, laird of Clan Ross, groaned into his hands. "Oh, God!"

Jilly looked at Monty and shrugged. "After being gone a year, that's not the reception I was expecting."

Monty looked a bit disappointed too. "I'm no' here to ask for the chair back, if that's what ye're worrit o'er."

Ewan shook his head and tried to stand, then thought better of it, but his butt missed the seat and he slid down the front of the Great Ross Chair. She averted her eyes when his sporran and kilt started to rise along with his knees as he sank to the floor.

"I've been drinkin'. Quite a bit, as a matter of information." The shaggy man peered around the dim hall. "Looks like they all ran away, the cowards."

No fires were lit. There were only the torches that Monty had lit when they'd come into the hall. Jillian had tucked her little flashlight into her sock for safekeeping. The last time she'd come back to the fifteenth century she'd realized the only things that traveled with her were the things she was touching, so she was careful to keep it in hand. But now they were out of the cellar, she had to keep it out of sight. She had no intention of being burned as a witch.

"Who ran away?" asked Monty as he approached the dais.

"My clan. No, yer clan. The whole bloody lot of them."

Jilly laughed. "It sounds like they're having their supper outside."

Ewan perked up. "Aye? Well, then. That's fine. Hello, Monty," he said, like he'd just noticed his arrival. "Did you see? Jillian has come back to kill me."

This time it was Monty's turn to laugh as he helped his cousin lift his backside onto his chair.

"And why would harmless little Jillian wish ye dead, cousin?"

Ewan leaned toward Monty's shoulder. "Because I've lost her sister is why."

His whisper was loud enough he might have been heard outside. Why did men always go deaf when they drank?

She tried not to panic. After all, Juliet was her age; it wasn't as if she were a child wandering aimlessly around a jousting tournament without enough to sense to stay clear of the horses.

"I'm sorry you've lost her." She tried not to sound worried. "Do you remember *where* you lost her?" For all she knew, the woman was outside having supper with the rest. She could hardly trust what Ewan said, as drunk as he was.

"I lost her out the hall door," he gasped, as if the hall door were the gate to Hell. "That ruddy bastard got away from us and went after her, but he didn't get her either. Do you ken why?"

Okay, the gunman didn't get her. It was a start.

Monty gave her a wink and put both hands on the arms of the chair, demanding Ewan's full attention.

"That's fine, cousin," he said. "So how do you ken the ruddy bastard didn't find her?"

"Because I've men watchin' the Gordon Keep. They came upon Gordon allies who were taking the lass with them. They'd have taken her back had they knows she was ours." Ewan turned a little green, but swallowed hard. A few seconds later, he looked at Monty again. "So the ruddy bastard didna get her. But alas, the Gordon bastards did."

Ewan started slipping again. Monty stood back and let him pour into a puddle on the floor.

"By way of information, Monty darlin'," Ewan said, "did I tell ye that I've lost your great nephew?"

Jilly took a deep breath and looked at her husband. It was their worst fear...

She'd lived a wildly exciting and wonderful year as the wife of Montgomery Ross, made doubly so by the fact that she'd gotten the best of both worlds, or both centuries at least. He was bold and beautiful and unrepentant. He saw things clearly, simply, like an old cowboy. He loved and never analyzed why he loved. He judged only himself. The dangerous life he'd come from made him enjoy every minute he had. Nothing was wasted, especially not a chance for a nap together—or whatever else they could think of.

And she'd been able to enjoy the gloriousness that was Montgomery Ross in the comfort of the twentieth century. She didn't have to worry about losing him to infection or disease. She had toilets and hot showers and fast food. The winters would not threaten the lives of their children. Neither of them would have to break their backs to put food on the table, or keep a sword close by to defend that table.

But her double blessings had come at a price, and it was Quinn who had paid it. Willingly. Eagerly.

The most she and Montgomery had paid was the worry. Was Quinn safe? Was he happy? Was he regretting the choice he'd made? Should they go back and ask him? History hadn't changed at all. They had no record of what had become of him.

Of course Jilly hadn't been nearly as worried as Montgomery was—not that they talked about it much—because her husband knew the world in which they'd left the man. He knew much more about the dangers than she'd learned in history books. And every time she'd seen a shadow cross Monty's face, she suspected he was thinking about Quinn, or Ewan, or Isobelle—the ones they'd left behind.

Of course, they couldn't have brought through the tomb everyone Monty had ever cared about. Ewan had a clan to run, Quinn had asked to go back, and Isobelle was lost to them. It just wasn't possible to make the world the way they wanted it, even with the help of a passageway through time.

The look on her husband's face when Ewan announced Quinn was lost? It was that same old shadow of worry, but multiplied by a hundred. Beneath that quite surface, she imagined the ground was crumbling.

She knelt next to Ewan and pushed his knee down and straightened his kilt.

"Ewan? Where did you lose Quinn?" She asked it so Monty wouldn't have to.

Ewan shook his head slowly. "Poor bastard. Can't remember where our land leaves off. Doesn't pay close mind to much, that one."

"Does he live?" whispered Monty.

Ewan nodded carefully. "For the moment, cousin, but nae for long."

"What do you mean?" her husband demanded. "Where is he?"

"He's in The Gordon's dungeon. And now Jules is there as well." Ewan peeked at Jilly, then looked away quickly. "Dinna let her hurt me, cousin."

Jules? Her sister's name was *Jules, not Juliet?*

The sound of it made her stomach do strange things. Or was it the baby? She thought she was going to be one of those lucky women who didn't get morning sickness, but maybe not.

She looked at Monty. Just the sight of him always seemed to calm her.

He stared at Ewan and took a deep breath, then let it out slowly. He certainly didn't look like he was freaking out. It was enough to give her hope. Things must not be as bad as she'd thought they were. Monty would know just what to do, just like he always did.

"Och, Ewan," he said. "No one is going to hurt ye. It'll be ever so convenient to collect them both at the same time. Ye've done well, cousin. In the morning, we can have this entire conversation again, aye?" Monty pulled the big man up, then hefted him over his back. "We'll just put ye to bed first. It's a fine way to hurry tomorrow along."

Jilly numbly followed as Monty headed for the archway and the stairs beyond.

Ewan grunted. "I doona wish the morrow to hurry along, Monty darlin'. 'Tis the day your great nephew is to die. If not by Gordon's hand, then by mine."

Jilly's heart stopped.

Monty halted and tipped forward, dumping his big cousin off his back and onto the floor. Then he fetched a pitcher of water from the high table and headed back for Ewan with murder in his eyes.

CHAPTER SEVENTEEN

Quinn swallowed hard. As much as he wished Jillian away from that place, he couldn't help but be thrilled to see her again. He'd never imagined his dream took place in a dungeon, but then again, he never thought his dream would become reality either.

"Come here, lass. Let me touch ye, just enough to know that ye're real, that I haven't conjured ye to comfort me in the dark." He shouldn't have said it. He couldn't have not.

Of course he had no intention of dishonoring his great uncle, but just like in those dreams, he seemed to have little control over his need for her. And now, awake, the need was much more intense. If it was the last thing he'd ever do—which it very well might be—he was going to hold her close and press his lips to hers. Just one perfect kiss. It was all he wanted.

It was all.

She moved along the bars. He could hear her hands bumping each one as she came slowly toward him. The anticipation twisted his chest and made him want to groan with the exquisite frustration of it. There, in the dark, she was merely the woman from his dream, not Jillian, his friend.

"Montgomery Ross?"

Her whispered question cut through his fantasy, sobering him.

"Nay. I cannot pretend that I am Monty. It is I, Quinn. Has my homely uncle returned as well?"

She stopped moving. Her small gasp came from only an arm's length away. He wanted to reach out and pull her to him, to give her no choice in the matter. But surely she would come to him, even as a friend, Jillian would come. They'd comforted each other before, when they'd been in the depths of despair—he still mourning Libby, and she rent in twain after leaving Montgomery in the past. Now, tossed in the enemy's dungeon, she would need a bit of comfort again. Why did she hesitate?

Why, oh, why couldn't he have let her believe he was Monty, if only for a few moments?

"Quinn?" Her voice broke, as if on a sob. "Quinn *Ross?* The one on the website? I thought Quinn and Montgomery were the same man."

He suddenly felt as confused as she sounded.

"Jillian. Dear Jilly. Have ye lost yer senses? Do ye not remember me? We spent the better part of two weeks together, greetin' over the loss of our loved ones. Do you remember none of it, then?"

"I'm...I'm not Jillian. I'm *not* Jillian. I swear to you, I'm not Jillian." She laughed, but it only served to worry him more.

He'd never been so desperate for light.

"Martin! Martin, can ye give us a wee bit o' candle? Just a quick bit of light, aye? Martin," he whispered as loud as he dared. "Can ye hear me?"

There was movement near the door. A few minutes later, the old man approached.

"Trusting a blind man with fire is terrible foolish," said Martin. "But lucky for ye, they're a foolish lot. But ye mustn't risk more than a moment or two before ye must douse it."

"Don't move," Quinn told the woman. He pressed himself against the cell door with his hands outstretched and clicked his fingers. He could not wait to prove this angel from his dream was not Montgomery Ross's wife.

An eternity passed, then a box crashed into his hands. He took it, gave Martin's hand a squeeze, then opened the box. He located the flint, the tinder, and a short nub of a candle only two inches long.

"God bless ye, Martin," he said, but the man was already shuffling away.

"I'd stay to have a peek at her, but I doona wish to interfere," Martin said, then laughed.

After a lifetime of tries, the candle took. By the time it did, he was worried that he'd imagined it all and there would be none but Skully in the adjoining cell.

His hands shook as he put a protective hand around the flame and turned. Each step he took gripped his heart tighter...

Tighter...

Tighter still.

There was a bit of shine to the woman's coat. Leather, like Jillian wore the first time she set foot in the Ross hall. A plaid dress, like the one Jillian was wearing when she brought Morna and Ivar through the tomb and into the twenty-first century.

His stomach dropped when he noticed the Western cowboy boots. How could she not be Jillian? Dare he hope the way she was dressed was but coincidence?

When he finally stood before the dimly lit form beyond the bars, he removed the hand that blocked the light from her face.

His own face fell. He could not help it from doing so, he was that disappointed. The only thing different about her was that her hair looked a bit darker than before, but it might only be the lack of proper lighting.

"Jillian." He wanted to demand why she would have lied to him, but it was hard enough to just say her name. He wanted to take her by the arms and shake her, to make her understand how her pretense had hurt him.

"I'm *not* Jillian. I'm her sister, Juliet. I go by Jules. Apparently, we're twins."

He shook his head. How could she tease him like this? Especially now, when he might actually hang in the morning.

"Ah, Jilly. Surely ye didn't find your way in here only to tease me." He held out the candle. "Here. You take it."

The thing was small. She tried to take it from his fingers, but couldn't do so without them losing the light altogether.

"Forget it," she said sharply and turned away, leaving him holding he candle up to empty space. "And I'm not Jillian, asshole."

He stood there in stunned silence. Was she telling the truth?

Then, with no more warning than a low keening to precede it, a painful scream shot through his ears and head and ricocheted through the dungeon. Jillian's scream. When he finally thought to shield his eyes from the candle, he found her, whimpering with her back against her cell door. She was staring at the corpse.

"I'm sorry, lass. I should have warned ye. I call him Skully."

The pet name was no help. She didn't seem to be listening on any account.

"He's harmless, lass. Look at me."

She took a few deep breaths, then turned her face. Eventually, her eyes turned too.

"And by the way," he said. "I believe ye're not Jillian after all."

"Oh yeah?" She took a deep breath and choked, then she pulled up a t-shirt from under her blouse and covered her face. It muffled her voice. "Why? Don't I scream like her?"

"I don't ken about that," he said. "But I do know she would have never called me an arsehole. Ever."

CHAPTER EIGHTEEN

The replica of Montgomery Ross, the man she'd prayed for, the man she recognized in the core of her being, reached through the bars again, his hands open, palms up. The candle was perched on one.

"Take the candle, lass, but for pity sakes, look at me, not Skully."

"Who is he?" She couldn't seem to let go of the bars behind her. She'd seen her parents in their caskets, but she didn't remember it clearly, only that they didn't feel real anymore. Other than that, she'd never been around a dead body before. Except for Nikkos, she reminded herself. But Nikkos had still been bleeding.

"It doesn't matter," the Quinn said. "Just pretend he's but a decoration for Samhain."

"Samhain? Oh, right. Halloween. Decoration. Got it." She still couldn't stop staring.

"Look at me, lass. Am I so disgusting you canna stand to glance this way?"

She heard him talking, but all she could do was shake her head. Disgusting? Hardly. But it was hard to face him when just a moment ago, looking at her face had somehow disappointed him. That Muir sister had noticed something that made her different from Jillian.

Apparently, he noticed it too. Maybe Jillian was a real beauty or something.

"I don't believe you," Quinn said. "I must be repulsive indeed."

Him? Repulsive? Yeah, right.

She'd only gotten a quick look so far, but repulsive he was not. He was obviously just being nice, trying to distract her. Calling him an asshole had been a little harsh—maybe—but being mistaken for someone else was new to her and damn hard to get used to. The fact that he'd been disappointed when he'd looked at her just added insult to injury.

You idiot, said the voice in her head. *He was disappointed when he thought you were Jillian!*

Oh my gosh! That's true, she answered back.

She smiled and turned. He grinned and held the candle up in front of his face. She was finally able to release her grip and move closer to the side bars to look her fill. He did look just like the picture on the website, and she told him so.

"Oh, that." He sounded a little disappointed. "Yes, that was me. A long while ago, I'm afraid."

She caught herself licking her lips and she turned away, mortified. Why didn't she just reach over and start running her fingers through his hair? Just because she was so intimate with the man in her dreams, didn't mean she could jump on this guy. But there, in the darkness, it was hard to believe it wasn't that dreamland where they already knew each other. She was just going to have to try harder to put that dream aside.

"Tut! Doona do it, lass. Just a decoration."

She nodded and brought her attention back to him, reluctantly. She'd almost forgotten about being scared shitless.

"Just a decoration," she said. "No biggy."

He nodded. "Happy Halloween, aye?"

Other than his build and his coloring, he really didn't look that much like Jillian's husband—at least the face she'd stared at through binoculars. There was something a little more intense about him. His cheekbones were a little higher. Or maybe it was just the darkness. Shadows do funny things to a face. She could look into his smoldering eyes forever, especially while he was staring into hers...

She realized he was waiting for her to say something. What had he been talking about?

"Right. Halloween," she said. "So, who is he?"

"A stubborn man, or so Martin told me." It wasn't the casual way he'd said it, or the slightly higher pitch that gave him away, but the pause before he'd spoken.

"You thought I wouldn't want to know he was stubborn? I doubt that. What aren't you telling me?"

He sighed. "He was a son to The Gordon."

She turned to look at the skeleton again. No way could she think of it as just a Halloween decoration anymore. He had been someone. This castle had been his home. And his father had let him die here, chained to the wall, in the dark.

A shiver went up her spine. No matter how cold-hearted a murderer Gabby was, he could have never been so cruel. Or could he? Poor Nikkos. *Like a son.* How his heart must have broken in that millisecond between Gabby pointing the gun and firing. But how many times, while he waited to die, had this Skully's heart broken? A bullet would have been kinder.

"Lass." Quinn Ross waved a hand to catch her eye.

She turned back to him. He shook his hair out of his eyes and looked into her soul again and she couldn't help but smile. She was like the candle, coming to life under his attention. It made her feel warm in a creepy dungeon that had no warmth. Too bad he was just a nice guy, trying to keep her calm.

"You didn't want me to know that the man—into whose dungeon we've been tossed—is ruthless enough to leave his son in this same dungeon to rot. Is that it?"

He smiled. His eyes crinkled and he winked at her. "Aye. That's just it."

That wink sent chills to all the places she'd felt warm just a second ago. Winks, she realized, were highly under-rated.

She was afraid her knees might just give out if she didn't look away. Unfortunately, Skully was the only thing to look at.

"What a very, very sad Halloween decoration."

"Aye, lass. Now, let's not waste what time we have left to us."

She could get used to being called lass. It beat being called Jillian any day. She took a deep breath and turned back to him, trying to think of something to say, to keep him talking.

"Why do you say that? You always say that."

She gasped when she realized it was true. He'd always said that—but in the dream!

How had her subconscious known she would end up there, having that exact conversation? How could she have dreamed about a man she'd never laid eyes on yet? She'd never even known about Jillian when the dreams had started, let alone the Castle Ross website where she'd found his picture.

Quinn's picture.

Gah! He must have thought she was so stupid. He wouldn't have any idea what she was talking about. But, holy crap! Quinn Ross—not Montgomery Ross— haunting her dreams?

It had been a shocker, running across that picture and recognizing him when he shouldn't have existed. She'd obsessed about him 24/7, for weeks, making herself sick until she'd turned her attention to escaping from her federal babysitters.

But he was real. And he wasn't Monty. And now he was going to think she was certifiable.

She closed her eyes and shook her head, waiting for the ceiling to fall on her head.

He laughed. Then he stopped short. Then he laughed again, and all without her looking up. He was delighted about something, and after a few seconds, she couldn't stand it anymore and opened her eyes.

He reached out with his free hand and took hold of her fingers, pulling her up tight against the bars, and suddenly, she felt like they were in his cell and not hers. The heat coming through the empty gaps was more than enough to make up for the cold bars pressed against her. He studied her face for a minute and didn't seem to find anything unpleasant, even though she hadn't seen a shower or a brush for two days and been dragged halfway across Scotland by Cheval. The last time she'd cleaned up had been at Debra's.

"I always say that?" he whispered. "We've only met, lass. When did I say it? And what did I say?"

She looked down, embarrassed. He'd been laughing at her after all.

"Speak to me, lass. I must know. Tell me the truth of it, if ye please."

It was charming, the way he begged.

She took a deep breath, stalling, wanting to wait just a minute longer before saying anything that might make him want to let go of her.

"You're going to think it's silly."

"Never." He lifted her chin with a knuckle, and then the contact was gone. She very nearly lowered her head again, just to feel that knuckle a second time. It felt wonderful, like her chin had been starved for attention.

How pathetic.

"Fine," she said. "I've had this recurring dream, see. It was about you—probably because of that picture on the website. But then I got to Scotland and saw Montgomery and I thought I was lusting after Jillian's husband. I was sick about it, actually."

"Lusting, ye say?"

She tried to pull away, but then she remembered how badly she wanted to *not* be in that cell with Skully, so she let him pull her close again, grateful that he still wanted to, considering how silly she was acting.

"I ask, Juliet, because I've shared this dream."

Oh, great.

"Uh huh," she said. "Sure you have."

No way was she going to stand there and make a fool out of her. But if she put up much of a struggle, the candle would go out and she would freak out.

She took a careful step back, but he only pulled her tighter. The light wobbled and she froze.

He shook his head. "You don't believe me. I understand why you wouldn't. I do. But I'm not playing with you. Hear me out, aye? In this dream, is it always dark?"

"Lucky guess."

"And is there always something between us, keeping us apart?"

She gave him one nod. No way would he guess anything else.

"And perhaps we only have a few stolen moments together because I'm supposed to die in the morning?"

Oh my hell! How does he know?

"What? Wait! What?"

He sighed. "Perhaps that wasn't technically part of our dream then. But I always supposed what kept us apart was the impression that you were Jillian and the love of Monty's life, and not a wall of bars."

"Wait. Just wait a minute. What about you *dying* in the morning? Was that a dream, or is it real?" She found her fingers digging into his skin, trying to pull him closer, but he didn't seem to mind, which was lucky, because she couldn't seem to stop. She felt so desperate, just like she always did, clinging to him like she was. It was exquisite torture, wanting to hold onto the dream, not wanting to wake up, but at the same time hoping she wasn't dreaming at all.

"The Gordon has decreed it," he said casually, like, "It's supposed to rain in the morning."

She stared at his broad chest and the neck just above it. Hang him? How could they? Were they blind? Then she remembered Skully.

"The Gordon is the bastard who left his son to die, right?"

"Right you are," Quinn said, but she had the impression, from the way he was staring at her, that he wasn't paying a lot of attention to their conversation. His eyes kept moving around her face, like it was a puzzle he was trying to solve. If someone handed him a pen, he might draw a little path from her brows, to her ears, back to her nose, then around to her chin. Her mouth was apparently the end game.

Please, let my mouth be the end game.

He looked back at her eyes and smiled.

She took a deep breath and sighed. "Then, we've just got to get you out of here."

She knew full well she was stepping back on the delusion train, but she didn't care. This was no time to be realistic. Wolfproof, bulletproof, and fireproof. Well, the last part she wouldn't have to wonder about if she managed to escape with him.

He laughed. "You have a grand plan, do ye?"

"Aye. I do." She couldn't help but mock his sexy Scottish brogue.

"Complicated, is it?" He tucked her hair back behind one ear. She was losing his attention again.

"No, not really." She tried to imitate his sexy smile too, to get him to look at her lips again, but she'd done better with the accent.

He raised one brow. No way could she copy that.

"Truly? Then I must hear this plan."

She grinned and wished she could wink, but she was afraid she'd look anything but sexy doing it.

"We scream," she said, "until they come to shut us up, then we overpower them and get away."

He laughed. Hard. It started to sound a little hysterical.

"Hey, don't knock it. I'll have you know every plan I've had lately has worked. For a while anyway. Obviously, this dungeon was not in my plans."

"And just how many plans have you needed lately, sweet Juliet?"

She was just about to correct him, to tell him that no one calls her Juliet, but she realized the chills currently shooting through her were due to the way he'd said her name—again, with that lovely brogue.

While she watched his lips, waiting to hear her name again, she told him how she'd gotten from point *a* to point *b*—from shaking the feds to stalking her sister with binoculars, from outrunning the Gabby's hitman to ending up in Gordon's dungeon. It sounded more like a list of people, and an animal, whose heads she'd damaged in one manner or another. The head butt she'd given the guard at the Castle Ross's gate made her sound downright violent, even when she called it a Glasgow Kiss.

He looked more than a little doubtful, and she was almost relieved he didn't think she could be so dangerous. Then she remembered the wolf's tooth and pulled it out of her sock.

"See? Proof." When he had no comment, she got nervous and started to ramble. "You probably thought I was making it all up—"

He dropped the candle and reached for her. His lips were on hers before the light sputtered out.

Just like her dream. And who knew? Maybe she was dreaming again. Her eyes were shut, his lips felt the same as they always did. She reached up and held onto his hard biceps as well as she could. They were huge.

The bars kept her from moving closer, but she raised her hands to his neck and was able to hang on better.

He pulled back enough to break the kiss.

"Stay with me," he whispered.

"You always say that."

"I mean here. Right here. Stay with me here, until morning."

"You usually say, *until it's over*."

"I thought I'd change it up a bit. Keep you on yer toes."

"I'm already on my toes."

"Well, then, I've got ye where I want ye."

And he kept her where he wanted her for a good long while. Finally, she had to ask for a time-out because the bars were bruising her face.

"You know," she said as they slid to the floor, still clutching each other. "If anyone studies the angle of the bruises on your face and compares them to the ones on mine, they're going to know what we've been doing."

"Well, here's our first test then. Looks as if someone is coming."

She looked over her shoulder and sure enough, the passageway was turning orange.

"Get ye back, lass. Cling to the far corner. If they believe we care for one another, they'll use it against us. Quick now!"

She crawled away like she was told, staying as far away from the Halloween decoration as possible.

"Juliet," Quinn whispered.

"What?"

"Your cellmate stinks to Heaven."

She smothered a giggle, then smothered another when she thought about how silly it was to be giggling in such a place, especially if she considered what might happen in the morning. But for the moment, the man from her dreams was smiling at her, knowing full well she was *not* Jillian.

Their visitors, when they stopped at her cell door, were not smiling.

CHAPTER NINTEEN

"Ye've been summoned by Himself, madam. Best get on yer feet," said the man with the torch. Two burley dudes who could have bounced for Gabby any day, stood to either side of the door while Martin fiddled with the keys. She wondered if he was fumbling on purpose.

She looked over at Quinn. He was leaning casually against the far bars, but his eyes didn't miss a thing—not a thing about her, anyway. With more than just a candle's worth of light, it was hard for her to take her eyes off him too, until he gave a slight shake of his head, then looked at the visitors.

"The mighty Gordon has taken to harassing women now?" He smirked. "I canna wait to see what the neighbors think."

The guard closest to him kicked at his bars. "Quiet Ross. You willna be about long enough to discover what the neighbors think of anything."

Quinn just grinned. "No, I won't be around, but you will. I hope they are kind to you men when the castle is overrun."

"Don't mind him. Watch her," said the other. "Her husband says she's a slippery one."

Jules looked at Quinn and shook her head. Then she looked back at the goons.

"Husband?" she said. "I have no husband."

They laughed at her while they watched Martin fumbling with the keys. One reached out, like he was going to take the ring away from the blind man, but Martin slapped it away. The guard narrowed his eyes, then waved a hand in front of Martin's face, only to be slapped again.

"Ye think I canna smell yer oxter each time ye lift that arm? Now back away. Ye've made me lose my count. I must start from the beginning all over again."

Her stomach was tied in knots but she didn't dare look at Quinn for comfort. She was absolutely petrified of who might be coming to claim her as a wife. Maybe someone along the road, maybe one of Cheval's friends, had taken a fancy to her and meant to cart her off to who-knows-where. If they did, who was going to help Quinn get away? And if Quinn didn't get away, there wouldn't be anyone coming to her rescue either.

Of course there was also the hope that Ewan had come looking for her. She'd just have to make sure they took Quinn with them. But the thing she was most afraid of was that the precious dream was over, that she'd never see Quinn again.

Was that what the dream had been—a warning to make the most of their few moments together?

Jules shook her head. That couldn't be it. It couldn't be all they would have. She wouldn't allow it. That dream was going to end the way she wanted it to end, and heaven help whoever got in her way!

Martin sighed and slipped a key in the lock. Her time was up. Quinn had dropped the casual pose and was gripping his own cell door, growling in frustration. She was glad she wasn't the only one.

But she couldn't give up hope. Maybe he'd find a way to escape after all. Maybe he could somehow help her. But just in case someone was there to haul her away, Quinn would need some clue as to where she'd been taken. If it was Ewan, then Quinn would know the Calvary was near.

"What's this husband's name?" she demanded as they dragged her from her cell. They had to pry her fingers off the swinging bars, but she didn't make it easy. "Just tell me his name and I'll go quietly."

"She will not. 'Tis a trick," said one.

"No! I promise! Just tell me, right now, who it is who thinks I'm his wife." They had to say the name while Quinn could hear it. She was terrified she'd just disappear, never to be heard from again. Medieval times. Scotland. She had no idea what the rules were, but she suspected that men could just claim a woman and haul her away. Probably not by the hair, though. Hopefully they'd progressed a bit beyond cavemen.

"Bond, something," said one man.

Bond? That wasn't even a Scottish name, was it?

She held her ground and rolled her eyes. "You don't remember his name?"

"Here, I do," said the other. "His name was silly. Said it was *Bond James Bond* he did. Now you promised to come peaceful-like." The bigger of the two men stepped back and waited for her to comply.

But how could she comply?

Bond, James Bond? It had to be Gabby's man. It had to! And if he was allowed to take her away, she couldn't help Quinn! She'd be dragged back to the twenty-first century and handed over to Gabby. Then they'd both be dead.

A little image surfaced in her mind of Quinn and her reuniting in the clouds.

No way! No effing way! She'd finally gotten her hands on him. It was like God had granted her exactly what she'd asked for, and now He was taking it back.

What had she promised? To give up her revenge on Jillian if she could just have a Highlander of her own. Well, she was going to make sure God stuck to his bargain. She just didn't know how she was going to do it.

She spun around and looked at Quinn, but he seemed as alarmed as she was. Of course, he was from the future and would recognize the name of Bond, James Bond. The taunt was clear. McKiller had tracked her down, gotten the ear of Laird Gordon, and they'd made a deal.

Maybe she wasn't bulletproof after all.

A guard tugged on her arm. "Come now, lass. There are witnesses and ye gave us yer word."

"All right. Just let me say goodbye to—" Wait! She was supposed to act like she didn't know him, or at least she was supposed to act like she didn't care. "I'm sorry, what did you say your name was?"

"Ross. Mister Ross. At your service, milady." He gave her a little bow, but his eyes never left her face.

"Oh, here now, Laird Ross," said the bigger guard. "Don't go about propositionin' a marrit woman. There now. Hold fast to her arms, just in case she bolts. With such a big bounder for a husband, it's understandable her being a mite skittish."

The guards laughed at her all the way up the steps and into a huge common room. All the while, Jules was aching to return to the dungeon. It was ridiculous, but she felt like every step she took was a betrayal of Quinn, that she shouldn't ever leave his side. She'd promised. She was supposed to stay until the end.

She had to go back. No matter what she was offered, she'd have to make sure they took her back to the dungeon.

***

The guards deposited Jules in the middle of the hall and let go. Their arms were poised to grab her again if need be. She rolled her eyes and ignored them.

One look at the men lining the room and Jules realized this would be like a practice run for the trial in seven days—the trial she hoped was *still* scheduled because she *still* intended to be there to testify. It had taken her three days to get into this mess. Even if it took her as long to get out, she'd still have time to make a flight to New York.

Yeah, it was like a practice run, but instead of just one cold-blooded murderer at the front of the room, there were two. The Dungeon Master and McKiller.

As the big redhead turned, she braced herself for the sneer she expected on his face. But she was wrong. He was frowning.

Still mad, huh?

He stood off to the left of a rough-looking throne in which sat a large balding man. The straggly strands of hair growing out the sides of that one's head were orange on the end. Once upon a time, he probably had hair just like his visitor.

McKiller stepped forward. "Are ye harmed, Juliet?"

He was an incredible actor. For a second, she could almost believe he was worried. But why should he care how she'd been treated? As long as he was able to take her back to Gabby, a bruise here and there didn't matter.

He held out his arms and briefly narrowed his eyes, like a warning to play along.

She shook her head. "Sorry. I don't know you, pal. Nice try though."

She turned around to go back to the dungeon, but Moe and Curly blocked her path. Finally, when her dirtiest look didn't affect them, she turned back to McKiller.

The redhead took a step toward her, but the one on the throne, presumably Laird Gordon, held out an arm, as if his reach were so vast he could hold the man back while sitting six feet away. He was draped in furs in spite of the summer weather. She wondered if they were the symbol of his power, somehow.

"Nay, Bond," Gordon said. "As ye so kindly pointed out, me hostage's wellbeing is me duty to protect. I canna have the likes of ye stomp into me hall and claim any woman ye like."

McKiller looked the laird over like he was trying to decide the least messy way to take him out, or the best angle from which he might break the old man's neck. His would-be victim gave him a look that screamed, "Go ahead, idiot. Make my day."

Finally, McKiller looked back at Jules.

"My men saw her taken by Cheval," he said. "Cheval agreed, with a bit of persuasion, to tell us where he'd left her. How else would I have known where to find my wife?"

He shifted his weight, to take another step, but thought better of it. He finally settled for glaring at Gordon. No one in the room seemed worried enough to defend the older man if the younger one attacked. Maybe they didn't care.

"How indeed?" said Gordon. "But can you explain why the lass would deny yer claim, then? She looks of sound mind to me."

Juliet smiled at the awful man and tried to forget, for the moment, that he'd let his own son rot in the basement.

She gave a little curtsy. "Thank you, sir. My mind is just fine."

Gordon lost his smile when she spoke. She guessed her accent sucked.

"Juliet, darlin'," said McKiller, smirking. "Didn't I say you'd stick out like a sore thumb?"

She lifted her chin. "I really don't know what you're talking about." She was feeling very Scarlet O'Hara at the moment. Maybe all women felt that way when men were fighting over them, but since it was yet another experience that was new to her, she could only guess.

McKiller's face turned a shade of red that clashed with his hair, and he lowered his head like a bull getting ready to charge. She couldn't fight her instincts on this one and took a step back.

"Laird Gordon," the man's voice boomed through the room that was slowly filling with an audience. "Clearly, someone among you has seduced my woman away from me. Who is it? Who of yer clan has shared private speech with my wife? I demand satisfaction."

As it happened, McKiller towered head and shoulders over just about everyone in the castle. Quinn Ross was the only man she'd seen in the last two days who might come close. That big mane of red hair made him look like the king of the lions demanding his dinner, and she'd be damned if every Gordon clansmen didn't take a half-step back too. Their laird called a man to him who leaned close to have a private conversation, clearly not interested in whether the lion got fed or not.

But what was McKiller trying to do? Get someone to fight him? No one knew her there. And no one in their right mind would want to fight the guy for her. Was he hoping Laird Gordon would give her over because no one had the guts to oppose him?

Damn it! She was not going to leave with him!

She put her hands on her hips. "You want someone to fight for me, is that it, Bond?"

He and the old man both looked at her like she was no more than a fly buzzing around their heads. The latter went back to his conversation. McKiller went back to puffing out his chest and glaring at anyone who didn't look away fast enough.

She decided she needed to make herself look a little more significant, so she marched over to a young kid and pushed him off his stool, then she climbed up on it.

"Can you hear me better now?" she hollered.

McKiller rolled his eyes. Laird Gordon looked at her like she'd sprouted an extra nose and he couldn't see it as clearly as he'd like. When the guy Gordon had been conversing with finally turned to look at her, he gasped. Gordon shoved him away with disgust.

"If anybody's going to fight for me," she paused for dramatic effect. "It's going to be me!"

Some laughed along with McKiller. Most sighed and turned away from her like they were disappointed she hadn't done or said something more exciting. Gordon turned slightly to say something to her so-called husband, but she had the feeling his was the only attention she had.

Well, if they wanted excitement, they were going to get it.

She hopped off the stool and grabbed a tankard out of a man's hand. Then she spun around and lent a little momentum to the most important pitch of her life. She had hoped to catch McKiller off guard, but he deflected the heavy cup. When it flew to the right and dinged Laird Gordon on the head, she suspected he'd done it on purpose.

Fifty people gasped before the tankard stopped spinning on the floor.

She tried bravado first.

"Softball pitcher. High school."

Bond just grinned.

She tried defense.

"I told you I was going to fight for myself."

Laird Gordon stood up. His head was so red she was worried it would explode and McKiller would grab her and flee in the confusion.

She tried distraction. She was good at distraction.

"Come on, Bond. Let's see what you've got. Let's say if I can knock you to the ground, just once, you have to go away and leave me alone."

The big man turned to the laird. "You see? She clearly protects someone. I demand to ken the man's name."

Well, something worked; Gordon sat back down.

"Who is it, woman?" the old man asked. "One of me sons?" His eyes sparkled. He had sons that he hadn't killed yet? And so many he could afford to lose one in a fight with McKiller?

Jules shook her head in disgust. "No. The only one of your *sons* that I've spent any time with...*is the one in your dungeon.*"

Someone roared, but it wasn't Laird Gordon. It was someone standing behind her. She ducked sideways, expecting to be attacked. But it was Percy, the one with long legs and a short kilt. He stood with his hands fisted and his face as red as his father's.

McKiller. He might be able to get away, or something. "How dare you," he hissed at her. Then he gave her a look that turned her blood cold—a look that said she'd pay. She'd been in plenty of danger in the last three days, but this time she didn't have shock to numb her. This time, she believed she was screwed.

"I'm sorry," she said, and meant it. Of course she'd been insensitive to the father. She hadn't meant to hurt the son.

"Father," he called out. "She is protecting your prisoner, Laird Ross. They've had hours of...*private speech*...since she arrived. She's spoken to none else."

No! Quinn was in no shape to fight anyone. He'd told her he was already suffering from a serious concussion!

Low murmurs filled the hall. Laird Gordon laughed at his tall visitor. McKiller glared at her, but she could tell by the lifted corner of his mouth he was pretty pleased with himself; the glare was just part of his act.

Laird Gordon gestured wide with one arm. "Oh, by all means, Mister Bond. Have yer revenge. Here, in the hall for all to enjoy. Be warned, he used to be a grand fighter. But of late, he's gone soft in the mind and likely the middle." He looked over her shoulder. "Percy! Return the hellcat to the dungeon. Bring up the old Ross laird. Perhaps we can dispense with the hanging and go straight to the burnin'."

Holy shit. It was Quinn they had planned to burn as a witch? Hang him? Burn him? Beat him to death? He had to get out of there!

Jules ran forward. She had to do something, to say something that would make them listen to her.

"Bond! I'll do whatever you ask! I'll go along quietly, I swear. Just don't hurt him!"

"Come," Percy barked behind her and grabbed her arm.

With one hand on her elbow, he bent her arm up behind her and steered her in a circle, then headed her back the way she'd come. She had no choice. She'd never taken a self-defense class that might help her get out of the hold he had on her. She tried to move faster, to gain a little slack, but he stayed right on her.

"Why can't I stay and watch?" Jules whined as loud as she dared. There was no way Gordon missed it, but he ignored her and hollered to someone to bring him a drink. If she provoked him, she might just end up chained next to his son. Then she wondered if it was that threat that kept the rest of his clan in line.

Once they were in the side passage, Percy took her wrist and released the painful hold on her arm. Only when the pain subsided did she realize how much it had hurt.

"Come," said Percy again, almost gently.

Had he already forgiven her? Was he regretting his outburst?

"Please," she said softly. "Don't let them kill him."

Percy didn't even blink.

She let him lead her to the stairs instead of trying to make a break for it. That had been the goal, after all, to return to the dungeons to be with Quinn. But they wouldn't be together for long. As much as she didn't want to be left down there in the dark, however, she held on to a little morsel of hope that Quinn might beat McKiller. Hi might be able to get away, or something.

Something. Please, God, anything.

She could worry about herself later. After all, in a place where so little was expected of a woman, she could surely catch someone off guard and get away. But would it be in time to do any good? And would she and Quinn ever have the chance to finish that dream the way she wanted it finished?

CHAPTER TWENTY

At the first landing, Percy handed her off to the tall guard, then followed them down the steps. Jules felt the others hesitate just a fraction of a second, just as she had, when the smell of a rotting body hit them. Continuing on, everyone walked a little slower, in no rush to be immersed completely in that invisible cloud.

Had Skully been the only one to die there? Probably not. And his bones looked far too bare for him to have died recently.

She shook her head to keep from imagining of what other atrocities the laird of Clan Gordon might be capable of. That head shaking put her off-balance, however, and she tripped. Percy, strangely enough, helped steady her.

The big guard returned her rather roughly to her cell. She felt rather than saw Quinn stiffen in the shadows. She took his lead and didn't rush to the bars like she wanted to. They were back together, but it would be short-lived. And she didn't want Percy to imagine more than he already had.

Or had he imagined anything at all? Maybe he'd been there, in the shadows around the arch, listening to their conversations. Maybe he'd known about the kiss.

Maybe when he'd offered up Quinn as a punishment for her cruel mention of his brother, he'd known precisely how much it might hurt her in the end.

And if that was so, ignoring Quinn now would be wasting her last chance to speak with him, because she knew, in the pit of her stomach, that no matter how this all ended, she'd never be granted that dream again. This was it. All those practice runs were over.

This time, she was going to have to say goodbye.

She pushed her tears back. There would be plenty of time to cry later, once she was alone.

She turned to face the cell door and stole a look at Quinn. His worry was plain, though he tried to mask it. Her insides begin to melt and those tears threatened to defy her. It had been so very long since anyone had worried about her. If she let herself cry, though, he'd only worry more, and he was going to need his head in the game. Especially if he'd gone soft, as Gordon said he had. Quinn was the one they should be worrying about.

"I have good news and bad news," she said cheerfully, ignoring the finalistic clang of her prison door. "Good news is I'm back."

Quinn glanced at Percy, then shrugged his shoulders and leaned against the far bars. He folded his arms, like he was bored.

She sighed. "By the way, I'm pretty sure Percy speaks English."

Percy didn't flinch as he took the keys from Martin in exchange for the torch. Then he moved the old man's arm to show him where the light must be held.

Still watching Percy, she said, "Notice how he wasn't even curious when his name was mentioned?"

"Is that the bad news?" Quinn had sounded casual, but his fingers were digging into his own arms.

Percy began trying the keys in the door of Quinn's cell.

"Not all of it," she said. "The other bad news is the guy who claims to be my husband *is* Gabby's hitman. When I insisted I didn't know him, he started ranting about needing satisfaction from whoever had been turning my head."

She knew she was wasting time, but how did she tell him he might be about to die.

"And then?"

Quinn was no longer leaning. His hands were on his hips and he was looking right at her. He still stood on the far side of his cell, though. She got the impression he'd already guessed what came next.

"Percy told him it was you. You were right. He knows that I care about you and he used it against me. I don't think he planned to, but he was angry because I mentioned...Skully."

Quinn nodded slightly, but didn't move any closer.

Jules couldn't take it anymore and grabbed the bars that separated them. They were out of time.

"He already knows, Quinn. He already knows."

A heartbeat later he was pressed against the bars, pulling her tight. She was so relieved she could have laughed. Percy and Martin disappeared in the background. It was only them. Together again. He was kissing her all over her face, missing her mouth in spite of her trying to help him find it.

"Your chances of escaping are much better above ground, right?" she whispered, since her mouth currently not in use. "I still think my stand-by plan is better than nothing—bash him on the head and fight your way out. His nose might be broken, so I'd try to hit him there first."

Quinn kissed both eyes, then pulled back a little. By the look on his face, he wasn't any more impressed with her plan that he was the first time she'd shared it. Then dread struck her in the chest like a boxing glove.

"You do know how to fight, don't you?"

He rolled his eyes and shook his head. "Of course I ken how to fight. Am I not a Scot? We're taught in Primary School. Now, go back to the part where you were lusting after the man in yer dreams, aye?"

A key clicked in the lock and they froze. Percy rattled it, but it did not turn. He tried the next key. For a dungeon with only two cells, there were a helluva lot of keys on that ring. But one of them was going to fit.

Their hearts were pounding like horses' hooves. She could hear her pulse in her ear where his hand covered it. She could feel his heart beating in his neck.

It was time. This was it. That last chance for a kiss. And if he kissed her like a damned butterfly, she was going to rip the bars apart and make him do it better.

"Kiss me, damn it," she whispered.

He smiled at her and winked, his eyes sparkling in the light from the torch that Martin silently held.

Obviously, Percy was too impatient to wait for a blind man to find the right key, but even Martin didn't take so long to unlock the doors.

She popped up on her toes and stretched her neck at the same time Quinn's mouth came down firmly on hers. He seemed to understand that she wasn't looking for butterflies. And except for bumping into the bars a few times, they managed to make more than their jailers disappear. His short whiskers were a soft brushed against her chin. His hand moved across her cheek and into her hair, like he needed to know the texture of it as badly as she'd needed to know the feel of his lips. When she finally had to stop to catch her breath and give her toes a break, she didn't back away, but leaned her forehead against his chest, and for the first time since she'd landed in Scotland, she didn't envy her sister.

Well, much anyway. At least Jillian would still have her Highlander tomorrow. Jules didn't know what she'd have beyond this memory.

He smelled good for having been in a dungeon for days. And his shirt was a little too tight, like it wasn't meant for him, but it was clean. She reached through the bars and ran her hands up his arms.

"Please tell me you can protect yourself."

"I can protect myself," he murmured.

"Really? Because Bond James Bond is in pretty good shape. He's probably planning to open up a can of karate on your cute arse, you know?"

"Cute arse?" He let go of her and turned, so they could both get a better view.

Him trying to get a good look at his own ass was going to be mental snapshot she would never forget.

"Very nice," she said. "Now please don't let him damage it."

He grabbed the bars again, just a few inches above her own hands and she realized what he was trying to do. Letting go of each other would have been painful and he'd ripped that bandage off before she had a chance to think about it.

"No worries," he said.

The haze from their kiss was fading, but the compulsion to renew it was as strong as ever. All she wanted was to kiss him again, but there was so much to say.

"If you can get away, go," she said. "Promise me you'll go. I won't be far behind. I have that plan, you see."

"Aye, a fine plan," he said.

She noticed he promised her nothing. She wasn't going to waste precious time arguing.

Metal clicked against metal. It felt like someone had just locked her heart.

The gate swung open behind him. His hands were still on the bars, but she dared not touch him again. She put on a smile and let her hands drop to her sides.

"Forget about me," she said. "Just concentrate on winning the fight. Don't let him hit you in the head."

A hand landed on his shoulder and he took a step back.

"Did Gordon say what I get if I win?"

She smiled and shook her head. "Me, I guess."

"Well, then. I cannot lose."

CHAPTER TWENTY-ONE

The guard held Quinn's arm while Percy tied his hands together behind his back.

"What's the harm in leaving her a bit of light, Percy?" Quinn asked.

The thin man said nothing, then left him to the guard and preceded them up the steps.

Their steps echoed in the stone stairwell.

"So," Quinn said. "I see you've made your decision then. You don't believe me."

Percy glanced over his shoulder. "Not just yet. We'll see how yer luck holds out with her husband." Then he snorted. "Ye manage to keep from dying by his hand or hanging on the morrow, and then I'll believe ye can change the future. For I'm certain the only thing yer future holds is a bit of dirt—or ash, o'course."

They entered the hall to a mixture of applause and whistles. A wet bit of something struck him on the neck as he was led forward to face The Gordon. The smell that followed told him it had been an apple. He was simply grateful to have something pleasant to breathe for a change. He was also pleased to note the laird's throne was not nearly as grand as the Great Ross Chair made by Monty's grandfather.

Percy made a slight bow to his father and moved away. The guard remained at Quinn's back. An impressively tall man with an equally impressive mane of red hair stood to the old man's left. He glared at Quinn, sized him up, then gave him a wink.

The Gordon's spawn laughed. They were queued up along the wall to his left as if they were waiting in line to kick him as soon as he was down. So brave.

No wonder The Runt will be able to take the reins here once the father is gone.

He tried to be as hopeful and fearless as Juliet. She seemed to see no complication so great that it couldn't be faced, bashed, then run from.

He laughed just thinking about the stories she'd told. If only half of them were true, he might have a sporting chance against the red beast if he but kept to her daft excuse for a plan. The only thing she hadn't considered was that he could never flee and leave her behind. Or perhaps she had considered it just before she asked for that promise—a promise he could not make.

Better get on, then. If he could best the man, he would at least have one more night in the dark with Juliet. Perhaps, once his date with the hangman was over, she'd be able to cajole her way out of the Gordon keep since she'd no longer be burdened with saving his hide.

He faced the laird of the clan.

"I've been told I'll be fighting this day," he said.

"Aye, ye will be." The Gordon leaned to one side of his large chair and grinned.

Quinn tried to think of something that might douse the old man's mood.

"Are you certain?" he asked. "What if I refuse the play?"

It worked. The Cock o' the North sat forward and frowned.

"Then the woman below will be sent home with her husband." He pointed to the tall one. "And ye will meet yer maker on the morn, as I've said. I suspected ye'd rather leave this world fightin', but if ye'd rather leave it like a woman, then so be it."

The redhead met his gaze, but he couldn't guess what the man was thinking. It was a fact, the man was trying to say something with his brows, but only the devil could know.

Quinn turned back to his host. "And if I beat this man?"

The Gordon grinned. "'Tis...unlikely."

The hall erupted in laughter.

"'Tis possible," Quinn shouted to be heard.

The laird lifted a hand and the hall went silent.

"I'm ever a man of me word, Montgomery Ross. I promised ye a hanging in the mornin', and if yer still alive when the sun shows itself, I'll not fail ye. If he kills ye, then ye'll be spared the hangin' is all. But you were the one to claimed to have The Sight. We'll still burn ye; we'll do it proper or not at all."

Quinn grinned. "I prefer not at all, of course."

"Noted." The Gordon sat back and relaxed.

Quinn couldn't leave it at that. "But surely I'll deserve a proper reward?"

Gordon frowned, then smiled knowingly. "Ye want the lass in yer cell for yer final night, is that it?"

The redhead's mouth dropped open. He looked fairly irritated at the turn of the conversation. Either he didn't care to hear that he might not win the battle—which meant he thought quite highly of himself—or he didn't care for the idea of Quinn having the lass alone in the dark. And that didn't make sense unless the bastard had similar intentions for Juliet.

Something was amiss with this one. Perhaps his journey through the tomb had left his brains a bit foosty.

Quinn shook his head and answered Gordon.

"Not at all. I want her released. I want her returned to Castle Ross and protected from him." He pointed at the hitman.

"Well, if he's dead, then she'll have no need to fear him, aye?"

Everyone within earshot seemed to appreciate Gordon's joke.

"I won't kill him," Quinn said. "I'll fight him. I might even beat him. But I'll not kill him. And I'll have your word the woman will be returned to Castle Ross, *unharmed.*"

Gordon waived an impatient hand. "Fair enough. Ye have me word. But I'll wager Bond James, here, will be taking his wife home this night."

And so the betting began.

Quinn stripped off his constricting shirt and heard a gasp to his left. Betha was suddenly pushed behind one of her brothers. He got only a brief glimpse of her wide eyes before they disappeared behind the shoulders of two Gordons.

Too little, too late, he thought. She shouldn't have taken her time about freeing him. No matter. He was destined to be in the Gordon's dungeon when Juliet was brought in. He understood that now. Fate had been planning their encounter for a good while. He only hoped Fate had something in mind for he and the lass that involved a great deal of time together.

That was worth fighting for.

Quinn took the excess plaid from his ancient kilt and twisted it, then wrapped it about his waist and tucked in the end. A length of cloth over his shoulder would just prove a convenient hand hold for his enemy, or so Ewan had taught him. The more Quinn had trained in the plaid, the more he understood why old soldiers preferred to fight without any clothing at all. Of course, if he attempted to fight in the Gordon's hall, in his altogether, he might find himself missing a vital part or two, all thanks to the armed audience in Gordon colors.

The big man noted how he'd wrapped his plaid and followed suit. Then he made a spectacle of giving up all his hidden blades.

Quinn met the man's gaze and lifted a brow. The man had a gun hidden somewhere, but it would be wise for Quinn to insist he set the weapon aside. What the Gordons would think of the gun, he could not say. But he could at least make sure the man couldn't use that gun on Juliet, whether to harm her or compel her to leave with him.

The man raised a brow as well.

Quinn made his hand into a pretend gun—a sign that would mean nothing to the onlookers.

The redhead frowned briefly, then gave his head a slight shake.

Quinn understood it to mean that he was supposed to keep his mouth shut about the gun. But why would he? Was this man not the enemy?

"Battle!" cried Laird Gordon, and suddenly any further discussion was ended.

The big man ran at him, threw his long arms around him and clamped his fingers together behind Quinn's neck. Then he pressed his forehead to Quinn's own.

"Quinn Ross," he whispered. "You haven't got any more sense than Juliet. Did the name James Bond tell you nothing?"

Quinn pushed him off, but ran back at him again, anxious to keep the man from calling him *Quinn* again. But how did he know? Ewan wouldn't have told him. Not if he'd come chasing after Juliet, to eventually see her eliminated. Ewan would have guarded the Ross secrets with his life.

Quinn was surprised, actually, that Ewan hadn't sent a marksman after him, worried The Gordon might torture those golden secrets off his tongue. After all, one man's life was hardly worth the price the clan would pay if the truth got out. And they'd pay that price for generations.

"Who told you my name?" He ground the question out through his teeth while he held his arm around the other man's neck. Getting behind the bastard hadn't been easy.

"Ewan Ross told me," the man grunted, then held tight to Quinn's arm and flipped him over his wide back and onto the floor.

The filthy rushes were a fine inducement to get on his feet again, and they began circling each other. The crowd made accommodations.

"Liar," Quinn said. "Ewan Ross would have taken my name to the grave. He'd tell no hitman—"

"You idiot!" the big man roared as he rushed him.

He wrapped his arms around Quinn's entire body, trapping his arms to his sides. Their faces were inches apart.

"Bond. James Bond. I'm MI6. Not some bleedin' hitman. The FBI lost her at the airport. I was sent to watch her sister's house. When Juliet ran from me, every time she ran from me, she never gave me a chance to explain."

Quinn gave the bastard a Glasgow kiss and heard the satisfying crunch of another man's bones. The redhead stumbled back, one hand on his nose, the other flung wide in search of support. Two Gordon brothers were knocked on their arses, as was Betha. She was lost under the pile, but they heard her screeching clearly enough.

"I don't believe you." Quinn spit at the man. "How long does it take to say *I'm MI6?*"

He moved back and gave the man room to get up. He also needed time to recover. That head-butt was the worst thing he could have done to himself. The world was spinning around him, slightly off axis. The crowd watched closely and he could tell which men had bet against him by the frowns on their faces.

Percy, surprisingly enough, was smiling.

Bond wiped a bloody hand across his chest as he stood.

Quinn smiled. At least he'd drawn first blood.

The man hurried forward, and as prepared as Quinn believed he was, he still was unable to avoid the big man's fist.

He spun around once and though his face was numb and his neck burned, he was pleased to find himself still on his feet. That was, until he realized that the other man was holding him up with a flat hand against his chest. Disappointing, that.

Bond's big fist pulled back and held. Quinn was pretty sure he could drop like a sack of wheat just before contact.

"I was warned she'd fight me," said the taller man. "that she didn't want protection. I thought she understood who I was."

Quinn couldn't afford to listen. If that fist connected, it might just kill him. The man had no knowledge of the beating Quinn's skull had already taken thanks to Gordon hospitality. He might kill Quinn whether or not he meant to.

The fist came slowly. Quinn dropped his butt toward the ground, and when he found himself sitting on it, he also found his head was still attached.

Lucky thing, that.

Bond grabbed his hair in one hand and pulled him to his feet. Standing behind Quinn, he leaned close and spoke low.

"Now quickly, I need you to act like you've passed out. I'm going to cut you. You're going to play dead."

"Kiss my arse," Quinn said, then spit blood on the floor.

The crowd laughed.

"Play dead, Quinn. Ewan's waitin' with horses. I'll insist on taking your body back to Ewan."

Bond pushed him away and Quinn spun to face him. They danced in a circle again.

"MI6? Truly?"

"MI6, ye dense bastard." The man rushed him and put his hands around his neck.

Quinn bore down to turn his face red, but he couldn't resist complaining.

"It's a bit too Romeo and Juliet, don't you think? My playing dead?"

"Well, just be glad you get to play the part of Romeo. I, for one, wouldn't touch her with a ten meter pole."

Quinn went limp, then was glad the man tossed him onto his face so those watching wouldn't notice any twitching.

"Here. Finish him," came Gordon's voice. "Through the heart, Bond James. I'll not have him rousing while he's roasting on the spit. The women doona appreciate it."

"I can imagine," said Bond. "Will you have my wife brought?"

"Aye. Percy. Fetch her."

Someone knelt on Quinn's back. "Sorry about this," the man said.

Hot fire sliced his back. There was no telling how deeply the blade had gone. He could only pray he'd put his trust in a true MI6 agent and not some lunatic whose mind was bent by a wee jaunt through time.

He dared not move, even when warm blood puddled on his back and tickled his side on its way toward the floor. If Bond James Bond wasn't MI6, Quinn was going to take him apart. Slice by slice.

He concentrated on breathing as slowly as possible—not easy when his mind was reeling. He only needed to think calming thoughts. Immediately, his mind went to Juliet and the panic dissolved.

His lungs were still working. Neither of them punctured, thankfully. His sweat was drying quickly on his face.

The murmurs of the crowd turned to chatter. A dog trotted over and started licking his face. He fought his facial muscles, forcing them to relax when the beasts tongue slipped past his lips.

He hoped the thing wouldn't start licking up his blood, and even the thought of it pushed him over the edge—he couldn't help it when his entire body shivered in revulsion.

"There now, there's a death rattle for ye," said Gordon. "Ah, here comes yer wife now. Let her see that her lover is dead and she should look to you now."

Dear Lord! Juliet! How could he just lie there and let her believe him dead? She didn't know yet that Bond was an agent. She would fight him. And how would she react when she thought she had sent Quinn to his death?

He couldn't stand it another second. He had to stand up and fight their way out. Use the fall back plan. Bash, fight, and run.

A boot came down hard on his back.

"Here, wife. Come. There is no reason for you to pretend. Tell Laird Gordon I'm your rightful husband."

He felt her coming, heard her slow steps, how she choked back a sob.

"I'll kill you for this," she whispered. "You've just removed any leverage you might have had over me. I would have done anything to have him spared. Anything. Now you're the dead man."

There was only silence while his heart beat loud in his ears. He couldn't help but be touched by the passion in her voice and be thrilled that her feelings for him might equal his for her. The pressure on his back never let up and he was lucky it didn't. He needed the reminder to keep his breathing slow in spite of his urge to shout for joy.

When Juliet spoke again, her voice had changed.

"Forgive me, Laird Gordon. We'll get out of your way now. I'm sorry we bothered you with our personal problems. Come, husband. We really don't need witnesses." Her voice was sticky sweet. Her accent wasn't pretty.

"Hold a moment, Lady *Bond*," the agent said. "We'll go when I'm ready. Laird Gordon, allow me to return Laird Ross to his cousin. Ewan will wish to seal him in the tomb with his sister witch. Ye can hardly wish to have the likes of him haunting yer home."

There was a drawn out silence. The only thing Quinn heard was the sound of the crowd's breathing.

"Why would ye do such a thing, Bond James? Do ye not believe the more pressing need is to meet out the woman's punishment and set yer house to rights? Perhaps there is something ye mean to hide from me?"

The agent laughed. "Nothing to hide. Ye've been right generous with me. I'll be the same. 'Tis the truth, Ewan Ross has something I need. I mean to trade the body of Montgomery Ross for it. I also meant what I said about Laird Ross's ghost. It is only my opinion that a man's ghost will likely be more bothersome than that of a woman, but I might be mistaken. Perhaps ye have a priest about who might have better advice?"

In the silence that followed, Quinn could imagine dry wood being added around the pole in the outer bailey. If his enemy remained unmoved, how in the bloody hell was he going to escape that?

"Devil take ye," Gordon snarled. "Away with ye, then. Take Montgomery Ross. And someone clean his blood from my hall. I won't have him coming back for it on Samhain!"

CHAPTER TWENTY-TWO

"Juliet Ross, brace yerself," the redhead whispered in her ear.

She was seated on his horse, basically in his lap, while Quinn's body was strapped over the horse her supposed husband had brought along for her. The head and arms of her supposed lover hung down the side nearest them. She tried not to stare at the large bloodstain on the rough sack cloth in which they'd wrapped the body.

"Quinn's not dead," the man behind her said carefully.

"Just what is your name?" she blurted. "I can't keep thinking of you as Gabby's hitman."

He didn't answer, so she turned to look at his face. It was located a bit higher than expected, so she tipped her head back. His mouth was hanging open.

"Your name?"

"James, actually. Did you not hear what I said?"

She faced forward. "Yes. I know."

"You know?" Quinn's words were muffled, but intelligible just the same. His carcass didn't move. The hands still hung limp.

"You're doing a fine job, Quinn. You still look dead." She knew if she was the one who had to play dead for miles and miles, she'd appreciate a little encouragement.

James gave a rude laugh. She decided to ignore him.

"How did you know?" came Quinn's voice again.

"I'm not an idiot," she said. "I figured it out while I was still in the dungeon."

"You did not," whispered James.

Jules shrugged. "You'd be amazed how much clearer things seem in the dark."

"Bull. Shite."

His breath on her ear made her shiver.

She shook her head and gave him a frown. "That tickles my ear."

"What?" Quinn demanded. If he wasn't careful, their distant escort might hear him.

"Hush," she hissed.

When she realized James had been tormenting Quinn on purpose, she glared over her shoulder. James grinned back.

She rolled her eyes and spoke loud enough for Quinn to hear.

"It was something Martin, the blind guard, said. That you didn't sound like a monster to him. That made me consider what else you might be. And I remembered you'd never actually come out and said you were going to kill me or deliver me to Gabby.

"There were only two possibilities when you chased me into Castle Ross. Hitman or cop. If you were a British babysitter—I mean agent—then you wouldn't be beating my boyfriend to death. Then there was the small detail of you winking at me every chance you got."

Quinn grunted.

James laughed. "Shut up, man. Twenty minutes and I'll let you sit." He then gave her a little squeeze around the middle. He was enjoying himself. For a few quiet minutes they were lulled by the clap of horses' hooves on wet mud. Finally, Quinn's voice interrupted again.

"Did she say *boyfriend?*"

James laughed. "She did."

Jules was mortified. The man was at least ten years older than her, and she'd called him her boyfriend.

Gah!

Somewhere, under all that burlap, he was probably rolling his eyes, wondering how he was ever going to get rid of her.

She'd plunged into a special kind of hell when she'd seen Quinn lying on the floor and for that second or two afterwards—until she'd convinced herself it was a hoax. She would have thrown herself across his body and started checking for vital signs if it hadn't been for the slow twitch of James' eye. Then, she was able to do a little method acting of her own. But had it been enough? Was someone suspecting, even now? Would Gordon send men after them?

Jules turned in the saddle. "Can't this horse go any faster?"

James gave her a little smile. "Oh, aye. But it will jostle our package to death in truth. We only need to get over that ridge. Just keep watching the ridge."

She realized his arm had inched up a bit from her waist. Then she felt his long fingers twitch. Maybe he was enjoying himself just a little too much.

"You can let go of me now. I promise this Wyoming girl can keep her butt in the saddle. And it's not like I'm going to run off, right?"

"Oh, right ye are. I beg pardon." He pulled his arm away.

He still sat too close, and she could feel his breath against the top of her head, but she was done complaining.

"James?"

"Aye?"

"Are you married?"

"Uh uh."

Quinn mumbled something she didn't understand, but James must have. He scooted his rump back behind the saddle, until their bodies were no longer touching.

***

As it turned out, they had to leave Quinn across the saddle for a lot longer than planned because at the top of the ridge, there were a dozen Gordons guarding the border. All of them watched James and her like they were suspected pick-pockets leaving a jewelry store. She could feel their stares while they headed down the other side of the ridge with their package in tow.

When the ground leveled out again, James finally turned off the road and into the woods. Remembering the wolf she'd faced, she didn't know if it was time to relax, or time to worry harder.

"This is the straightest shot toward Ross lands. They would expect us to leave the road here," he said.

As her eyes adjusted to the shadows, she realized they were on a well-worn trail. A minute later, the hairs rose at the back of her head and on her forearms. They were no longer alone. She frantically looked around for a stick and discovered they weren't surrounded by wolves, but by Highlanders all decked out in blue paint like they were headed for a Colt's game. Then she remembered. War Paint.

Shit.

They didn't have time for this. They needed to get Quinn off the horse and treat his wound, not defend themselves again.

She took a deep breath and prepared to pull out her best bravado, when James gave her a little squeeze. He'd scooted close again.

"Don't move," James said clearly, and she knew his warning was for Quinn too.

The biggest painted man urged his horse forward until he was in their faces. He held a heavy sword in one hand, reins in the other. He glanced from James to her and back again. His expression told her nothing.

"Hello again, ye ruddy bastard," he said.

James laughed. "Ewan, is that you? Only my own grandda calls me that."

"More like he's the only one to say it to yer face." Ewan suddenly grinned and his paint cracked around his lips. His beard looked like he'd cleaned the blue off his fingers with it.

To Jules, he looked beautiful. And only when her body relaxed did she realize how tightly she'd been wound. She nearly fell off the horse, shaming the state of Wyoming.

Ewan looked at the other horse. He had to know whose body it was.

"And where's me cousin, then?" he asked anyway.

Quinn groaned.

Ewan nearly jumped off his horse. "Jesus, Mary and Joseph!"

"He's not dead," James announced, like he should get credit for that.

"But I *am* bleeding," Quinn mumbled.

James had promised that as he was tying Quinn's body to the horse, he'd been sure to place pressure over the wound in his back, promised that pressure was the only thing they could do for him until they met up with Ewan. He'd also promised the hole wasn't deep, but that didn't keep Jules from worrying.

Frankly, she was surprised he hadn't passed out, hanging over a horse, all that blood going to his head.

Jules swung a leg over her horse's head and jumped down, but when she ducked beneath its chin to get to Quinn, a big man was blocking her way. She tried to step around him, but he was already lifting Quinn's body off the horse and onto his shoulder.

"Quinn!" It was pitiful, really, but she had to let him know she gave a damn that he was bleeding.

The big man turned to look at her and she tried to read his expression through the slashes of paint. He looked an awful lot like—

And he looked just as shocked as she was.

"What are *you* doing here?" she demanded. She could feel herself blush, for all the things she'd fantasized about this man in spite of the fact he was technically her brother in law.

"Juliet, is it? We've come to bring ye safely home, lass. To the arms of yer family."

And just like that, her insides started falling apart, like she was a human sized pastry that had just had all its filling sucked out. Pieces of her broke away like crust, including the words she'd intended to say to this man once she got up the courage to knock on his door, the words she'd laid out in her mind to make damn sure his wife suffered enough in five minutes to make them even. If they were going to be nice to her... If they were going to be nice to her, she was doomed. None of the mental weapons she'd prepared would be effective against *nice*.

She fought the urge to turn and run, not sure her legs would cooperate and damned sure she didn't want to leave Quinn.

"Monty Ross," came Quinn's muffled voice. "Keep yer bloody arms to yerself. She's mine."

The big man put Quinn's feet on the ground and steadied him, then began unwrapping him, carefully, frowning at the wide bloodstain as he pulled it away. Quinn grasped at the plaid at his waist when the unwrapping might have gone too far. Jules couldn't have looked away if she'd tried. His back was a bloody mess, but the hole looked small. And she was relieved to see he'd stopped bleeding for the moment.

"I've yet to touch her, Nephew." Montgomery laughed. "And I can't tell ye how pleased I am to find yer still alive."

Quinn ignored him and turned to face her. The way his eyes crinkled, she figured he was pleased to find her so near. She gave him the same smile, but what pleased *her* was the fact that he'd claimed her.

Too bad it was only for the moment.

Leaving him behind was going to suck. If she was smart, she'd start preparing herself now. But she didn't want to waste what time they had left.

Who was she kidding? It was already sucking. The reality that they would never see each other again, after she climbed back in that tomb, made her feel hot and sick on the inside. The cool air of shadows surrounded her. A few deep breaths of it helped.

When he reached for her, she stepped up to him quickly, ecstatic there were no longer any bars between them. And as he pulled her to his bare chest, her fingers started tingling. She couldn't tell if that tingling was due to the fact her fingers were finally getting a little oxygen or if they were anticipating the touch of Quinn's chest.

His breath caught.

She pushed him back to look at his face. He smiled and gave her a wink, but she could tell he was in a great deal of pain.

"You can hold me later," she said and tried to step back.

He held her fast. "I believe I'll hold you later as well," he said, then bent down to kiss her. It was a glorious kiss with no bars pressing into their faces. "You promised," he whispered. "'Till the end, aye. 'Tisn't the end yet."

He kissed her again and she heard the chuckle of more than one man, then the gasp of a woman.

"Montgomery! He's bleeding!"

The woman's voice sounded a little too familiar. Jules hadn't considered that her twin would sound like her too.

Quinn looked down into her face. He was worried.

"Ready or not, aye?"

Tears welled in her eyes, but not because she was afraid. She was just so relieved he understood her so well.

"I'm a coward," she whispered. "Who knew?"

Quinn laughed. "I suppose you could bash her on the head and try to fight your way out."

She sighed. "Yeah, but that plan's getting a little old."

Quinn nodded. "Will you let me handle this?"

Jules smiled, grateful, and got a wink as a reward. He pushed her hair back behind her ears, straightened her coat, then pivoted so they both faced the woman waiting behind him.

Binoculars hadn't done the woman justice. And she'd been right. Jillian Ross *was* a beauty—like a Photo-Shopped version of the chick Jules saw in the mirror each morning.

"Holy shit," she said at the same time Jillian said, "Holy crap."

No one laughed.

"Jilly?" Quinn gave the woman a little bow. "This is my... This is Juliet. She's mine. I'm certain the pair of you will find the time to get to know one another, but just now, I need you to tend to my back, aye?"

Jillian's pale face stared at her. It was like looking at a ghost. Jules was frozen in place.

"I'm bleeding, Jilly. Remember?" Quinn lowered his head to get the woman's attention.

Jilly noticed him again, nodded, then hurried away to one of the horses. When she came back, she was carrying a first aid kit.

Jules suddenly felt...extra, like she'd been holding someone's place in the world and now that someone was there to take it back. She was nothing more than a seat-filler, and the appropriate thing for her to do at the moment was to get the hell out of the picture.

CHAPTER TWENTY-THREE

For a half hour, James paced around their little group while Quinn was cleaned and sewn up by her sister. The woman seemed to know what she was doing, so Jules let her at it. But she couldn't bear to stand near her.

Quinn seemed to understand. At least he didn't complain about her not holding his hand while a needle was poked in and out of him.

They still hadn't spoken. Quinn had needed all of Jillian's attention. But the woman kept glancing over at her. She paced about twenty feet away, between two trees, feeling like an orphan looking through the dining room window at a real family sitting down for Thanksgiving.

She felt a heavy arm descend over her shoulders and glanced up, sure she would see James there, trying to make Quinn jealous. But it was Montgomery.

"Ye see, Jillian?" the man called to his wife. "I've got her. She's not going anywhere." In a lower voice he said, "For the love of God, don't go anywhere."

Jules laughed.

Quinn's head snapped around. He looked at Montgomery, then at her. There was a question in his eyes and she knew just what he was asking. *Was she remembering the dream? Imagining it was Montgomery on the other side of the bars?* The fact that he would worry made her tear up.

She looked intently into Quinn's eyes and shook her head slowly, clearly.

He smiled and nodded. Then she looked from him to Jillian and back, asking him the same silent question. He laughed and shook his head.

"What the bloody hell was that about?" Montgomery asked it none too quietly.

"Private joke," she said.

"Ah. And just how much privacy did you and my nephew enjoy?" He'd sounded like a protective father, not a brother in law.

"Oh, we didn't enjoy it."

Quinn frowned, then called out. "The hell we didn't."

Jillian made Quinn lift one arm, pushed it up a little higher, then gave him a good frown. Then she bent back to her stitching. A second later, Quinn cried out.

Montgomery laughed. Jillian slapped her patient on the shoulder, like it was his own fault he'd gotten hurt.

Quinn held very still, but spoke loud enough for everyone to hear.

"I'd be better able to concentrate, Jillian, if a certain great uncle of mine would just remove his hands from my woman."

Jillian straightened and dropped the bloody rag she'd been holding. She glanced in Jules' direction, but not up at her face. Tears poured from her eyes and she walked away, in the opposite direction, into the trees.

Montgomery's arm disappeared from Jules' shoulders and he ran after his wife. She didn't go far, though, and collapsed at the bottom of a tree, bawling into her hands.

"Jillian! You will be all right, do you hear?"

"No. No, I won't," she sobbed quietly, but her voice carried in the moist air.

"Is it the babe? Do you wish to lie down?"

"No. The baby's fine. But..." She was crying too hard to finish.

She was pregnant?

Well, hormonal or not, Jules knew the crying was her fault. If she were anyone else, she might have been able to run up to the woman who was supposedly her sister, throw her arms around her, and start celebrating. But she just wasn't like that.

Jillian Ross wasn't just a stranger; she'd been the bane of Jules' existence. And she couldn't just pretend it wasn't true. She had to show a little loyalty to herself, to remember what she'd come here to do. She was finally close enough to speak to the chick. It was time to suck it up and do it. After all, Jillian was already crying—she couldn't make it much worse.

Her pounding heart propelled her across the clearing and she didn't stop walking until she was standing in front of her sister. Montgomery was squatting beside his wife, drying her tears with her own hair. He stood and gave Jules a grateful smile, then started to walk away.

"Wait. You probably don't want to leave her," she warned. "Not when you hear what I've come to say."

Monty's brows rose, but he looked more curious than worried. He shared a glance with Jillian, then leaned against the tree. Within comforting distance maybe.

"First of all," Jules began, "I want to thank you for taking care of Quinn. I don't know anything about stitching wounds. I'm probably a lot better at inflicting them. I'm sure you'll agree in a minute."

Jillian put a hand on the ground and got to her feet. "I guess if you plan to hurt me, I shouldn't take it sitting down," she said. Then she wiped a sleeve across her face and lifted her chin.

It was all too painful to watch, like Jules was seeing herself move, hearing something she might have said under the same circumstances. But she shook off the empathetic impressions and got back to the script she'd practiced on the hillside.

"My parents... Our parents died in a car crash..." She couldn't go on. After all this rehearsing, she couldn't tell this ghostly version of herself that it was her fault her parents died. Maybe, now that she wasn't alone anymore, she could see through that red, angry fog and admit that it hadn't been Jillian's fault. All the fault should be laid at their grandmother's feet.

"My grandmother," Jillian began. "Our grandmother told me my parents died in a car wreck. She never said anything about a sister. She said we had no other family. I've known about you for about thirty-six hours."

Her sister swallowed, then gave a little smile, but it didn't stay long. She must have read something on Jules' face that told her not to start celebrating. It must have been the shock. When Jules was able to speak again, she couldn't seem to turn up the volume enough to hear herself clearly. What she did hear clearly was her heart pounding against the wall of her chest.

"You don't remember me?" She didn't know if she was more hurt or outraged. She'd considered the possibility, but it hadn't seemed possible that Jillian's memory would be worse than her own. The second time she spoke, she was nice and clear. "You're claiming you don't remember me?"

When her voice bounced around the trees and back into her face, she glanced over at Montgomery, to see if he was going to come to his wife's defense, but he was gone. Jillian followed her gaze.

About twenty feet away, the missing husband had his arms over the shoulders of Quinn and Ewan and the three of them were sneaking quickly away into the mist.

James, who now stood guard over the horses, seemed to realize he'd been abandoned. He turned aside and whistled softly.

"Cowards," she and Jillian said in unison.

Neither of them laughed.

"To answer your question," Jillian said, "no, I didn't remember you. Since the Muir sisters told me we were twins, I've remembered just a few things. Little, stupid things. I didn't even remember your name, although Jules sounded a lot more familiar than Juliet. I should have been able to remember your name. I'm so sorry."

"I would have given anything to forget yours," Jules mumbled.

Jillian's mouth opened like she'd just been punched in the stomach, but she recovered quickly for someone who'd just been bawling her head off.

"First blood goes to you," said her sister. "Fine. So I'll tell you what's been bothering me for the last day and a half. If you've known about me, remembered me, why the hell didn't you come looking for me before now?"

Jules' mouth opened with an indignant grunt. "Are you kidding me? I spent my life looking for you! You stupid, self-centered bitch! You never looked back! *You never looked for us!*"

To her horror, that little outburst opened a floodgate of her own wild emotions. She couldn't catch her next breath and was at the mercy of her own contorting body. The only way to breathe was to bawl.

Quinn came out of nowhere, but it wasn't *his* arms that came around her, it was Jillian's.

"Get out of here," her sister barked at him.

Jules was grateful he went. Even her hand spread wide couldn't hide her gaping, howling mouth, and she turned toward her sister and buried her face against her so no one else could see the ugliness. There was just too much pain for her to handle on her own. For once, just this once, she'd lean on Jillian, but just until the tide in her chest turned.

Jules hadn't noticed when they'd made it to the ground, but as her surroundings crept back into her awareness, she realized they were seated right hip to right hip facing opposite directions, with their heads on each other's right shoulders. Jillian flipped a small square of plaid over her arm and Jules hurried to blow her nose on it before anyone told her it was meant for something else. Scots were funny about their plaids, weren't they?

Jillian let go of her and pulled back to look in her face.

"You said, *You never came looking for us*." She took a deep breath. "Who is *us?*"

Jules wasn't sure she could talk, but she tried.

"Mom and Dad," she said.

Jillian frowned. "But they died, when we were three."

"No. They died when just before our tenth birthday. We looked for you for six years. It's what we did. Then, after I was old enough to drive, I was always looking for you too. By then I was pretty mad and wanted to take it out on somebody. It wasn't until I was snooping in an FBI agent's stuff that I found the file they had on me. They'd known about you, and about grandmother. Suddenly I knew right where to find you."

Jillian was shaking her head and tearing up again. "I don't understand. Why would Grandmother have lied to me? Why would she keep me from my parents? Were they abusive?"

"No! No, they were wonderful." Jules realized she'd been so angry for so long she'd forgotten how lucky she'd been. "It was Grandmother," she said. "She was crazy. Mother refused to believe her conspiracy theories so Grandmother took you away. Supposedly, she was protecting you from something that was supposed to happen in the future. Now that I know about the tomb, I'm not so sure she was crazy. But how did she know?"

"It's a long story. Let's just say, she misunderstood something she heard. I'll tell you all about it another time. And you can tell me what our parents were like."

"Deal," Jules said.

Jillian leaned back on her hands and looked at the toes of her green boots.

"I remember a little girl who I thought was just my reflection in a mirror," she said. "And a bear named Necklace."

"White bear with purple legs and arms?"

"And head."

Jules shook her head. "It wasn't Necklace. It was Jewels. Your bear was Jules. Mine was Jillybean. They're in a box, somewhere."

"Grandmother called me Jillybean."

"So did I." Jules swallowed back a wave of tears rising in her throat.

Jillian smiled. "I can't believe you kept them all this time."

"Yeah. Neither can I."

They sat in silence for a minute. It was a comfortable silence. Jules could almost imagine she heard her sister's thoughts.

Someone cleared his throat on the far side of the tree. "Does this mean you two are ready to—"

"Go away!" they shouted together, and this time they laughed.

The guy was gone so fast Jules didn't know if it had been Quinn or Monty who'd tried to interrupt them.

"So. Is there anything else you wanted to get off your chest?" Jillian asked. "You know, in case we need to cry some more before I finish stitching up Quinn?"

"No. I think—well, at least I hope—I'm done being mean to you."

Jillian laughed.

They heard a scuffle, then a strange thunk, then silence.

"Jillian! I'm bleedin'," Monty called.

Jillian shook her head and didn't move.

"Then stop fighting with Ewan," she called back.

They giggled, then waited.

A few minutes later, there was another plea for attention.

"Quinn's bleedin' again!"

That time, it sounded like Quinn's voice, but they both jumped to their feet and went hurrying around the tree. Monty and Ewan didn't look too happy to see them. They both passed a coin to first Quinn, then James.

"How much did you lose, husband?" Jillian walked over and prodded Monty's arm with a sharp fingernail and he winced.

"Naught," he said.

"But I saw you pass coins," she argued.

Monty looked at Quinn and grimaced. Quinn shook his head so slightly Jules wondered if she'd imagined it—if it weren't for the guilty way he avoided eye contact when he reached for her.

"What did you bet on?" she asked him.

"Nothing of import," Monty claimed.

"What did you bet on, husband?" Jillian ran her dangerous fingernails up Monty's chest and by the time she reached his neck, his defenses were forgotten.

"The first wager was determined by which was made of sterner stuff and wouldna greet first." He cleared his throat. "Knowin' ye fer the strong woman ye are, I bet on ye, wife." He grinned like he expected a reward.

Jules figured *greet* meant *cry*. Well, at least Quinn had bet on her. He'd lost, but he'd bet on her. She made a mental note to reward him later, but saw nothing wrong with hugging him tight right then.

"And the second wager was whose blood would bring ye runnin'," Monty continued. "I must admit to being a wee disappointed in ye, mavournin'."

"Be disappointed later, uncle," said Quinn. "For I meant what I said. I am bleeding again."

***

Jules resumed her pacing between the same two trees while she waited for Jillian to finish with Quinn. He'd already pulled out a stitch, and didn't mind getting poked again, but something about it bothered Jules and while she paced, she realized what it was.

What if he got an infection? Here. Now.

Could she convince him to go back to the real world with her? Was she wrong to even think it? Wrong to ask him?

But there was something else bothering her too. Something more immediate. Another foreboding.

She spun on her heel and met her sister's gaze. She suspected the frown on Jillian's face matched her own. Whatever the foreboding was, her sister felt it too.

"Montgomery," Jillian called. "We need to leave. Now."

She said something to Quinn. He nodded. Then Jillian shoved her supplies in her little first aid kit and headed for her horse. Jules could only think to go to Quinn. He raised an arm and waved her to him, smiling, oblivious to whatever it was she and Jillian were feeling.

She took two steps through the pine needles when she was stopped by James' bellow—the alarm she'd been dreading to hear for months.

"Gun!"

CHAPTER TWENTY-FOUR

A dozen thoughts flew through Jules' mind while she ran and lunged for Quinn.

Would she hurt him when they collided? Could she protect his head? Had the Gordon's been watching and decided to perform their own execution? Or had a hitman been following her after all? It wasn't impossible to think a Skedros might have tagged along, might have jumped into the parade line through the car park and into the tomb. It didn't matter that it was fourteen hundred something and guns might not have been invented yet—James was there, and James had one. Therefore, it was possible someone else did too.

Jules had spent far too many months in close quarters with FBI agents not to react as she did. With all the false alarms and dry runs, she was programmed to hit the ground when anyone yelled *gun*. But Quinn was another story. Maybe his twenty-first century senses had dulled over the past year. Of course he still knew what a gun was, but he might not react so quickly. Not to mention he'd been sitting on that ancient log with a hand in the air like he was just asking to be someone's target.

Just as Quinn reached for Jules-The-Flying-Squirrel, something pinched her in the waist. Hard. The impact of her body slamming into Quinn's hardly registered at all. But when she landed on top of him on the far side of the log, she felt it.

Below her, Quinn gasped for air. The wind must have been knocked out of his lungs, so she needed to get off him so he could breathe, but she couldn't seem to move.

"Let me up," she panted. "You can't breathe."

He shook his head and held her close. "Dinna move, love. We're pinned. An arrow, I'm certain."

She put her chin down but couldn't see anything. If the arrow went into her waist, then into him, it could have hit just about anything depending on the angle.

"Dinna panic, lass," he whispered. "And be still. He's still out there, aye?"

"Enos!" Ewan bellowed the name over and over. "The threat has passed, Enos. Stand ye doon!"

"Ewan?" A different man's voice then. "How the hell was I to recognize ye with all that paint?"

"How do ye think, ye big bastard?" Ewan's voice again. "Ever seen the Ross tartan afore?"

Jules and Quinn only looked at each other while they listened to a short fist fight. Only when it ended with a satisfying thunk, did she dare speak.

"Enough!"

"Sounds like Monty," Quinn said.

"Sounds like you," she whispered, then gave him a peck on the lips when it looked like her comment hadn't pleased him. "You're going to be fine," she added, ignoring how bossy she sounded.

He was even more handsome than he'd been in dungeons or dreams. She could have stared at him all day, but he would need stitching again. She supposed she would too. And without anything to numb her!

Her head fit nicely against his collarbone. At least the arrow hadn't gone through either of their hearts because they were both beating hard up against each other.

"Is anyone hurt?" James this time.

"Will ye stay with me, lass?" Quinn's question brought back all the dreams and all the emotions in them. It was a little painful, but she reached up and pushed his hair out of his eyes. For once, she was going to look into them while they had their conversation.

"Until it's over?" Jules shuddered as the dream echoed in her ears and sharper pain shot through her shoulder— like lightning, branching off in mean directions. She could see it doing the same to Quinn.

"Nay, lass. This will never be over. You and I will never be over. We're meant."

Monty peeked over the log and laughed. "Ah, here they are. Moonin'— Dear God! Juliet's been hit!"

***

Other than the day Jillian and her grandmother had gone missing—and granted, she didn't remember much more than her mother bawling and ranting and pulling on her own hair—this day had been the most emotional of Jule's life. And considering she'd also witnessed the murder of a dear friend that was saying a lot.

As it turned out, the man who'd shot her had been ordered, by Ewan, to kill Quinn. Ewan had tried to explain why, but Jules seemed to be the only one in the bunch that didn't understand.

"Mayhap ye'd have a better understanding after ye've spent more time in my century, aye?" said Ewan, standing over her where she leaned against an equally traumatized and bleeding Quinn. Jillian had done what she could. The little round holes were clean. The arrow had been removed. And she was certain that nothing organ-ish had been affected in either of them. They'd been extremely lucky.

She shook her head. "Spend more time here? No way am I sticking around until it all makes sense. You people will never make sense."

Quinn tensed and she realized what her little statement would have sounded like to him. She looked over, ready to explain, but he was watching a long lanky man walk toward them. A bow was slung over his bare and bony shoulder. She tried not to stare at the creature-like tufts of hair that filled his armpits.

"Jules," Ewan said, "this is Enos."

Enos, the man who had nailed both her and Quinn with one shot, gave her a little bow and mumbled something she didn't understand. An apology, she assumed.

She gave him a little smile and a nod, having no problem forgiving him for following orders. If Quinn would have died, however, she was pretty sure she would have exacted all kinds of vengeance on his ass.

The man moved on to Quinn, gave him a fierce-looking frown, snatched up the two pieces of arrow that had been pulled from their bodies, then walked away into the trees. She wasn't too comfortable with him being out there, somewhere, with that frown still on his face, but Ewan and Montgomery didn't have a problem with it, and they knew the strange man best.

Ewan had decided that since she probably wasn't going to forgive him, he should be the one to stop her bleeding. She didn't understand what he was talking about until he came at her with a glowing red knife. She understood perfectly when she woke up to the smell of burned flesh.

It was then that she realized Jillian was a mess. Her sister had serious bed head, like she'd been trying to pull her hair out. Her eyes had thick red rings around them, and her nose didn't look much better. She'd insisted then and there that if Jules died she'd die too, which Jules found very touching in revenge-free kind of way.

Unfortunately, that made Montgomery freak out and he scooped up his wife and disappeared for a while. When they'd returned, Jillian was noticeably recovered, although she was wearing half of the paint from her husband's face, and it was Montgomery whose eyes and nose were red.

Jules thought she'd cheer everyone up by announcing that she was determined to live, but she didn't hold out much hope for Ewan.

Quinn suggested Ewan start spending more time at prayers.

***

Never before had Castle Ross looked as much like a home to Quinn. But never before had he ridden toward it with a lass in his arms who made him want to live and love and laugh again. Well, at least not on horseback. And not for a very long time.

"We have a wee problem," Ewan pointed out as they started down into the glen where Castle Ross stood waiting for them. The ridge was covered with wildflowers of blue and yellow, waving slowly in the breeze above the pink heather, calling to question the chance that anyone could have a problem on such a lovely summer day in the Highlands.

"What problem, Ewan?" Quinn asked.

"Weel. We're returnin' with two living Montgomerys and two green-toed faeries. How do we explain it?"

"Green-toed faeries?" Jules turned to her sister.

Jillian pulled up her skirt to reveal her green ostrich boots she'd been wearing when she first traveled back to the fifteenth century.

Juliet grinned, then pulled up her own skirts. Her boots were grey, but they, too, were ostrich. They were a close match, all but the more intense black of Juliet's hair.

They'd been crying off and on for hours, with very little said between them, and Quinn wondered if they were somehow speaking in each other's minds. It was hard to explain it otherwise.

Jillian had insisted on stopping as soon as they reached Ross land, so they could have a chat and the wounded could rest. Then they'd walked into a wee clearing, stood toe to toe, and said nothing at all. Their arms had flown round each other and none of them had been dry since—the rain notwithstanding. Neither had he received much attention from his wee lass. Of course, she was also injured, but he could have used a query or two concerning his own health.

Just then, Juliet twisted the seat before him and looked up.

"Are you okay?" Her hand came up to pat the bandage that covered the hole the arrow had made.

"'Tis a scratch," he said, mollified.

He pushed her black hair behind an ear so he could see more of her lovely face. How could he ever have believed she was Jillian?

"And how do you fare, my Juliet?"

A pink shadow rose beneath her smooth cheeks.

"It doesn't hurt like I thought it would." She laid her cheek against his chest and sighed as if she were truly happy, in spite of her wounds.

"We must get you seen to. As much as I appreciate Jillian's forethought when bringing a Primary Aid Kit with her, you still need doctoring. And you'll not be leaving my side. I won't stand for it."

She turned forward and nestled back against him. He preferred to think of it as a sign of agreement.

"You have a bigger problem than that," James said as he spurred his horse even with Quinn's. He nodded toward the woman in his arms. "I'm not leaving this place without Juliet Bell."

Quinn's spine stretched in spite of the pain it caused.

"I'll not allow her out of my sight," he announced to anyone wanting to know.

Jillian's horse appeared to his right.

"Well," she said. "I'm certainly not leaving her here." Then she turned in the saddle and gave Monty a look that demanded he say something. The look also suggested it be something that would please her.

The big man gave a nod and moved his horse up next to his wife's.

"And I'll not be leaving without Jillian, no matter how confusing it might be for our clansmen." Monty tried not to smile, but failed. Then he laughed and pulled Jillian from her saddle and across his lap. "Was that heroic enough for you, love?"

Jillian rolled her eyes but appeared to be pleased with her new seating arrangement.

"I almost forgot!" she cried suddenly. "Two months ago, I got a package from Grandmother's attorney." She turned to Montgomery. "Remember?"

He only shrugged.

"He said he'd tried to find the woman it was meant for, but she'd disappeared. Since it was his last duty as executor, he was passing it on to me for safekeeping. He said if a *Ms. Bell* ever showed up asking about Grandmother, I was to give the package to her. He also said it was up to me whether or not I opened it, but that's all he said. I knew I wouldn't be able to resist taking a peek, so I put it in a safe deposit box in Edinburg. Too far away to tempt me, you know?"

She turned to Juliet.

"I never realized you had a different last name. I'd have remembered sooner. Maybe, whatever she wrote to you, will better explain why she took me. I still can't believe she didn't tell me about you, or our parents. I can't believe I never remembered." Jillian reached over the empty saddle of her own horse and squeezed Juliet's hand. "We'll go to Edinburg just as soon as we're home."

Home.

Quinn's chest tightened and felt a bit hemmed in. He couldn't help feeling like a greedy bastard, but he was tired of everyone trying to take his woman from him, if indeed she wished to be his.

He pulled back on the reins and his horse stopped, then began backing. "Give us a moment, if you please," he said to the rest who had begun to slow their mounts.

He guided his horse off the road and close to a stand of birch trees, hoping the rustle of their silver leaves would somewhat mask their conversation and give them a sense of privacy. Monty raised a brow that warned the distance would have to do. It was irritating to have the man take on the role of Juliet's protector when Quinn was completely capable of filling that role himself.

Juliet turned in the saddle, looked about at the trees, then up at him. "What now?"

Quinn smiled at the way she'd braced herself, like she was ready to defend them both at the drop of a hat. There was also a small flame of fear in her eyes, as if she worried he was about to shoo her from his saddle.

"Ah, my love. Tell me what you're thinking. None of us seems to be able to give you up, but it is you who must decide where you will go and with whom, aye?"

Of course *he* had little choice. The Gordons believed he was dead and if word reached Laird Gordon that he'd been tricked, that the man he believed was Montgomery Ross yet lived, there would be all out war between the clans. Blood would be shed. Lives would be lost. And there was no need, thanks to a certain enchanted tomb that could take Quinn away.

But he wasn't about to point it out to Juliet. She needed to decide if she wanted him with her after they reached the other side of time itself. He would not force her to change her life to accommodate him if he wasn't truly the man she wanted.

"Tell me what you want, lass. And don't think to spare me."

She nodded, then hung her head. She fiddled with her fingers, but he doubted she was paying them much heed. When he forced her to lift her chin, her eyes were full of tears, and it frightened him.

"What is it, lass?"

Finally, she spoke.

"They all act like I'm so special. I'm not used to that. The Feds only treated me well because I have something they need. My parents always treated me like I was the consolation prize, not the prize. And Gabby only... Only..."

"Gabby what? I've heard ye say he's like a father to ye. Do ye miss him that much, lass?"

"No. I don't miss him. I miss who I thought he was, but that was just a fantasy. I hate him for taking that fantasy away, I guess. I hate him for killing Nikkos. In that second, after the shot, I realized I'd lost a brother and a father. How can I forgive him for that?"

"It is the same sometimes, with Libby."

"Your wife?"

"Aye. Sometimes I can't forgive her for leaving me."

Jules looked down again. "Plane crash, right?"

"Right. But even though it wasna her fault, I'm still angry that she's gone."

She scrubbed at her fingers. "You want to hear something sappy?"

"Sappy?" He didn't understand.

"Yeah. You know, corny?"

"Perhaps you should just tell me. I'll brace myself, just in case."

She nodded. "Okay. Well." She took a breath and looked up. "I feel...less angry when... When I'm with you. See? I warned you it was sappy."

He smoothed a fingertip along the side of her face, scared that she might dissolve if he pressed too hard. What had God seen in him, to deem him worthy of such a lass?

"Ah, love. I feel less angry within your presence as well, but that's not the reason I must stay near you."

She took a deep breath and sighed. Then she waited.

"I stay near ye, lass, because in my dream, it's all I wanted. And when I woke from the dream, only to find ye there, in the dark with me, you were all I wanted still. And the feeling only grows stronger each time I touch you, or look at you, or hear your voice. It was not just a dream, lass. It was the telling of our future. The question is, do you want to share that future?"

She was crying again, but this time he had a cure for it. A hundred soft kisses across the whole of her face would fix her up fine.

"Give us a moment, he says." Ewan laughed. "Ye've had yer moment. Has she decided then?"

"Another moment if ye don't mind," he called back. He ignored the groans of the others and looked into Juliet's eyes. "What do ye say, lass. In which century are we to reside? For it was no exaggeration. I go where you go, if you'll allow me."

She shook her head and his heart stuttered.

"I have to go back. I have to testify. Gabby's a murderer. If I can stop him, I will. If I stay here, with you, who knows how many people will die because I didn't show up on the stand? I'd end up like Lady Macbeth, wandering around the castle trying to remove blood from my hands—blood only I can see. Can you understand?"

"Aye. I do. But do you wish me to go with you, lass?"

She shrugged her shoulders. "I thought it would be too selfish of me to ask. It would kill me to leave you behind. Please, come with me. Please." She leaned up and kissed him, not giving him a chance to reply.

In truth, he couldn't be more pleased. He'd often believed that he'd done what he was supposed to do for history's sake. He'd helped the Rosses transition from one laird to the next. He was only filling space now.

But since meeting Juliet in spirit, and then in person, he'd realized that filling space was no longer enough for him. And if she were consulted, Libby would agree. He had much to give, and just because he mourned Libby still, it did not justify turning his back on the rest of his life.

"Aye, lass. I'll come." Then he covered her one ear and held the other to his chest so he could shout. "Jillian! Just how many people to you reckon we can fit in Isobelle's tomb?"

CHAPTER TWENTY-FIVE

One week later...

Jules had choked down a dry biscuit breakfast with absolutely no coffee for washing it down. She was thrilled to be going back to civilization before lunch.

If Quinn wouldn't have agreed to come along, she suspected she would have stayed behind with him. She would have had to learn to live with herself for not putting a stop to Gabby, but she couldn't have forgiven herself for leaving her Highlander behind. Besides, Gabby's sins were not her own. Neither were her grandmother's.

And like Jillian said, the tomb wasn't the most reliable mode of transportation. There was no guarantee she could have come back for him later.

Her sister led the way to the workroom where they would begin their journey back to the world of caffeine.

"I'm sorry, Ewan," she said. "We'd stay longer but we need to get these two to a doctor, just to be safe."

Ewan squeezed Jillian. "Never ye mind, lass. I'm sure we couldna stand to feed ye, and that was before you starting carrying Monty's child about.

"Children," interjected one of the Muir sisters.

Montgomery blanched. Jillian bit her lip. The Muirs
just laughed.

Jules could never remember the sisters' names. It
spooked the hell out of her that there were Muir twins
everywhere. And standing there in the cellar, with Jillian,
Quinn and Monty, and the Muirs, it looked like a reunion
that excluded anyone who wasn't genetically duplicated.
James and Ewan stood off to the side, looking nothing
alike.

The last time she'd been in that room, she'd been
filled with bitterness, disagreeing with Ewan over the
sainthood of Jillian Ross. But the second Jules had let go
of that bitterness, something else had flooded in and
filled the gaps. If she liked sappy, she'd say it was love.
But she wasn't sappy. Okay, not *too* sappy. If she had to
put it into a single word, she'd call it...home.

Into the arms of yer family.

Montgomery's words were still stuck in her head and
she had no wish to unstick them.

Now, they were safely ensconced in Castle Ross.
The tomb's entrance was waiting patiently. The prying
eyes of Clan Ross had been swept from the building and
a state of mourning had commenced in honor of Laird
Montgomery Ross who had died of battle wounds at the
hands of the Gordons.

Quinn had once again assumed the role of the dead
body and had been led through the streets of East
Burnshire. The real Montgomery had ridden with his
plaid over his hair and blue paint re-applied to his face. A
few people noticed Jules and her sister and murmured
"Muirs!" Jules figured it was as good a disguise as any.

All of them standing in the workroom had been
moved by the respect shown for Montgomery Ross by
hundreds of clanspeople who'd had to stand in the
pouring rain to do so. Although, if Ewan shed a tear, it

wouldn't have been distinguishable from the rain pouring down his upturned face as he led the procession.

The emotions wrung from Jules that day had been emotions she didn't believe herself capable of feeling. And no one had even died.

What a wuss.

She looked at Jillian and couldn't help but see her now as the little girl on the other side of the table, soaking crayons, thinking the same things she thought. She remembered a lot of laughing.

The importance of that day, long ago, when the laughing had stopped, was fading.

In the morning, Clan Ross would bury a box that Ewan and Quinn had built and filled with stones. The Muirs had suggested it might be bad luck for Montgomery to have a hand in it.

No one had argued.

During the course of the past week, she'd even forgiven Ewan. She'd had no choice.

For some strange reason, Quinn had insisted that Daniel try his hand at sculpting Jules' face. Apparently, the young man had a talent for it. Quinn had even found a stone for the guy to use, insisting that he'd do as fine a job as the Italian had done on the likeness of Monty. Ewan had moped around in front of her the entire time she was forced to hold her pose. Finally, she'd forgiven him just to get him to leave her alone.

Jillian and Quinn had acted freaky every time they'd checked on Daniel's progress. Jules had started getting jealous of them excluding her from some inside joke, but Quinn promised he'd share their little secret as soon as they got back home.

While they'd waited for Daniel to finish, their wounds had healed nicely. She was going to have to get a tattoo to cover up the scars made by Ewan's cauterizing job, but they would be a permanent reminder of the way she and Quinn had met. It had been a pretty hellish vacation from reality, but she didn't want to forget it.

Also, while she'd posed for Daniel, she and Jillian had talked about their lives. Now she knew the old wives tale about twins was true, that Jillian's pain caused her pain and vice versa. And even if there wasn't that supernatural connection, she couldn't bring herself to break her sister's heart. For all Jillian would ever know, their parents had simply died in a car wreck. She would never know they'd been on their way to check out another lead on their missing daughter and her lunatic grandmother.

They'd had plenty of chances to giggle like sisters since Daniel's new bride, Annie, kept sneaking into the hall to lure Daniel away. They had giggled about Quinn, about Monty, and giggled a helluva lot about the comparisons between Quinn and Monty. When Daniel had swaggered back into the hall, they'd giggled about him too. It was like they'd been making up for all the years they'd had no one to laugh with.

And now Daniel's sculpture—which he called The Green-Toed Fairy, even though it was Jillian's boots she'd been wearing half the time—was finished. Ewan was forgiven. And there was nothing left in the fifteenth century left undone.

It was time to go home.

"All right then, get ye gone." Ewan turned to Monty. "I'll miss ye, cousin. Perhaps when ye're needin' some peace from all yer bairns, you'll come here. I'll keep a barrel below the hole. Always. And the next time ye come visit, I'll tell ye all about yer grand funeral."

Monty shook his head. "No, my friend. Carry on as we'd already decided. The Ross lairds must keep their course, so everything stays right for the future. Guard our secrets. The clan is all."

"Aye, cousin. The clan is all." Ewan gave Monty a knock on the shoulder. "Up with yer sorry arse, then."

Monty hefted himself up into the hole where Jillian waited for him.

James gave Jules a wink, then followed Monty. "Oh, aye. Plenty of room still. Come on, Juliet."

She shook her head. "Quinn first. I'm not taking a chance on this elevator leaving before he can get in."

Quinn laughed and jumped on the barrel, then he looked over her shoulder in horror. Monty and James already had a hold of his arms and were lifting him up.

"Wait! Stop! Let go!" he shouted.

Jules didn't know what terrifying creature might be behind her, but she lunged for the far side of the barrel where the Muirs and Ewan stood, sure the adrenaline shooting through her would help her fly. But hands grabbed her from behind. She struggled until she saw the flash of a blade, then felt it pressed against her throat. She'd felt such an edge before, when she'd awakened in Debra's bed.

Back on the barrel, Quinn held out his hands. "Percy! Percy, don't hurt her. You can have whatever you want. Just don't hurt my lass."

"Just what a man likes to hear," the young man snarled in her ear. "In truth, I've come to tell ye I've made me decision. I've decided to believe ye, that ye are able to change history. When the big red bastard turned aside to stab yer heart, so no one could see how deep the blade went, I kenned ye'd cheated death yet again. It's a charmed life ye live, aye?"

"History is written by the folks that write it," Quinn said. "I can write whatever history you wish. Is it your ambition to replace yer father, then? Or make certain the Gordon clan will be ruled by your children? Whatever you wish. Just let her go."

Quinn had slowly lowered his body until he was squatting on the top of the barrel. He started to lower a leg to the ground, but pulled it back when Percy hissed.

The knife bit into her skin but she didn't dare make a sound, afraid Quinn might attack to save her, afraid Percy might feel threatened enough to start slicing and dicing. Besides, with his injuries, Quinn might not be able to move as quickly as he'd expected to, just as she hadn't been able to get to the other side of the barrel as fast as she thought she could.

"I'm no' daft, Quinn Ross," said Percy. "I'll not take yer promise and let ye flee. Besides, it's no' the future I wish to change, but the past."

Quinn frowned. "I canna change the past, Percy. What's done is done."

The man behind her grunted, maybe even sobbed. Jules almost felt sorry for him. She reached up and laid a hand on his elbow. He jerked away from her touch, but luckily, not with the hand holding the knife.

He stiffened.

She thought she was screwed.

"I don't believe ye," he spat. "If ye can change the future, ye can change the past. And for yer sake, ye'd best think of a way to do it. Or for her sake, that is."

She could hear Monty and James shuffling around inside the hole. They were probably going out of their minds not being able to come out and fight. But Quinn was in their way, and he couldn't move without pissing off Percy.

She needed to distract him.

"What is it, Percy?" she asked calmly. "What is it you want to change?"

She could feel his chest at her back, shaking as he tried to compose himself to speak.

"It's all right, Percy. Take your time," she said.

Quinn nodded. "This is about your brother."

Percy sucked in a breath and held it. When he let the air go, it came out in a rush.

"William. His name is William. We're forbidden to say his name. *William*," he said again, like it was a relief to say it. He sobbed, sucked in another breath. "He'll never be allowed to leave the dungeon. My father's no better than Montgomery Ross, refusing to bury his dead. Keeping them close. Killing us all."

He was losing it. She had to help his focus.

"You want to bury your brother?" she asked.

She didn't know if she was trying to distract him or help him.

Percy grabbed her hair and yanked her closer to him. He pushed the blade up against her skin, obviously no longer caring if she got cut.

"Eegit," he hissed. "I want him to never go into the dungeon in the first place! I want Quinn Ross to stop it from happening. Six years ago. Ye'll find him six years ago. I've been here for days, listening. I heard enough from ye all to ken ye can move from one year to the next. So ye must go back. Go back and stop me father. Bring William to...now. Hang a plaid from yer battlements when ye have him, and I'll return yer woman. Fail to save him by Samhain, and that day she begins to die— the same death me brother suffered, alone and with nothing. In an oubliette. Ye'll ken not where."

Jules was pulled back off her feet, then carried out of the little room. Percy paused to slam the door shut, then held her with an arm crushing her neck while he jammed something against the door.

"Percy. Please. Don't do this."

"Enough!"

He dragged her down the corridor, in the wrong direction, barely allowing enough space in the crook of his elbow for her to breathe. Arguing further was impossible. In his other hand, instead of the dagger, he held a large torch that dripped fire with every step. At least, when they hit a dead end and had to return, there was a chance the others would have made it out—a chance they could save her.

He stopped.

Here is the end. We'll have to go back.

But then she heard metal bang against wood, like a ring handle on a door. The giant door in the great hall had that type of ancient handle. She'd held onto it while she'd teased James into following her away from the keep.

A moist breeze brushed past her face in the wake of a small round door. It looked like the end of a wooden barrel. She strained to the side, but saw only darkness beyond.

A tunnel?

Was this where the modern Muirs had hidden from James once they'd sent her up into the tomb?

Percy reached through the opening and set the torch in the wall so he could drag her through. The threshold was high and she struggled to keep her feet beneath her while he pulled her to the other side. Percy released her neck and grabbed her wrist. She tried to wrench it free while he pulled the round door shut. He hardly noticed.

"Those Muirs came sneaking down the hall while I searched for the entrance to yer enchanted tomb. They had to have come from somewhere, and I knew if I waited long enough, they'd lead me to their secret. Let's hope the torch lasts long enough to reach the other end, aye?"

CHAPTER TWENTY-SIX

Once they broke through the door, Quinn followed closely on Ewan's heels. Montgomery brought the second torch and led the women.

Daniel turned from his post at the top of the stairs just as Annie's blue skirts swished around the corner.

"Why did you not come to let us out, when he got past you?" Ewan shoved at the man, nearly knocking him over.

Daniel shook his head. "No one's passed me, laird."

"Oh? And how would ye know if yer tongue was down Annie's throat and yer eyes were shut tight?"

Daniel straightened his spine and lifted a haughty nose. "She but came to ask how long before I'd be home, yer lairdships. Not a soul has come up those stairs since the lot of ye went down them, may God strike me dead if they did."

"All's right, Daniel. All's right." Ewan turned to face his following. "Did he get lost, do ye suppose?"

"The dungeons," Quinn said. It was the only other place they could be. The cellar twisted a bit, but didn't go much past the workroom beneath the tomb. Even in the future.

Montgomery led the way. The Muirs brought up the rear, too stubborn to leave off, Quinn supposed. When it was clear that no one had been in the dungeons for a good while, one of the Muirs, Margot he thought, began to wail, which was odd; they never carried on. Oh, they were difficult to best in an argument, but he'd never seen one shed a tear, not in either century.

Montgomery and the rest looked about the dusty hallway, waiting for someone to explain the matter with the woman. Mhairi wrapped an arm around her sister's shoulders, then turned a look on Quinn that scared him to the bone.

"What?" he asked. "What is it? What do you know?"

Mhairi shook her head. "He must have found the tunnel. Mayhap there will be footprints, so we'll ken for sure."

"What tunnel?" he asked, then turned to Monty. "Is there a tunnel?"

"None that we could ever find." Monty nodded to Mhairi. "Show us."

She gave Margot one last pat, then Mhairi took Monty's torch and started back up the passage. They all followed close on her heels. Margot had recovered enough to keep up. Soon they were passing the broken door of the workroom. Then beyond.

At the end of the tunnel, where the walls had been shored up with odd bits of barrels, beams, and planks, Mhairi reached out a hand and pulled on a metal ring attached to a barrelhead.

Much to his surprise, and apparently to the surprise of all, the barrelhead swung open on silent hinges. A tunnel gaped beyond.

Quinn moved forward, but Mhairi fairly jumped into his path, her arms spread wide. Margot moved around behind her and did the same.

Mhairi shook her head. "Ye cannot enter, Quinn Ross. None of ye can enter here. The tunnel is cursed. We've only showed it to ye so ye can see if Percy took Juliet this way."

Quinn tried to push around her, but she blocked him again.

"Mhairi, I care not for faery tales, or ghosties. I'm going in. Look there." He pointed to the dirt floor beneath the hole. Their footprints, clear as day. Juliet is draggin' her feet, smart lass. Now let me pass."

Mhairi shook her head again. Margot moved closer behind her sister, as if she truly believed that together they could stop him.

"The tunnel taketh and giveth," said Margot, over her sister's shoulder. "As Percy and Juliet travel beneath the hillock, the tunnel is taking from them. It takes all."

Quinn froze at the last, not because he was afraid to enter, but afraid of what the cursed tunnel was doing to his brave Juliet.

Monty had hold of another torch and held it high, peering at the sisters as if he thought they might not be real. The firelight reflected off twin streams of tears—one running down Mhairi's right cheek, the other running down the left cheek of her sister.

Muirs did not cry.

Quinn swallowed the bile rising in his throat and turned to Monty. "Do ye understand a word of this?"

Monty shook his head and looked behind him, to Jillian. His wife hurried forward and slipped beneath his arm.

"Mhairi," she said. "Please. Help us understand. What is the tunnel taking?"

The woman nodded, her graying hair swung forward and back. But she looked for a nod from her sister before she answered.

"Age."

The word hung in the air.

Jillian frowned, as did they all. "Age? Do you mean that the tunnel will make them younger?"

Mhairi sighed, then nodded.

Margot came around her sister's shoulder and together they dropped their arms.

"Takes the years, dries the tears," they chanted in unison. "Quiets laughter, lulls the fears."

Tears poured a fresh trail down Mhairi's right cheek. Her sister tried to console her while keeping a steady eye on Quinn.

"They'll lose ten years by the time they reach the other side," she said. "But it takes the memories of those ten years as well. Young Percy will be younger still. He won't remember his purpose, so your lady fair will be in little danger. But I'm afraid young Juliet won't remember... Well. You." She patted him on the arm, then stepped back to guard the tunnel once more.

Quinn listed to his left as his heart turned heavy like a stone. Monty left his wife's side to shore him up.

Jillian stepped up to the sisters. "What if we can stop them from getting to the other side?"

Mhairi shook her head. "I doubt Percy would come back just because ye ask him, nicely or no. Besides, the tunnel is not so long. They are well beyond halfway."

No. That couldn't be. It couldn't be too late!

Quinn's strength rallied with the silent denial.

"No!" He pushed his way toward the opening. He was right; even three women were no match for him. Someone grabbed hold of his waist but he was progressing. His fingers were but an inch or two from the frame when a gentle hand came to rest on his outstretched arm.

"Quinn."

It was Jillian.

"Quinn, if you go, you'll forget too. Think of the memories you'll lose." She shook her head. "You'll lose Libby."

As quick as a lightning bolt, he lost all the strength in his arm and it dropped.

Libby!

James was suddenly at his side, but Quinn noticed little else as he conjured Libby's face in his mind. All those memories had become so clear since he'd met Juliet. He remembered all the little creases around Libby's eyes, the dip below her nose. The sound of her laughter.

Trouble was, he remembered the same of Juliet.

Tears filled his throat and rose behind his eyes as he realized he would give up the past, even the memory of it, if he might save his Juliet even a little horror.

"Goodbye, Libby," he whispered and lunged.

A large hairy arm rose between himself and the road to his woman. And worse, it held fast.

"Quinn," James said calmly, as if holding him back was taking no effort at all. "Don't give up on her. She's slippery, that girl. She might get away from him and head back."

James was right. She always had that back-up plan. Any moment she might come running back into the light, having bashed poor Percy up the side of the head.

"If she does," Mhairi said, "the tunnel giveth the same. It will give ten years from stem to stern, but it gives naught more. She'll gain the age she lost, but the memories will not be restored. 'Tis a wicked curse. One meant to protect Clan Muir. What foe cannot be bested as a child? What better punishment for a fleeing enemy than to age him quickly without the benefit of wisdom?"

Margot pushed past his body and put her hand through the middle of the opening. She rubbed her fingers as if testing the texture of the darkness.

Chills assaulted Quinn's spine and spread beneath his hair. He tasted metal on his tongue.

"'Tis finished," Margot said. "They are through."

Quinn refused to believe it all. Of course they'd always called them Muir witches, but they'd never done anything so ridiculous before. They were just trying to keep him from following after Juliet. But why?

"Quinn Ross, how can ye be so unbelieving when ye've traveled from yer time to ours?" Mhairi was behind him, shaking her head.

"Come," Monty barked. "We can cut them off if Percy tries to take her north. Younger or not, he might think to take her back to Gordon land."

He halted before his wife. "Jillian, my love. Ye'll stay home, and ye'll keep away from that tunnel. Mhairi, Margot? I trust ye to see to it. Doona fail me. Someone stay here, in case Juliet comes back this way."

"Aye, yer lairdship. We'll watch her like our own."

Monty had taken half a dozen steps, but stopped short. Quinn nearly plowed through him.

"I expect the pair of you to do better than that," Monty shouted. "Remember she carries my child."

***

Jillian should have followed the men out of the cellar. The Muirs dried their faces and turned their clever smiles upon her. When they wrapped their arms around her shoulders, the feeling of deja vu should have sent her running, and praying, all the way to the twenty-first century, but she could never leave Montgomery behind. She'd done it once. She would never do it again.

"Jillian, dear. We have a great deal to talk about," said Margot.

"Aye," added her sister. "And not much time."

***

Monty was about to lead them all out the kitchen door when Ewan put a hand up to stop the thing from opening.

"Monty, ye're dead," Ewan said. "No one can lay eyes on ye who doesna ken the truth. And neither can Quinn be seen. The funeral's in the mornin'. I doubt the clan will believe that Montgomery Ross is dead while two men walk about who look just like him, aye? Our clansmen are no' blind. Nor are they daft."

Five minutes later, in ridiculous disguises, he and Monty waited by the door for Ewan and James to bring round the horses.

"She's a fine lass, Quinn," said his uncle. "Almost as fine as my Jillian."

Quinn realized he'd been chewing off his fingernails and stopped.

"Oh? I admit your wife is a fine woman. There was a time I wished I would have been worthy of her myself."

Monty's smile dropped.

Quinn held up a hand to discourage the other man from swinging at him. His head had only begun to heal from all the pounding of the week before.

"But Jillian was never for me, Monty. She was always as a sister, though in my dreams I believed myself to be falling in love with her. But when I laid eyes on Juliet, I realized she was the one I'd been dreaming of. The Muirs had a hand in that dream, but I cannot begrudge them for it. Which reminds me, if that tunnel is as cursed as they claim, it should be destroyed. I find it hard to believe that danger has lain below our feet all these years."

"Och, aye, nephew. We'll see to it as soon as Juliet is safe."

CHAPTER TWENTY-SEVEN

Quinn allowed Ewan and Monty to take the lead. He was a poor hand at finding his way beyond Ross lands, but it was more than that. As desperate as he was to have Juliet safely in his arms, he was afraid of what they might find. He hoped someone else might catch sight of her and Percy before he did, so he might have some kind of warning. It was cowardly, he knew, but allowing the love of his life to be buried had almost killed him once. He was certain he couldn't survive doing it again.

How unworthy he was.

They'd been together for nigh a week and he'd never even asked her age. He had no idea how old the lass would be if she'd truly had ten years removed. If she'd been thirty to begin with... But she hadn't. He was sure of it. And what teenager would want a thirty-five year old man waiting about for her to grow up and fall in love with him?

She wouldn't.

Then he realized the answer rode before him.

"Monty! How old is Jillian?"

His uncle turned but did not slow his horse. "Doona think it, man. Just keep prayin', aye?"

"Easy for you to say," Quinn mumbled.

"Twenty-three," said James. "The yanks forwarded her file, aye?"

Quinn gave the agent a curt nod in thanks.

That would make her thirteen.

Oh, God!

He could not wrap his mind around it. He could not conjure an image of her at thirteen, but hopefully, Monty could, so they'd know what kind of lass to be looking for.

Blasted Muirs! Blasted tunnel.

But wait!

If Juliet was now thirteen, he'd just have to go through the tunnel as well—and twice! He'd make Monty promise to pick him up and send him through again. He'd be fifteen.

Perfect.

But would he remember to fall in love with her? Aye, there was the rub. If he weren't going to end up with Juliet by his side for the rest of his days, would he take that chance? Was he willing to live the horror of being a teenager—again—for the chance of winning Juliet's heart?

"Please, God. Help me."

He whispered the same prayer a dozen times while they came 'round the northern tip of the wee mountain. Ewan dropped to the road and peered closely at every hoofprint.

"Nothing fresh. They've not come through yet." Ewan remounted and headed southeast.

None but Muirs from that point until they crossed back into Ross land. It was an odd bit of land that jutted from the sea to the hill that separated their clan homes. As if Fate had decreed the witches have access to Ross lives. They certainly had enough to do with their history, and their legends. But in modern times, Muirs had become a sept of Clan Gordon.

How he hoped he wouldn't be around to see that bit of history unfold. He could almost pity the formidable Gordons.

As the road turned due south and slowly filled with people, Quinn began searching faces. A boy there. A young lass there. The Muirs were a friendly lot, smiling and nodding as the four horsemen cut their way into their home ground.

An old man stepped back to give them a wider path. He looked at Quinn, then Montgomery, and back again, then slid a finger along the side of his nose as if it meant something. A heartbeat later, Quinn noticed the man again, only on the other side of the road, touching his nose in the same manner.

James leaned closer.

"Twins," he said. "There are many."

Quinn was relieved he wasn't losing his mind, but the presence of more Muir twins in their midst left him unsettled. Again, he tasted metal and wondered if it was new or just the phantom of the time before.

The taste was gone. Memory then.

A young lass with black hair turned away from her mother to watch their passing. Quinn looked closely, to see if her eyes were green. The lass smiled and shook her head as if she'd read his thoughts.

Another chill ran up his spine when he noticed something else. He glanced at James to find the man staring at him with eyes wide.

"It's quiet," Quinn told him. "Why do they not speak?"

But he was afraid he knew the answer.

James shivered. "'Tisn't possible."

Monty, being Monty, pulled his sword from behind his saddle. The Muirs stopped making eye contact and wandered their way off the road. A hundred yards later, the four horsemen were alone and Quinn was grateful for it.

Monty and Ewan fell back until they were four abreast.

"We will go slowly now," Monty said, "to be sure we doona pass them in haste. I think ye should prepare yerself, nephew. I believe Margot and Mhairi might have been telling the truth. If anyone could devise the devil's own tunnel, it would be these people, or their ancestors, aye?"

Quinn had been coming to the same conclusion.

Ewan laughed. "He's been to Muirsglen before, aye?"

Monty grunted and faced forward with an unkind stare.

"I drugged him a year ago, when Jillian took Morna and Ivar into the future and left him behind. I thought he would kill himself with grievin', wear himself out walking the path from the Great Ross Chair, to the witch's hole and back again. More than a dozen times a day, mind. And he wouldna eat. So I drugged his drink. Had him taken to the Muirs to keep him away while I had the cellar filled in. Turned out for the best that I only filled it with barrels of whisky, because the lass came back for 'im."

James laughed, then laughed harder when Monty glared at him. As they rode on, the rest of Morna and Ivar's story came out including a few details that had never been included in his script for the tourists of Castle Ross. Monty also explained how they'd gotten Isobelle out of the tomb.

A few minutes later, Monty and Ewan shared a horrified look, and Quinn knew just what they were thinking.

"Don't worry about it," he told them. James here will keep the secret like the rest of us. Who would believe him anyhow? When he starts telling someone that he's spent time in the fifteenth century, they'll stop listening."

James frowned. "But what about Isobelle? Only a wee while ago, we were all ready to go back into the tomb and never return, and no one made mention of her. Did she die?"

Monty turned away, silent.

Quinn didn't feel as though it was his place to speak of Isobelle.

Ewan shifted in his saddle, then finally, he spoke.

"We dinna ken where she is, James. Our man Ossian went with her, to get her safely settled. We received word from him once, that he and his travelling companion had decided to make a go of things in Spain. We sent a letter there, only to have it returned. A note had been written upon it, claiming the pair had disappeared in the night. We've heard nothing since."

James shifted in his saddle. "And she wasn't a witch, ye say?"

"Nay," said Ewan. "Bewitching to be sure. Red hair, like yers, but nary so many curls. Turned men's heads since the day she was born. Always causin' trouble."

James turned to Monty. "Allow me find her for you, Laird Ross."

Monty wiped an arm across his face before he turned back.

"Why would you say such a thing? This is not yer time. You canna locate her on the internet. She could be anywhere in the wide world—a world that is not so small as you might think at this point in history."

James grinned. "To tell the truth, I'm not quite ready to go back yet. If this is the only chance I have, I'd like to see more of your time. I may as well see Spain and look around for your sister while I'm at it, aye?"

Monty shook his head. His brow was a threatening thundercloud.

"It willna matter," he said. "The tomb's a bit touchy. Only seems to work with Jillian and now, with Juliet. A Muir creation and not to be trusted. For all we ken, we're stuck here for the rest of our days," he turned and looked at the Muir clansmen who were once again making use of the road. "Here, among so many Muirs. A tomb. A tunnel. Only God kens what else. We'll none of us be safe."

James let the subject drop.

No matter what Monty had said, Quinn had the feeling the man was just touchy about anyone getting a look at, or getting their hands on, his sister. Even if it meant he might see her again. After all, hadn't he become immediately protective of Juliet? It seemed it was just Monty's nature.

He hoped Jillian's baby was a boy, or boys rather, because he pitied the lad who came to court any daughter of Montgomery Ross.

They reached the glen and headed for the side of the hill where a couple of youths might have emerged and perhaps had their presence noted.

"Keep a sharp eye. A young lass and a younger laddie," said Monty. "I've no ken how old Percy was, only that he was a mite younger than our lasses."

Quinn nodded. He was also hoping that since these Muirs seemed to read their minds, there might be some among them to lead them in the right direction.

Juliet, sweet. I'm coming.

The village spread much further than expected. From a distance, it hadn't looked like much. As they came nearer, a small city unfolded like a wild rose in bloom. Patches of mist clung to it like morning dew in defiance of the midday sun. Would the mist ever lift completely from a place that sheltered witches?

A tall fort stood at the Eastern edge of town and Quinn wondered if perhaps it hid a good sized castle behind the wooden facade. At one point, they passed through the gates of an ancient wall that likely contained the entire settlement in decades past. Into his mind popped a fanciful image of a city wall that might hide everything and everyone within it from the eyes of their enemies standing ten feet away.

He shuddered.

Ridiculous. He needed to find a handle on his imagination.

An entire clan of witches? *Nonsense.*

They split up. Monty took James and followed the edge of the hillside. Quinn and Ewan dismounted and led their horses into the village, following the flow of its citizens who seemed much too busy to stop and read the minds of strangers. He was relieved to hear the rather normal hum of voices and laughter.

Eventually, they followed a curve and through a light cloud, they saw a well at the top of the street. Two dozen women stood in line awaiting a turn with the bucket. While they waited, they were all turned their attention to a young woman who stooped before a youngster while she washed his face. The lad was seated on a low stone wall beside a large white-washed cottage.

Quinn froze.

The woman wore Juliet's leather coat over her plaid gown. The mist made the colors unclear. Her hair was not nearly so neat as Juliet's had been, and the color was dark, but again, unclear. When she turned to the side, to take a bucket of water from another woman, she didn't look a day less than twenty.

"But that can't be!" Quinn's voice stretched across the distance between them, daring her to turn and prove him wrong. But she didn't turn.

The boy might have been Percy. He looked like a lad of ten wearing his father's clothes. His sleeves hung nearly a foot past the bend of his wrist. For once, his plaid covered his knees. When the lad turned and noticed Quinn, there was no hint of recognition. His attention returned to the woman washing his face. She took a handful of his hair to hold him still while she scrubbed.

Turn. Please, turn.

And yet he dreaded her turning. What if she looked at him, as Percy had done, and she would see a stranger. If she, too, turned away from him, what then? Who might stand beside him for the rest of his life and remind him to breathe in, and then out again? Because he would need reminding.

But if he couldn't find the strength to move his bloody feet, he would never know.

CHAPTER TWENTY-EIGHT

Juliet laughed at something the lad said and for Quinn it was magic enough. Just enough.

He kicked a foot forward, then the other one, as if he were kicking his way out of his own grave. His boots stomped loudly on the packed earth of the street. With no attention to spare his horse, he dropped the leads as he went, determined to face Juliet again, no matter what reaction he might see there.

"Juliet!" he cried as he strode, feeling like a man walking into a wall of spears aimed at his heart. If he stayed back, he'd be safe—he'd never know if she'd forgotten him. But what would it matter? He'd win her heart all over again, even if he had to enlist the aid of a Muir witch to slip him back into her dreams. Even if he had to bide his time while she grew a half-dozen years.

The lad pointed at him. Juliet turned, her eyes following the small filthy finger. Then she straightened and waved to Quinn, waving off that wall of spears.

She knows me!

When he heard Ewan laugh, only then did he realize his distant cousin was still at his side.

"Quinn," she called, and in her smile, he saw the reflection of all the relief he felt himself.

No one would need to bid him breathe again.

"Quinn! Ewan! Come and meet this young man. His name is Percy. He's a terribly brave boy who saved me. I was lost in a cave, and he saved me."

"Jillian Ross!" Montgomery's bellow filled the misty air.

Quinn turned in the direction of the sound and saw Jillian running from the road to the right, toward her sister. The Mhairi and Margot appeared next. Montgomery, on horse, was headed up the street behind them. James followed.

Jillian and Juliet embraced as the older sisters slowed and stopped behind them. Quinn was a little disappointed she had yet to throw herself into *his* arms. He closed the distance to make it easier for her to do so, but she only winked at him and turned back to her sister.

After a flurry of conversation that was too fast for Quinn to understand, Juliet stood speechless while Jillian moved over to the little wall and bent to speak with Percy. The Muirs patted Juliet on the shoulders and laughed.

Quinn prepared to shoo them away just as soon as Juliet gave him permission to do it, but it looked as if Montgomery wanted that pleasure all to himself.

"Mhairi Muir," he shouted as he dismounted. "Ye're done for, do ye hear? That goes for yer sister too. But ye'll be placed in separate dungeons. Mayhap even separate centuries."

The very pale laird pushed the twins aside to get to his wife, then physically wrenched her attention from young Percy—he took her by the shoulders and gave the slightest shake. "Why would you risk such a thing, Jillian? Why?"

Though Quinn was thrilled to find Juliet untouched by the tunnel's curse, he, too, was shocked by the risk Jilly had taken.

The woman smiled and patted Monty's chest. "There was no danger, husband. Because the tunnel holds no curse for *Muirs*. My grandfather Wickham was a Muir if you remember. Just a drop of Muir blood is enough, so the children were never in danger either."

Monty suddenly looked around, then sat abruptly on the short wall next to Percy. It took him a moment to catch his breath.

"Children, ye say? Ye ken it for certain?" He smiled, but he still looked a little sick. "That's grand, aye? But Muirs?"

The last bit he whispered to Jillian but everyone in the vicinity of the well heard it and laughed.

Jillian shook her head. "Only a little bit."

Monty moaned. Percy offered him a filthy wet cloth and the man took it and pressed it to his head.

The look Jilly then turned on Quinn made him wonder if there was more room on the wall, next to the lad.

"Quinn," she said. "I've just broken the news to Juliet that our grandfather was a Muir. It's the reason the tunnel had no effect on her. But I think she might need a little consoling too."

Juliet stood just out of reach looking a mite green, but he couldn't seem to cover the distance. His knees had dissolved—his legs just didn't know it yet. Any second, he was going to be a lifeless pile of pudding in the dirt. He could only look at her, helpless.

Finally, Juliet stepped up to him and took his hand, and just in time too. At least he was still standing—that was, until James pounded him on the back.

"She might be a Muir," he said, laughing, "but she doesna look too young to me, laddy."

Quinn's mind sputtered.

A Muir? He was in love with a Muir twin? And possibly a Muir witch?

His feet bid him run. His heart bid him stay. His body made the decision and leaned toward her.

No. I am but in love with a lass...

He gathered her into his arms and the world around them quieted. Her leather sleeves were cool against his neck as she wrapped her fingers in his hair and pulled him close. When their lips were separated by only a breath, she spoke.

"Are you sure you want to kiss a Muir?"

He pulled back an inch and gave her a frown.

"Do you suppose we could discuss your lineage another time?"

She shook her head. "No, actually. I'm not going to fall in love with a guy who thinks I'm some kind of jinx."

Her fingers started slipping away, so he grabbed her around the waist and lifted her, to encourage her to hold on a bit tighter.

She squeaked.

His heart tripped but his legs held up fine.

"First of all," he said, "it's far too late for that. You're already in love with me."

"Oh?" She raised a brow, but her eyes were still locked on his lips. A good sign, that.

He ignored her interruption and went on.

"Secondly, how can I curse your Muir blood when it brought you to me? And now that same blood has seen you safely through the accursed tunnel? Fine blood indeed."

Juliet studied him for a long moment, then nodded. "Okay. You can kiss me then."

He reluctantly lowered her to her feet and bent to kiss her, but pulled back and searched her face.

"No arguments?" he asked.

"No arguments."

She gave a little grunt of frustration as she was poised on her toes for that kiss.

"Swear it."

She frowned and lowered back onto her heels, suspicious.

"Just what am I swearing to?"

Ewan poked his nose between them. They both recoiled a bit from the man's beard.

"He wants yer vow, lass," he said. "That ye love 'im. Ye made no argument when he claimed that ye've fallen in love with 'im, aye?"

Quinn glared at Ewan until the man backed away with his hands raised. Then he turned to Juliet, lifted her hand, and gave the back of it a long gentle kiss. He stared into her eyes and willed her to know that he'd prefer to be kissing her lips.

"No arguments?" he murmured.

She shook her head and bit her lip. "You won't want me."

"Too late for that as well, Juliet."

"But what if I already had a child?" she asked. "Would that make a difference?"

His brows rose. There was no stopping them.

"I'm surprised to hear it," he admitted. "But only because you've never mentioned a child before now. But no, it would make no difference."

He dropped down on one knee, never more sure that he should do so. Ewan snorted off to his right. Quinn would have taken a moment to gather his courage, but he needed none. It was the simplest thing he'd done since he'd agreed to change places with Monty a year ago.

"Marry me, Juliet."

She sucked in a breath and held it for a moment. Her consent was already written on her face, dancing in her eyes. But then she sobered enough to give him pause.

"But how would you feel," she paused, "about raising a boy that wasn't your own?"

Quinn grinned. That was her only worry?

"He's mine already. Now take pity, so we can get around to that kiss."

She looked to the ground and bit her bottom lip again.

So, there is more?

"And what if he were a *Gordon*?" she said. "Could you find it in your heart to love a Gordon?"

She'd whispered the last, as if fearful someone might hear her words and be offended by them. Then he understood.

He leaned to the left and peered around her hip at the childlike version of Percy Gordon. He looked quite the orphan in his ill-fitting garments. The problem was, the child was no orphan, and even if he'd forgotten the past ten years of his life, he would still remember who he was and the fact that his father was laird of the mighty Gordon clan.

Quinn pushed up off his knee and pulled Juliet aside so none could hear their conversation but the odd Muir witch or two that might be eavesdropping on his thoughts.

One of the sisters, likely Margot, laughed loudly and led her sister over to the well.

Quinn tasted metal, but it no longer frightened him, knowing the cause. He only wished it would go away before Juliet tasted it from his own lips. First, he had to explain why she couldn't simply claim Percy Gordon as her own.

He opened his mouth to speak, but she beat him to it.

"I'm not sending him back to that bastard," she said. "And I'm not going to tell him that his beloved William wasted away in that dungeon. If he goes back, he'll have to suffer that loss all over again. And they're not going to believe who he is—they'll probably burn him as a witch like they were going to do to you!"

"Juliet. Sweet. We're going to have to send him back through the tunnel. When he gets to the other side, we'll explain to him what's happened, help him all we can before we're on our way."

She stepped back from him then, horrified. Slowly, her head began to shake.

"No," she said. "He's a child. You send him back through that tunnel, and he'll be a child in a man's body. And he'll have to learn it all again, including what his father did to William. I won't let you do it."

He thought it best to hold his tongue for a bit. The village square was no place to discuss such things, even though anyone with the Muir name likely knew about the tunnel and its workings.

He turned to James.

"Would you mind rounding up the horses?"

James grinned and headed down the street.

"Quinn Ross!"

The gathering crowd parted and an ancient man made his way forward with an equally ancient walking stick that must have weighed thirty pounds. Patches of white hair covered less than half of the hundred-year-old skull. Each time the stick lifted seemed a miracle. Each step he took seemed a victory over death itself.

"Quinn Ross," he said again, with the strong voice of a much younger man. "This lad's fate is out of yer hands and now into mine."

Juliet was suddenly at Quinn's side again, clutching his arm like he was her personal walking stick—or the stick she planned to use to beat back an old man if he was foolish enough to get in her way.

"Who are you?" she demanded.

The old man looked her over, then stared into her eyes. His own glittered as if he were quickly reading over a document, and yet those cloudy orbs never moved. Quinn had to suppress the urge to push Juliet behind his back, for he knew she wouldn't appreciate his protective instincts when her own instincts were demanding she protect Percy.

"I'm laird here," said the ancient one. "And any who come through the tunnel must be weighed and measured."

"Are you kidding me?" Juliet's volume made it clear she'd misunderstood.

Quinn would have laughed at her, but he didn't care for the idea of the old man making any sort of judgment concerning his woman, let alone young Percy. He glanced behind him and was pleased to see that Monty was up off his arse and ready to fight. The lad was tucked in behind him and Jillian. Monty gave Quinn a slight nod. Ewan stood at the ready with the old Muir sisters behind him, as if they belonged to Clan Ross and not in the midst of these mind-reading strangers.

When Quinn once again faced forward, the old man was watching him closely, his head tilted slightly to one side as if he were somehow weighing and measuring Quinn. Or maybe the heaviest rock in the old one's head had shaken loose and rolled to one side.

"Our land. Our rules, Quinn Ross," he said.

Quinn leaned forward. "Stand back, laird. We'll be taking ours and going."

Although he never noticed the movement, the clansmen had shuffled around to form a tight circle, shoulder to shoulder, in front of them. There was nothing threatening in their eyes, just as there is nothing threatening about the pawns on a chessboard. But there was no doubt, they'd been moved into position.

Quinn's hand went to his sword, but the weapon would not release its sheath. One look at Monty and Ewan told him they suffered the same problem. The fact they'd tried to arm themselves didn't seem to concern the crowd, or their leader. They only waited and watched, pleased with the entertainment.

Margot moved around Ewan and came forward. She stepped in front of the old man and gave a little bow.

"Father," she said. "These young women are of Muir blood. Surely they can be allowed to go on their way."

"Our ways, Margot." A gnarly finger raised and pointed at Juliet. "That one's been in the tunnels. Even my auld nose can smell it on her, aye? And the lad as well."

Quinn resisted the urge to give Juliet a sniff. If they'd ever gotten around to that kiss, she might have tasted of metal. But he didn't care if she had liquid silver running through her veins; she was his.

"And mayhap it's me yer smelling, father. I was there, on the far end of the tunnel. I ken this lass was forced inside. Surely, she shouldna be punished for it?"

The old man smiled and nodded. "As you say, daughter." He looked at Juliet. "Come forward, Juliet. And bring yer sister."

Quinn tried to reach for Juliet's arm as she stepped forward, but his hand never rose. Jilly moved forward to stand next to her. Monty strained behind his wife, but couldn't stop her either. A fizzy chill ran up Quinn's spine and poured fresh metal into his mouth.

"*Haud yer wheesht,*" he heard whispered into his mind.

"Granddaughters to be sure," the old man greeted, taking one of each lass's hands. "I'll allow ye to go, and take yer mighty warriors with ye, but ken that ye'll always find a home here, and shelter, and protection. As will yer sons," he told Jilly. "No matter the century, aye?"

He gave Juliet some sort of blessing, then turned and did the same to Jillian, pulling each low so he could end his benediction with a kiss on the forehead. When he was finished, he dropped their hands and took a step to the side, then craned his neck to see Percy.

Monty stood at frustrated attention when the boy stumbled around him as if being pulled by some invisible rope. Quinn, on the other hand, was able to move just fine and so he did. He rushed forward and planted his body between Percy and the old laird.

The latter tipped his head back on a wrinkled neck and looked Quinn in the eye.

"What foe cannot be bested as a child?" he said, echoing Mhairi's words from earlier that day. Only now, that foe was no longer a concept, but a physical child! Quinn was horrified that the Muirs, a clan that had just proven how easily they could control an enemy, would conceive of such a curse—a curse that would end with the slaughter of children! It made no difference that those children might have been full-grown sword-wielding soldiers a half an hour before!

They were mad! All of them. Perhaps Margot and Mhairi were the sanest of the lot!

Mhairi!

Quinn looked in Ewan's direction and found the old woman meeting his eye.

Please, Mhairi. Help us!

Mhairi, bless her, nodded.

A heartbeat later, he held both Juliet's hand and Percy's, and they were pushing quickly through an unresisting crowd. There was no time to wonder whether or not Mhairi was responsible.

They burst down the street with Monty, Jillian, and Ewan on their heels. The Muir sisters remained somewhere inside the mob. James waited at the bottom of the slope with horses ready.

Thank you!

He sent the thought to God, and to Mhairi and Margot, and hoped they all heard, somehow.

CHAPTER TWENTY-NINE

It was dark when Ewan led his strangely disguised guests back into Castle Ross. He sent James on some errand and led the rest of them into the big hall, then went to work starting a small fire in the hearth. Thank heavens he'd sent everyone from the building until after the funeral—the funeral where, thank goodness, there would be no body in the coffin.

Jules was just grateful they were all accounted for, including Percy. It was easy to admit she was in love with Quinn and wanted to spend the rest of her life with him—when he'd gone down on one knee, she'd been so thrilled she could hardly breathe. But she couldn't live with herself, or anyone else, if she couldn't find a way to end that little boy's suffering. The funny thing was, she'd decided to help him however she could before he'd ever become that little boy.

When he'd taken her from the workroom beneath the tomb entrance, when he'd said his brother's name and sobbed, she'd been backed up against his chest. She'd felt that sob rack her own bones, but she'd also felt it in her soul. His heartbreak had become hers. And she knew she had to fix it somehow.

All that business about the oubliette was just a bluff. He'd have never hurt her in the end. It was almost like she'd been able to read his mind—

Okay. There was no way she was going to follow that thought to the end. No way. No matter what the old man had said, she wasn't one of those freaks on the other end of the tunnel.

As they all settled around the hall, she peeked at her sister and was kind of relieved that Jillian wasn't looking her way, thinking the same thing. She turned away quickly though, just in case, and stared at Percy who was staring up at the sculpture of Montgomery. With ten years of memories wiped away, he wouldn't remember anything about the statue or the tomb standing close by, or even the entrance to the tunnel.

Once she and Percy had taken a dozen steps into the tunnel, he'd forgotten she was his hostage and let her go. He'd wanted to know why they were in a cave. She could have suggested they turn around and go back to the round door, but she'd had an indescribable impression that they should keep going, that whatever they'd begun *had* to be finished. After that, and about every twenty paces, he'd ask who she was and where they were. By the time she'd given him some kind of story, he'd start asking all over again. By halfway, she realized he'd been shrinking. It had scared the shit out of her, but she couldn't let him know. He was so scared. So confused. So trusting.

The last time he'd asked who she was, she'd seen the light ahead. She'd told him they were in a cave, that she'd been lost and he'd come along and saved her. Once in the sunlight, she'd asked him his name and where he was from. He knew he was Percy Gordon and that he lived by the sea. He didn't remember much else. No mother was waiting for him. He had brothers much older, but he didn't like any of them.

That was the moment Jules had recognized as her chance to end his heartache. If he didn't remember loving William yet, then losing his brother wouldn't break his heart. And if she took Percy with her...

She suddenly realized why she'd been so set on saving the boy.

Deep down, she'd felt like erasing his father's betrayal would somehow make up for Gabby's betrayal of Nikkos. But it wouldn't. Nothing was bringing Nikkos back. And nothing could erase what had happened to William Gordon. All she could do was keep Percy from reliving the loss. She only wished she could have done the same for Nikkos.

She thought of William's body still waiting in Gordon's dungeon and wondered if he knew she would be preventing Percy from ever loving him again. But if he knew that, he'd also know that Percy would be spared, wouldn't he?

"Sorry, William," she muttered. "I hope you understand."

"What was that?" Quinn whispered in her ear.

Jules was sitting on a bench with Quinn standing behind her like he thought that hundred-year-old man might run through the door any second and drag her away.

"I said I'm not leaving without Percy," she whispered back.

"Well, of course we're not leaving without him," he said. "Who knows what those blood-thirsty Muirs might do if they ever got their hands on him?"

She jumped to her feet and faced him, then grinned like an idiot, trying to show him how grateful she was.

"Does this mean I can have that kiss now?" He pulled her close and barked his shin on the bench. "Why is there ever something between us, Juliet?"

She climbed over the stupid bench and stepped up close. Just as Quinn's mouth touched hers, Monty cleared his throat nearby. They ignored him and kissed like they'd been waiting all day for a chance to do it. Her lips were going to be bruised.

Thank goodness!

The second time Monty cleared his throat, he was a foot away.

Quinn pulled back. "What is it, Uncle? I ken she looks a great deal like yours, but this one's mine. Yours is over there." Then he pulled her close again.

This time, their lips didn't even touch before she and Quinn were pushed apart. His hands slipped out of her reach.

"I beg pardon, nephew," Monty said cheerfully, "but as Juliet's brother of the law, she is mine until such time as I hand her to ye, aye? And I doona see a priest about."

"In truth," said Ewan as he squatted before the hearth poking at the flames of his fire, "James has gone to fetch Father McRae, just in case mind ye."

Jillian started laughing. "Poor man! He's going to think he's marrying *us* again, Montgomery."

Monty didn't seem to hear because he and Quinn were locked in some kind of staring contest, like they were summing each other up. Was Monty daring Quinn to back out? Maybe run away before the priest showed up?

Jules felt the smile slip off her face when the word *marrying* finally registered. She heard a whimper and realized it had come from her own throat.

Quinn noticed her distress and pushed Monty out of the way to come to her. He hugged her to him, then ran his fingers along her hair.

"Don't listen to them, lass," he crooned. "We'll marry when you're ready and not before. I've more family who will want to be in attendance, aye?"

More family? The idea was shocking enough to get her mind off a rushed wedding.

What a difference a week made. No family, no ties. Now plenty of family with more waiting in the wings? It seemed like a pretty picture, but with one, unwanted face looming on the back row.

Gabby. The father figure. Smiling for the camera.

It was one *tie* she needed to sever before she'd be ready to tether herself to this family of Scots.

"We need to go, Quinn. I have to get back to New York in the next thirty-six hours, or I'll have to hide for the rest of my life. None of you will be safe if Gabby comes looking for me. I have to make sure he gets put away."

The color drained from Quinn's face.

"You will be safe," he demanded. It sounded a lot like the time Monty had shouted at Jillian that she would be fine, when she'd been crying beneath the tree.

"Here we are!" James led in a priest wearing a floor length robe. The man looked a little nervous, like he thought Satan might rear his head out of the giant mass of curls on James' head.

"Face the wall, Father McRae, if ye please." Monty's voice boomed around the room.

The priest did as he was asked, like he was invited to face the wall on a regular basis. Then he fainted dead away.

Everyone looked at Monty because it had to have been his voice that scared the man.

Ewan laughed.

"Och, forgive me," he said. "The man's likely been planning the words to say o'er yer grave, and here ye are, orderin' him about."

CHAPTER THIRTY

Standing in the tomb once more, just to the side of the hole and surrounded by all those who were supposedly traveling with her to the twenty-first century, Jules lowered the necklace onto her collarbone, just as Jillian had done a minute before.

Again, nothing happened.

The torchlight still rose through the hole. Ewan still gawked up from barrel below.

Jules huffed. "I don't know why I need to do this. I wasn't wearing the necklace when I came through the first time. Neither was James."

She didn't mean to sound cranky, but the six of them had been standing there for a while, and with five hands clamped on her arms, for fear she'd leave without them, she was feeling more than a little claustrophobic.

Quinn's arm, wrapped securely around her waist, gave her a little squeeze. When she looked at him, he winked.

Percy was squished between them with one hand on Juliet's arm and one wrapped around Quinn's wrist. The poor kid was scared to death.

"Each time I've done it," Jillian said, "it happened right when the silver was lowered onto my skin."

"Perhaps there are too many people," James suggested. "I can stay behind—"

"No," Monty growled.

There was something going on there that Juliet didn't know about.

Jillian perked up. "I know what it is! The *Muirs*. There were always Muir twins nearby."

Everyone turned to stare at her. No one bothered to say it out loud, that there were Muir twins already inside. Jillian wrinkled her nose and shrugged her shoulders.

"Well, we're not *old*," she said.

"By Muir standards, we're far from old ourselves," came the voice of one of the sisters. It was hard enough for Jules to tell them apart when she could see them. It was impossible to tell anything from their voices.

"Mhairi, Margot. We're ever so glad to see ye," said Monty to the hole in the floor. "What have we forgotten, ladies? We're all hangin' on to Juliet for dear sweet life. She's wearing the torque, as Jillian has already tried, but it doesna seem to be working."

"Och, Laird Montgomery, haven't we said it had naught to do with the torque?"

"Aye. Ye did. I remember now. But there must be something more."

"Aye, laird. There's more. But we must have yer promise before we help ye on yer way."

Everyone's eyes bugged out a little, all but Percy's. They all suspected that making a promise to the Muirs might not be the wisest move. But Jules was desperate. She was going to lose her effing mind if she didn't get out of there.

"What is it?" she hollered. "What's the promise?"

"The tunnel. You must all promise that no one will ken of it."

"An easy promise to keep," said Quinn.

"But ye must all vow, and Ewan as well, that the tunnel will never be destroyed."

Monty was already shaking his head.

Jillian bent and looked through the hole. "Why, ladies? Why can't we destroy it? What if our children wander inside?"

"They would need to be shown the way. If ye keep the first promise, ye'll have naught to fear."

"Why?" Jules had the feeling they weren't telling them everything. "Why can't we get rid of it?"

There was a long pause. No one moved. No one let go of her.

"Someone else moves within the tunnel. Cursed. And yet there is hope, as long as the tunnel remains."

There hadn't been anyone inside the tunnel but Percy and her. Or had there? They'd been watching their feet the entire way.

A shiver rose through her and she looked at Jillian. Her sister felt it too. The tunnel shouldn't be destroyed.

"We promise," they said in unison, then laughed. No one else in their little circle seemed to think it was funny. Under the circumstances, Jules resisted the urge to call out, "Jinx!"

"We need to go now, ladies," Quinn called out. "What is it we've forgotten?"

"Wrought with love and sacrifice, Quinn Ross. Love. And sacrifice."

One of the sisters laughed. *"And shame upon ye, fer thinkin' we're a blood-thirsty bunch. The lad would never have been harmed—but what better way to make ye determined to take him along than to forbid ye?"*

Quinn stiffened at her side.

Jules gave him a little squeeze. When he met her gaze, she gave him a wink.

"Enough love in here to choke a horse, I'd say." She turned back to her sister. "What about the sacrifice?"

The seconds ticked away. No one spoke, though it was clear by their frowns they were all thinking. Then suddenly, James laughed.

"Sorry, Monty, lad. I ken ye dinna trust me near Isobelle for some reason, but it seems there's no other choice." James looked Jules in the eye. "Give 'em hell, Juliet Bell."

One hand loosened its grip on her arm, then disappeared, and with it, the light from below. She was standing in the darkness with the echo of James' laughter fading from memory. Monty and Jillian released her. Quinn and Percy still held tight. A second later, a flashlight came on. Monty held it in one hand, his other was locked around Jillian's forearm in a deathgrip.

There was an empty gap in their little circle, where James had stood.

"Son of a bitch." Monty glared at the empty space.

Jillian laughed. "Well, at least your cursing is improving."

"Jillian, dear!" came a sweet shaky voice from below. It had to be one of the old Muir sisters who'd first sent Jules into the tomb.

"I guess we've arrived," she said.

It was a little shocking that she'd felt nothing at all. Inhaling in the fifteenth century, exhaling in the twenty-first.

Quinn finally let go of her wrist and tapped Percy on the shoulder.

"You can let go now, lad."

"Jillian? Did ye find yer sister?"

"Yes, I did," Jillian said with a smile.

"Well, then, there are a couple of surly gentlemen who suggest that she comes out with her hands where they might readily see them."

***

Up at the manor house, Jules the Prisoner, was held in the upstairs bathroom—or rather, the upstairs loo—for two reasons. First, no one trusted her not to escape before things were settled, and secondly, Quinn refused to let anyone lay a hand on her, let alone allow two agents to hold her by the elbows. The loo, with its small transom window through which no adult human could escape, became the only option.

She didn't know what those good old boys from New York had told them about her, but the men sent to apprehend her treated Juliet Bell like she was trouble. The fact that James hadn't turned up with the rest of them hadn't helped. What did they think, that she was a cop-killer. A bobby-killer?

It wasn't funny, but you know, it kinda was.

"James would have thought it was funny," she mumbled.

The bathroom door whipped open and Jules had to back up against the side of the toilet to allow enough room for Quinn and Monty to squeeze inside and shut the door behind them.

"What's going on?" she asked.

"I made a few calls," Quinn said. "They are British Secret Service. One of them is James' supervisor. He had no problem believing that James would take a leave of absence and head to Spain after making sure we were home safely. A couple blokes climbed into the tomb, but came back out again, thankfully."

"Aye, thankfully," said Monty. "Get on with it then," he said to Quinn.

"Get on with what?" she asked.

Quinn's face reddened. "Och, my uncle here doesn't believe you mean to wed me."

Monty snorted. "That's a fact. I doona believe it."

Jules didn't know whether to be offended or not. Of course Monty didn't know her well, but did he really believe that she'd take the money and run?

"It doesn't matter what he believes, though, does it? It matters what *you* believe," she said to Quinn. It kind of hurt that he doubted her, after all they'd been through.

"Och, now, Juliet. Of course I believe you. I just want Monty to shut his gob and stop his teasin'. If you'll just tell him..."

"Wait." Monty pulled out a plaid scarf he'd had dangling from his waistband. "If she's going to make a promise, she'll need to bind it. Hold up her hand."

Quinn inched around to the far side of the toilet and took her hand right hand in his right hand, then lifted it up. Monty stepped forward and started wrapping their hands together. Jules was just glad the toilet lid was down.

"What in the hell are you doing?" she demanded.

"Binding yer promise," Monty said simply, like she was stupid to have asked. "Ye canna break a promise that's been bound, lass."

Quinn just smiled at her and shrugged like it was the most natural thing in the world to be holding hands over a toilet asking her to promise that she would marry him.

"Of course I'm going to marry you," she said, "but only if you don't make a habit of doing silly shit like this."

Quinn looked at Monty. "Yes, I pledge to marry the lovely foul-mouthed lass. Will that do?"

Monty frowned, then nodded. "I bear witness to it."

Jules rolled her eyes.

The scarf was pulled away and Monty stuck only his head out the door.

"I think you should kiss me, lass." Quinn leaned forward.

She shook her head. "I am not kissing you over a toilet."

He huffed and stuck out his lovely bottom lip. She was incredibly tempted to reconsider.

Monty laughed quietly. "Stop yer moonin' and come on. We're not supposed to be in here. Juliet, ye'll stay put."

Quinn gave her a wink and then backed out of the room, grinning, pulling the door shut behind him.

She hurried to the door and pressed her ear against the thick white paint. She thought she heard men giggling on the stairs.

Men.

She shook her head and climbed into the footed bathtub. If they were going to make her wait, she was going to sleep and it wasn't going to be on the toilet.

CHAPTER THIRTY-ONE

The bathroom door burst open.

"She's gone!" a man shouted.

"No, I'm not," she hollered and sat up in the tub.

An agent jumped sideways with a gun pointed at her.

"Nevermind," he hollered toward the door. "She's here."

He kept his gun trained on her while she stretched her shoulders—the tub was far too short for her to have slept comfortably.

Then she laughed as the pins and needles worked themselves out of her muscles. Out of all the things that had frightened her in the last ten days, the guy with the gun was the least frightening of all.

"He's awake," another man said from the hallway. "He says it wasn't her."

The agent sneered at her but holstered his gun. Then he went out and shut the door.

"What?" she called over the side of the tub. "No apology?"

About five minutes later, the door opened again.

The squatty one must have picked the short straw. He stood back with his feet braced apart like he thought she was going to rush him. He looked so nervous, she hoped they didn't allow him to keep real bullets in his gun. Thankfully, he hadn't drawn that weapon, yet.

She climbed out of the tub and stretched.

Squatty nodded the direction she was supposed to go. She wanted to yell *boo!* at him as she passed, but she was afraid she'd get shot for it. Some laughs just aren't worth dying for, but she couldn't help holding up her hands and shaking them.

"Uh, oh. Where'd my handcuffs go?"

Squatty's eyes bulged and she thought he was going to pee himself. Then he frowned. He must have remembered she hadn't been cuffed in the first place.

She chuckled while he nudged her down the wide hallway and into a large study. The very handsome middle-aged man in the suit sat behind the desk and smiled. He'd been the same man who'd been sitting in the great hall when they'd all been escorted out of the cellar.

She smiled back.

Behind her right foot, something snorted, and she jumped. But it wasn't an animal—it was Quinn. He was lying on his stomach with his hands cuffed behind him. His head was up, though, and he winked.

She was thrilled to see him and worried about the handcuffs, but with as nervous as everyone seemed to be, she didn't dare kneel next to him. Since their little conversation in the bathroom, he'd taken the time to change into jeans, but he still had on the loose yellow shirt he'd been wearing since they'd returned from Muirsglen. And he was barefoot.

Nice jeans, she thought, but she'd have to study them later.

She turned back to the suit. "What did he do?"

The man's smile turned into a grin. She didn't trust him worth spit.

"Assaulted one of my men," he said.

"Allegedly," Quinn said cheerfully.

"Well, I'm not about to disbelieve my own agent, Mr. Ross. And I doubt he bloodied his own nose."

Quinn laughed. "Is he certain it was me?"

A man walked in from the hallway with a small bag of ice held to his face.

"Oh, I'm quite certain it was you," he said, and drew back a foot, just a little, to kick Quinn, but stopped when Jules pointedly cleared her throat. He stepped away from her and moved to the window like he thought she might sully his suit. But she would have done more than that if he'd have finished that kick.

Montgomery barged in behind the injured man, ignoring the policeman hanging around his neck. Someone from the hallway hollered for a stun gun. The policeman jumped down and backed out the door.

"What the devil have ye done to me nephew?" Monty took Quinn by the shoulders and helped him to his feet. "Well?" He turned a threatening frown toward the suit.

The suit just grinned. "Just one moment, sir, while Chambers here gets a good look at *you*. Perhaps he's not so certain who struck him after all."

Chambers looked from Ross to Ross and back again.

"Shit," he said, then stormed out.

The suit nodded to another man who stepped forward to take off Quinn's cuffs.

Quinn smiled. "Thank you, uncle."

"Not at all. But be quick about this, if ye can. We're waitin' that special supper on ye." Monty threw Jules a wink, then left.

Someone in the hallway shouted, "Halt!"

Another shouted, "Tase 'im!"

"Shite!" shouted a masculine, but high voice.

There was a loud thud, then a knocking.

After a second or two of silence, they heard Monty's laughter moving away.

The Suit rolled his eyes and mumbled something about hoping someone got it in the ass.

"Please, Ms. Bell, take a seat," he said. "Let's get on with it so I can save the remainder of my men from well-meaning Highlanders."

Jules plopped into one of the two chairs facing the desk. She thought Quinn would take the other one, but he came to stand behind her instead. She was surprised how glad she was to feel him so near. Then it hit her—she wasn't alone. And if she played her cards right, if she tried to be as nice to these Scots as they were to her, she might not ever be alone again.

"It's not Bell. It's Ross," Quinn said. "Juliet Ross. My wife."

Jules bit her lip. She couldn't believe he was lying to a government agent.

The suit raised a brow and brought his fingers together. His elbows rested on the arms of the large red leather chair.

"Married?" he said. "We have no record of it. Let me guess. This wedding was rather recent?"

"We're handfasted," Quinn replied. "You understand handfasting, Lord Dunbar?"

This guy is a Lord? And what the hell is handfasting?

Dunbar threw his head back and laughed. "You know that won't matter."

"It matters to me." Quinn bent down and whispered in her ear. "That business we conducted in the loo, lass, was Scottish marriage the old way. Yer mine now."

All Jules got out of it was *loo* and *marriage*. He'd married her in the bathroom? Was he effing kidding?

There was no time to find out.

"And I'm certain," Quinn addressed Dunbar again, "the legality of handfasting would have to be addressed, as would any extradition of a British citizen, would take a wee while to sort out."

She really didn't know what the hell he was talking about. She wanted to go back to the states. And she needed to go now.

"Look," she said. "I have to get to New York, to testify. If we don't get moving, it will be too late."

If anyone could get her there in time, it should be these guys.

Dunbar stopped playing with his fingers and leaned forward. "I'm afraid your testimony is no longer necessary. The defendant was murdered."

"Defendant? You mean Gabby?" Her heart sped up. It was all she could hear.

Gabby was dead? Her Gabby?

"Gabby Skedros is dead?" She was finally able to ask it out loud. "You're sure?"

"I'm afraid so." Dunbar watched her closely. "He was poisoned. Of course you wouldn't know anything about that, would you? You've been in Scotland since you landed nearly two weeks ago?"

He'd said it, but he didn't believe it. His condescending tone made her nauseous. He was no different than the Feds she'd dealt with for months, trying to make her feel like a guilty prisoner, instead of the witness they were supposed to be protecting. But with Gabby dead, she wouldn't need protecting anymore.

"I didn't want Gabby dead," she said. "I wanted to look him in the eye when I testified. I wanted to tell him what a coward he was for shooting a defenseless boy. I wanted to assure him that Nikkos would have hated him in those seconds before he died. I wanted to show him he would never get the chance to betray me like that. I was going to betray *him*. For Nikkos."

Quinn's hand rested on her shoulder and she reached up and touched his fingers. She wanted to double over and puke out the hate she'd been carrying around for a man that was already dead. She didn't need to hold onto it anymore. She could let it go. And she did. In a flood of silent tears.

She didn't care who saw, or what they thought. She had to let it out.

She had Quinn. And she didn't want that stored up hate anywhere near him.

Jules thought of Percy and the fact that he would never have to taste that intense hatred of his father. And she wouldn't either. She was done. It was over. She and Percy would move on.

Quinn cleared his throat. "If her testimony is no longer required, why the need to restrain her?"

Dunbar's smile helped her get a grip. She could almost hear the rattle of his snake's tale.

"Assault of a Federal Officer is a serious charge," he said pleasantly. "An FBI agent by the name of Dixon is demanding her head, or at the very least, her extradition."

Quinn laughed. "What did she do, bash him on the head?"

Jules laughed as she wiped away her tears. How well he knew her already.

Dunbar opened up a laptop and turned it to face her. Agent Dixon's mug flashed up in a Skype frame.

She stopped laughing, but didn't lose her smile.

"Hello, Dickie," she chirped.

The man's face turned red. It was always red. Easiest man in the world to goad. She couldn't believe the FBI took him on.

"Yes, Lord Dunbar," Dickie said. "That's her. Be careful. She's very dangerous. I'd suggest a full set of chains and perhaps a muzzle for transport."

Quinn reached over and spun the laptop away from her. "Lord Dunbar? May I have just a moment's time to defend my wife?"

Dunbar smiled and nodded. "You may have five minutes. Then we'll take her and go in spite of your handfasting. If you want to spend that five minutes defending her, be my guest, but—"

Quinn was already gone.

She could hear him running down the hall and then...nothing.

Well, at least he was hurrying. Maybe he'd even get back in time for some macking before they hauled her out. And she needed to remind him that he would be in charge of taking care of Percy while she was gone. She just hoped she wasn't going away for a very long time.

She refused to panic. She'd gone from witness to defendant so fast her head was spinning. They were going to have to give her some time before they could expect her to take them seriously.

But if she really was going to face charges, it would be Dickie's word against hers. She'd only been defending herself from the slime ball. Surely the ass had treated other witnesses like he'd treated her. She just had to insist the FBI look into that. But it might take some time. She just hoped Quinn's and Percy's lives wouldn't move on before she could make it back.

Of course, she'd have plenty of money for the ticket, but that hardly raised her heart rate anymore. Money was everything ten days ago. Now there were so many more things in line ahead of it.

Well, not things—people.

Quinn came back in the room breathing hard. He gave her a wink, but didn't come to her for some quality goodbyes. He walked around the desk and shared a very private whisper with Lord Dunbar.

Lord Dunbar cleared his throat, like he was trying to cover up the fact that he'd almost laughed. Then he nodded and turned forward.

"Proceed, Mr. Ross," he said.

Quinn spun the laptop to face her again, then stood beside her.

"Agent Dixon, are you there?" he asked, even though the man's face was filling the screen.

"Yes, I'm here," he said, like he was doing everyone a favor by squeezing this conference call into his schedule.

"Is this the woman who assaulted you, sir?"

He took Juliet's head and moved it until it was up close to the monitor.

"Yes. That's her."

"You're certain?" Quinn's hands wouldn't let her sit back in her chair and she was dying to ask him what he was doing. Dunbar had one hand over his mouth and he was turning as red as Dickie.

Suddenly, Quinn let go of her head.

"Just one more moment, if you please, Agent Dixon." He spun the laptop away again, then went to the doorway and pulled Jillian into the room. He gestured for Jules to get her ass out of the chair, then sat Jillian in her spot. He wiped the smile off his face and spun the laptop back.

"Hello, Dickie," Jillian said.

The agent's face darkened again. "What is this?"

"Just tell us what you see, Agent Dixon," Quinn said.

Jules backed up against a bookcase to make sure she wasn't part of the picture. She'd needed something to lean on anyway.

"I see the face of my assailant. How many times do I have to say it?"

Quinn butted in front of Jillian and grinned into Dickie's face. "That should do it, I think." He spun the laptop back to face Lord Dunbar. "My lord?"

Dunbar cleared his throat and sat forward in his crisp expensive suit to address the screen.

"Agent Dixon. You have just positively identified two different females, and I refuse to extradite a handful of British citizens just so you can take your pick. I strongly suggest you drop the charges against Juliet Bell—that is, Juliet Bell Ross—and if you feel we have erred, please invite your American superiors to contact me personally. I, for one, am certain they will find today's events to be quite amusing."

Lord Dunbar snapped the laptop shut and gave Jules a wink. Then he turned to Quinn.

"You might have made an entertaining barrister, Mr. Ross."

"Once upon a time, my lord, I was."

Dunbar laughed. "With a wife like yours, that experience should come in handy."

Quinn gave a little bow.

"And Mr. Ross?" Dunbar got up from the desk and gestured for his men to leave the room ahead of him. "I'd make it legal before Dickie there comes to call."

Quinn tilted his head back and gave Jules a look through narrowed eyes.

"Oh, I intend to, my lord. I intend to."

Quinn reached out a hand and drew her away from the bookshelf and over to the window. Jillian joined them and together they watched eight cars fill with suits and policemen before moving down the drive toward the remnants of Castle Ross.

"They've prepared a little wedding supper for us, Mrs. Ross," he murmured as he nuzzled her behind the ear.

Chills flooded her body, but it wasn't quite enough to make her forget.

"*Mrs.* Ross? You must be talking to Jillian because I sure *as hell* didn't just get married in a bathroom."

Quinn cleared his throat. Then cleared it again.

"Don't worry, sister," said Jillian. "We'll make sure he gets it right." She walked to the door, then paused. "Don't take too long with your apology, Quinn. Supper's still waiting. And my sons and I are starved." She patted her stomach. "Tomorrow, we can run to the city and get that package from Grandmother's lawyer."

Jules nodded, but food and a mysterious package weren't enough to get her attention when she was about to be left alone with her very own Highlander, and there were no bars or benches between them.

The door snapped shut, but Quinn took two long strides and opened it again.

"Pity, Jillian!" His voice boomed in the hallway. He sounded way too much like Montgomery for comfort. "Have pity! Eat without us!" Then he stepped back and slammed the door.

Jules laughed. "You watch. Monty will be up here before I can forgive you enough to kiss you."

Quinn walked back to her slowly, freezing her with a look that made running away impossible...and unthinkable. She also found it hard to breathe.

"Don't believe it," he said. "That man was a witness to our ceremony. He gave you to me. I've already explained, you're mine now."

He gathered her into his arms and her hands found their way around his neck. His thick black hair caressed the backs of her fingers, inviting them to play. His face turned deadly serious as he lowered his forehead to hers.

"Pity, Juliet. Have pity." He smiled then. "My uncle will be busy fighting Jillian for a small share of supper. Have you ever seen your sister eat?"

They laughed and sighed, then they got down to apologizing and forgiving. The apologizing was quick and sincere. The forgiving took a very, very long time.

THE END

Excerpt from GOING BACK FOR ROMEO

PROLOGUE

Castle Ross, East Burnshire, Scotland 1494

Odd.

The stone closest to Laird Montgomery Ross's foot looked to be the same shape as the hole remaining in the side of his sister's tomb, but he refused to reach for it.

"Nay. I'm not ready to be finished." Monty whispered his complaint to God, for surely it was God's hand that wrought such an appropriately shaped thing.

Behind him, one of the priests cleared his throat. Monty knew without looking it had been the fat one who could not cease rubbing his hands together, even while Monty's sister was led inside her would-be grave. The bastard had been rubbing them for a fair two days, since he'd arrived to try Isobelle as a witch. No doubt they were itchy for the feel of a woman's neck since Monty had cheated them out of wringing his sister's.

He could let the priest live, or he could be silent, but Monty could not manage both.

"If you canna seem to clean those hands, Father," he said without turning away from his morbid creation, "I'd be happy to rid you of them before I finish my task here. I'm sure my sister wouldna mind the wait."

A gasp of outrage was followed by silence, although the Great Hall was filled to the corners with his clan. Those who could not find space inside would soon enough hear of each stone lovingly placed as their laird buried his sister alive within their very hall, upon the stone dais, behind the great Ross Chair. Hopefully they would remember Isobelle's bravery and not how oft his tears mingled with the mortar.

None breathed, none dared rub their hands. How could he possibly continue? How could he not?

"Nay, I wouldna mind a bit, if you're quick about it, brother mine." Isobelle's voice echoed eerily from the tomb and she smirked at him from within the tiny patch of light the same shape as the odd stone. "In fact, toss the bloody things in here with me and I'll leave them at the gates of hell. Himself can collect them when he arrives."

Her unholy laughter no doubt had even the dogs wishing they could cross themselves, but it was music to Monty's ears. The Kirk's men allowed her no blanket, but she'd have the image of revenge to keep her warm.

"Isobelle!" Morna screamed. Monty's other sister stood off to his right, restrained by her puny Gordon husband. "'Tis all my fault. Forgive me."

Isobelle's sober face came forward to fill the hole as she searched for Morna, giving Monty one last glimpse of red hair.

"Morna, love. Dinna greet. The faery will come to make it all right again. Watch for the faery...and keep away from your husband!"

"Silence!" the robed bastard roared.

Isobelle laughed again, backing away from the hole. After all, what could the man do to her now?

Monty would not ruin her trust in the blasted faery, but if the creature ever placed its magic toe on Ross land, it would be dead before it ever took a breath of heathered air.

'Twas time.

He looked at the stone.

'Twas meant.

"I love you, sister mine." His words were quiet, for Isobelle alone.

"And I you, Monty. Blow us a kiss."

When he raised his crusted fingers to his lips, his palm filled with tears but they washed none of the nightmare away. He blew a kiss that was instantly returned.

"I'm stayin' right here, pet. Ye're no' alone."

"Get on, then." The whimper in her voice was slight. "I'll have a wee nap if ye'll but douse the light."

With a final wink she disappeared.

Monty reached for the stone, dipped its edges in muck, and pushed it home, breaking his heart in the doing. After long moments of stillness, his hands slowly opened and dropped away.

From the corner of his eye, he saw Morna swoon, but someone else would have to catch her—someone without mud or blood on his hands. Morna wouldn't welcome his comfort anyhow. She claimed it was her fault, but he knew both sisters blamed him.

If he'd have known the outcome, would he have acted differently? What kind of bastard would not?

There was no stopping the twisting of his face, the sob from his chest. He turned his head to the side and bellowed, "Out!"

Nearly everyone fled or slithered from the hall, all but The Kirk's henchmen who would stay until they believed his sister dead. Only then did he hear the muffled sobs of Isobelle. She sounded as if she were deep in the ground.

His heart shuddered with cold. Dear God, what had he been thinking? His plan was madness; she would never last. Not enough time. He had to get her out!

He reached for the odd stone...and was struck soundly from behind.

CHAPTER ONE

Castle Ross, Present Day

This wasn't the first time Jillian MacKay had felt a holy-crap-moment coming on. She wouldn't worry about it now, except for two things. First, her premonitions of holy-crap-moments were never wrong. And second, she was only minutes away from testing The Curse of the Ross Clan.

Jilly was alone for the moment, poised to enter the Great Hall of Castle Ross, the right heel of her green boots rocking nervously while she waited for the tour group to catch up to her. No sirens sounded. No trumpets announced that a simple girl from Wyoming was about to do anything noteworthy, even though, for the first time in her life, she thought she may actually *be* about to do something noteworthy.

She took a deep breath. Then another. Then tentatively stepped into the dimly lit Hall, turned to her left, and froze.

Holy, holy crap.

Silence stirred from its dreamy corner and rose to fill the Hall, pushing into every nook and cranny. There was no echo of her steps on the wood floor, no muffled voices of the tour group nearing the massive outer door—as if this moment was so pure, so important, that sound could not be allowed to sully it.

And all she'd done was look at his face.

Other books by L.L. Muir

The Curse of Clan Ross Series
Going Back for Romeo
Not Without Juliet
Redeeming Isobelle*
Wicked, Wickeder*, Wickedest*—What About Wickham?
(to be released in installments)

The Scarlet Plumiere Series (Regency romance)
Blood for Ink
Bones for Bread*
Two more books are planned for this series*

The Secrets of Somerled Series (Young Adult Romance)
Somewhere Over the Freaking Rainbow
Freaking Off the Grid *
Arma-Freaking-Geddon*

Other stand-alones
Lord Fool to the Rescue (Regency)
Christmas Kiss (Time travel)
Where to Pee on a Pirate Ship (Middle Grade)

*at the time of printing, these books have not yet been released

About the Author

L.L. Muir lives in the shadows of the Rocky Mountains. Like most authors, she is constantly searching for, or borrowing pens. She manages her characters in a waiting room in her head where fights often break out over whose story should be next in line.

If you like her books leave a review—all the Muir Witches will be most appreciative.

She loves to hear from readers. You can reach her through her website—

www.llmuir.weebly.com.

Made in the USA
Middletown, DE
30 December 2017